THE RED COAT

by Lyla Clarke

Order this book online at www.trafford.com
or email orders@trafford.com

Most Trafford titles are also available at major online book retailers.

Note for Librarians: A cataloguing record for this book is available from Library
and Archives Canada at www.collectionscanada.ca/amicus/index-e.html

Printed in Victoria, BC, Canada.

ISBN: 978-1-4269-0876-7 (sc)
ISBN: 978-1-4269-0877-4 (dj)

*Our mission is to efficiently provide the world's finest, most comprehensive book publishing
service, enabling every author to experience success. To find out how to publish your book, your
way, and have it available worldwide, visit us online at www.trafford.com*

Trafford rev. 10/2/2009

 www.trafford.com

North America & international
toll-free: 1 888 232 4444 (USA & Canada)
phone: 250 383 6864 ♦ fax: 812 355 4082

DEDICATION

I DEDICATE THIS BOOK TO all of the amazing women who have enriched my life: my grandmothers, mother, aunties, sister-in-laws, nieces, friends, and my daughter.

Of my friends I say a special thanks to the memory of Sonja who trusted in the power of words, as do I. Sonya, I do BELIEVE!

This book would never have come about if it weren't for eight simple words asked of me many years ago by my good friend, Maryjane.

"What would you do if you weren't afraid?"

"Write a book!" that little voice in my head screamed. And so I did.

Thank you, Maryjane, for your words of encouragement and for constantly challenging my antiquated ways of thinking. Your twisted sense of humor and ability to objectively simplify issues   have enriched my life and made me push myself into uncharted territory.

I believe that every person we meet influences the people we become. I am lucky to have many friends and family members that fill different spaces in me. Some bring me laughter, some a conscience, some challenges, some simple companionship. I cherish every one of them.

Jennifer and Kerri: your generous words of encouragement pushed me to finish and to *finally* send the final draft off to the printer.

Thank you, ladies. I love you all.

Thank you to my husband, Greg, daughter, Elizabeth and son, Graeme. You inspire me to pursue this dream of mine.

SONYA (BODNAR) SARGEANT
November 15, 1940 - November 12, 2006

ACKNOWLEDGEMENTS

I WOULD LIKE TO ACKNOWLEDGE the very generous help of Forestry Officer Tim Loran. Tim is the Provincial Forestry Forensic Specialist for the Ministry of Environment in Saskatchewan. His extensive knowledge of the job and expertise in rappelling and cold water diving were invaluable to the credibility of the storyline. Any mistakes regarding the duties or responsibilities of conservation officers in this book are mine alone.

The cities, towns, and various locals in this book are real. However, most of the characters are figments of my imagination. The exceptions to this are my Aunt Doreen, Uncle Ken, and her sons. Also, the anecdote regarding Thor the mountain lion is based in truth. There is a plaque relating his real story in the information pavilion at the top of the gondola at Lake Louise, AB. I simply embellished his story for the sake of mine.

I would also like to acknowledge the contributions of my three readers: Jennifer McLaren, Maryjane Shirreff, and Julie Robson.

I couldn't be happier with the cover created by Pamela Silver, a graphic designer. As fate would have it I work with her sister. When I mentioned I was looking for someone to do cover art, Pam's name was immediately brought up. The emails flew back and forth and a cover I love was born. Hope we meet soon, Pam.

A special acknowledgment must be directed to my editor, "Auntie Doreen" Neuls. Her days of tireless devotion to reading and to editing and then re-editing and then re-editing again will be forever appreciated. Fortify yourself, Auntie. Book two is on the way!

PROLOGUE

December 2009

Something was gently swaying in a burlap bag soaked in blood. The bag was tied like a hammock, between two large aspen trees on a small natural plateau, on the southwest slope of Shunda Mountain in the Canadian Rockies. The plateau was small, but level, and had provided the perfect feeding ground to lure a young pregnant cougar for the last couple of weeks. The serenity of the afternoon was uninterrupted except for the gentle breeze that ruffled the unfurled ends of the knotted nylon ropes hanging from the two trees. The warm afternoon sunshine and heat radiating from the bundle kept the blood from freezing in the crisp mountain air. The syrupy globules silently oozed from the warm bundle while it gently, ever so slightly, swayed. They seemed to transform into rubies frozen into the pristine, iridescent snow below. Thea scented the latest meal left for her and stealthily crept down the mountainside.

CHAPTER 1

Hᴀɴᴅs ɪɴsᴛɪɴᴄᴛɪᴠᴇʟʏ ᴄʟᴇɴᴄʜɪɴɢ ᴀɴᴅ body stiffening, she braced for the unavoidable collision. The lights from the oncoming truck and the swirl of snow created an aura of illumination around Thomas' head as he continued to badger her. While she held her breath he stopped yelling and turned towards the thing that was obviously commanding her attention. Her body jolted as the horror unfolded. In slow motion a spray of shimmering shards of glass exploded from the driver's side window onto the front seat. When Thomas turned back towards her his handsome face was gone. What remained was a bloody caricature emitting an inhuman keening.

With a strangled cry, Annah forced herself awake and sat bolt upright in bed. Tears streamed down her face and shudders wracked her body as she gulped and gasped for air. Unconsciously clenching and unclenching her hands she tried unsuccessfully to force the vividness of the dream back. Previous experience had proven that her sleep for the night was over. With a ragged sigh she briskly wiped her cheeks trying to erase the memories along with her tears. Dragging her nerve-racked body from bed she staggered to the kitchen to start the coffee, and then to the bathroom to try to revive herself with a pounding shower. Despite her best efforts to regain control the tears continued to flow. Thankfully, the shower drowned out the whimpers that increased to sobs which continued to wrack her body. Seemingly boneless, she slid down the wall, lay spent, and curled in a ball on the floor of the tub. There she lay until the water ran cold forcing her out of her stupor. Shivering, but finally back in control, she stepped from the tub, turned off the now ice cold shower and briskly rubbed herself dry.

As Annah reentered the kitchen wrapped in her robe she glanced at the clock; six o'clock in the morning. Not as bad as other nights had been. The kids would be up in an hour. Annah had just enough time to whip up a batch of muffins and get them baked for breakfast. Baking always seemed to have a calming effect on her and would help her to organize her thoughts. As she measured and folded and filled the muffin cups she resigned herself to the fact that she may never get over Thomas' death. Some mornings she could pinpoint an incident from the previous day that probably precipitated the nightmare. This morning's review came up with nothing. She might actually have to go see a shrink one on one, rather than just continuing with the group therapy. Sleep was far too valuable a commodity at this point in her life for her to risk losing any more. She'd talk to Jennifer tonight after dinner and see if she could refer her to someone. That decision made, she focused on the tasks ahead and so Annah's day began.

⌒⌣

"All Performing Arts student's need to proceed to Auditorium Two for the afternoon performance."

Annah put a hand over one ear as she tried to listen to Nanny on her cell phone.

"I can't talk to you right now. I'm on my way to a lecture and I can't hear you. The halls are packed and admin is paging. I have to go. I'll call you later."

Annah closed her phone, with a sigh, as she swung her backpack in front of her and readjusted her armload of books to put her cell away. With her head bent, she rounded the corner of the hall leading to her locker and proceeded to crash into two men walking, talking, and drinking coffee. The inevitable occurred. Coffee, cups and all, books, and cell phone erupted like an explosion in the crowded campus hallway. Fellow students, that were following Annah, deftly skirted around the disaster and hurried off to their respective classes. Annah and the tallest of the men bent down to retrieve her coffee-covered books, while the other man paged a janitor to corridor three. He then backed up from the mess, crossed his arms, chuckled and commented that multitasking was beyond some students' capabilities.

"Some girls just can't walk and chew gum at the same time!" he added.

Annah gasped and with her luminous green eyes flashing, she reclaimed her articles from the first gentleman, noticing with a start, that his eyes were the same silver blue as her son's. She slung her backpack over her shoulder and with a saccharine smile apologized.

"Please, excuse my clumsiness, Gentlemen."

With head held high, Annah walked between the two men. She felt them turn around and watch her leave. With a mischievous glint in her eye she took five steps, did a pirouette, and then with a flourish and an exaggerated bow to them, she gracefully rose and proceeded down the hallway to her locker.

If that man thought he could get the better of Annah, who juggled the responsibilities of full time student and single mother of two, he was sadly mistaken, she thought as she grinned to herself. While Annah was patting herself on the back, he turned on his heel and proceeded to swagger down the corridor, not realizing she had bested him. Instead of impressing the visiting speaker, as was his intention, she had made him look like a fool. While the *tall* one, with the ice blue eyes, who just happened to be the visiting speaker, shook his head, grinned, and mentally tipped his hat to her. He stopped smiling when he realized he was hoping that this wouldn't be his only encounter with her. Officer MacGregor was too old for saucy little schoolgirls, with flashing emerald eyes, a bouncy blond ponytail, and firm little derrière.

By the time Annah had wiped down her books and stowed away her unnecessary supplies she was late for her next class. As luck would have it, when she opened the door to the lecture theatre she discovered that the lights were off. A slide presentation was underway. Turning to pull the heavy hydraulic door closed behind her as quickly as possible, so as not to disturb the other students, she stood at the top of the stairs waiting for her eyes to adjust to the darkness.

A smooth deep voice from the front of the theatre below her, amplified by a microphone, requested, "Please find a seat. You'll find my presentation riveting if you concentrate on *it*, rather than on not falling down the stairs."

A few chuckles could be heard in the darkness. The voice sent shivers of sexual awareness running down Annah's spine. Thankfully, by now Annah had some semblance of sight, and she sank into the first available seat she could see.

"Thank you," said the voice, "Now, shall we proceed?"

Without waiting for a reply the voice continued. Although Annah could not see the speaker, she knew this must be the infamous Conservation Officer MacGregor. Professor Canning had been talking about him since the first class Annah had ever taken from him three years before. He had been so impressed by this man's accomplishments that many of the students wondered if this man was either a God or Professor Canning's secret lover. Though he had been repeatedly invited to speak, until today, no one had actually seen or met this man, and some were wondering if he really existed. Although the speaker's tone hinted at arrogance, by the way he detailed the things he had seen and done; Annah could not help but be drawn to him. Not only was his voice compelling, but the stories he told and the pictures he showed were fascinating. Obviously one of his many talents included very competent amateur photography. The slides were vivid and in some cases actually breath-taking.

He explained that he had been a conservation officer for 15 years. He had started out on the prairies in Saskatchewan near Fort Qu'Appelle. From there he took a transfer to the Canadian Shield around Lake of the Woods. His last transfer had taken him to Nunavut in the Canadian Arctic. All three locales were very different environmentally. No graduating student knew for sure where he or she would get their first posting and therefore, listening to this speaker was extremely informative as well as entertaining. His stories contained a great deal of dry humor and even some self-depreciating anecdotes. Unconsciously, Annah leaned forward in her seat and became totally immersed in his world. All too soon the presentation drew to a close.

The lights came on and Annah resettled in her seat. She opened her binder and started to jot down notes from the information she had just heard.

Unbeknownst to her, when she had opened the door to the theatre, the light from the hallway had caused the speaker to look up just as it shone on her face and he had recognized the tardy student. The voice from the front asked the question, "Who can tell me the ratio of black bear to humans in the Lake of the Woods area, specifically west of Kenora, Ontario?"

Annah finally looked up at this point and realized the voice had moved to the podium. With a gasp she recognized the speaker. It was none other than the "tall man" and he was looking right at her. Hands were going up all around her. Dread filled her as she realized by the tilt of his head, the recognition in his eyes, and the expectant look on his face that he was going to ask her for the answer.

"Can the young lady in the back with the purple sweater give me the answer?" Officer MacGregor inquired.

The second before she had seen his face she knew the answer. Now she drew a total blank. After several long seconds had dragged by and other students began to turn around in their seats to stare at her, Annah finally managed to speak.

"I'm sorry, Sir, but I can't seem to recall," she stammered. Blushing furiously, she could feel the eyes of several fellow classmates, specifically the other girls, focused on her. She was so angry she could have spit nails. She was positive he had called on her to show her she wasn't quite as smart as she thought she was even though she had shown she could maintain her dignity in embarrassing situations. The more she thought about it, the more she fumed as she knew that some of the male students in the class believed that women didn't belong in this field. The three other women in the class shook their heads with disgust. They believed their positions in this male dominated class were tenuous at best, and Annah had just made things worse.

Officer MacGregor seemed surprised by her answer but recovered quickly and redirected his question to a male student from the front row. He, of course, answered the question correctly and the lecture continued. Two of the girls continued to glare at Annah. She knew the other women felt they had to achieve higher marks because they tended not to do as well as their male counterparts with the physical side of the program. Few women applied for this degree and even less actually graduated. She knew she had a responsibility to earn the respect of her male companions so those future female students had a more even playing field in which to compete.

Officer MacGregor had unknowingly added to the resentment growing inside Amber, one of the other female students. The female students had formed a study group and for the past three years they had challenged each other to stay ahead of their male classmates. What had begun as ten women was now down to four. Annah was about to be the first woman to ever be excluded from that group. With the responsibilities that Annah had at home she wasn't always able to attend last minute cram sessions for tests and Amber's resentment was growing.

Annah closed her eyes and rubbed her temples. Focus, focus, focus her mind chanted. Breathe in..... Hold it.....Breathe out. Annah opened her eyes, straightened her spine, and focused on the remainder of the class.

Officer MacGregor had been watching the interaction between the other women who all sat together. It was obvious they were not happy with Annah. He instinctively knew he had caused a situation, even though he didn't know the politics of exactly what was going on. He knew he was baiting Annah when he had asked the question but he hadn't thought for one minute that she wouldn't be able to give him the answer. First, she had been shocked as she recognized him. Secondly, she was embarrassed that she was late. Thirdly, he had seen her eyes widen in fear as she realized she couldn't answer. Shame followed because he had unsettled her to the point of causing her to lose her focus. Then he saw the fury which he had glimpsed earlier in the hall: the flashing emerald eyes, the clenched hands, and the puckered brow.

Finally, just as suddenly as the fury settled in, she closed her eyes, unclenched her hands, rubbed her temples, and took a deep breath. When she opened her eyes and straightened in her desk he knew she was back in control. This was a woman, not a girl like the others in the class. She had now shown him twice that she was capable of handling herself in difficult situations. That was a valuable attribute for a conservation officer. As he had watched the emotions wash across her very expressive face, his reluctant admiration of her inner strength increased.

The remainder of the lecture was uneventful. When it was over Officer MacGregor watched the girls approach Annah. One of the girls struck a pose beside her desk and with a long-suffering look of regret was obviously expressing her displeasure. One of the others looked on haughtily, while the third looked at the floor and shuffled her feet. Annah rose, collected her supplies, and with a single comment smiled and walked away from them. The leader made a face and turned to her cohorts with a sneer and a gesture aimed at Annah's back.

Suddenly Officer MacGregor realized a student was standing beside him waiting.

"You shouldn't have picked on Annah just because she was late. She's one of the best all around students in this program and you made her look stupid in front of the other girls. She works harder than most of the rest of us on her studies and she has a family to take care of, as well."

"That wasn't my intention," Officer MacGregor stated. "And what do you mean she has a family to take care of?"

"Annah's a widow with two little kids, as well as being a full time student. She and the other girls have formed a group that studies together. Amber, that's the one that just flipped her off, has a chip on her shoulder the size of the Grand Canyon. She figures the girls don't get a fair shake here so she's always pushing herself and the rest of them to overachieve. The four of them always finish in the top ten for academics. Annah is the only girl who also always finishes in the top ten for the physical training. This is the first time I've ever seen Annah as the focus of Amber's wrath. You should probably apologize, you know. I think Annah's got enough on her plate without having a falling out with the group. I know their support of each other does help them to do better."

"You're right. What's her next class?"

"Field training," the student replied. "On second thoughts, maybe you should just stay away from her. It could make things worse if Amber sees you."

"And why is that?"

"Amber's jealous of her. Annah has already earned most of the students and Profs respect, while Amber is still struggling to achieve that. Annah's not only smart and well trained but she's also kind and funny. She isn't a threat to most of us. Some of the guys resent the girls because they think they're taking jobs away from them. However, most of us are cooler than that," he replied.

"Anyhow, I actually wanted to ask you some questions about the posting in Nunavut. Have you got time?" the informative young student asked.

"Certainly. I'm done for the day. Ask away."

Officer MacGregor promised himself he'd find out how to get in touch with the girl named Annah to apologize privately. And, he knew just the guy who could get him the information he needed to keep that promise.

CHAPTER 2

Wɪᴛʜ ᴛʜᴇ ᴜɴᴜsᴜᴀʟ ᴇᴠᴇɴᴛs of the day, her lack of sleep, and the stress incurred by her morning exam, Annah was exhausted. Her day, however, was not over yet. Nanny Bea was leaving for the weekend in half an hour, so Annah needed to hurry home. She had hoped the workout on the training field would give her the extra energy she needed to get through the evening out that she had planned. So far that extra energy burst wasn't happening. Annah raced home with five minutes to spare. As she opened the back door, two squealing kids physically assaulted her, while a huge calico cat went shooting through her legs.

"Whoa!" Annah exclaimed. Nanny Bea stood in the hall, arms crossed, with a grin on her face. Simon was plastered onto her leg and Summer wrapped herself around Annah's waist.

"Well, that was quite a welcome. You would think someone was happy to see me."

Annah knelt down and hugged her children tightly. The extra energy she had been seeking suddenly flooded into her. This was what kept Annah strong. These two were the catalyst to keep her going night and day. The unconditional love shining from their two glowing newly spit-polished faces was Annah's reward for working so hard.

With tears glistening in her eyes Annah peeled the two off of her and stood up.

"Well, I'm off then," stated Nanny Bea. "The children have all kinds of exciting news to report. There's a parcel for you on the table that I picked up at the post office this afternoon." Nanny waved at it as she buttoned her coat and picked up her overnight bag.

Annah hugged Nanny Bea goodbye on her way out the door and wished her a fun weekend. Taking each child by the hand she led them over to the sofa and sat down sandwiched between the two giggling and wiggling siblings. Every day they followed the same routine. It was the favorite part of Annah's day.

"Now, tell me all about your day. Today we will start with Simon," Annah declared as she turned to look at her son. Simon was four and half and went to playschool on Fridays. He had Annah's same wheat colored blond hair and heart-shaped face. But, his eyes were a cool silver blue ... like the dashing Officer MacGregor. Dashing.....for God's sake! He wasn't dashing, he was just rude. And why was she thinking about him anyway when her son was trying to tell her about his day. *Focus ... Focus..... Focus.* You would think she had hit her head when she bumped into him today. Annah decided she needed a good night's sleep more than she had originally thought.

"I went to school today," he stated seriously. "We learned about cougars and the teacher said you have ta' take me to the zoo so I can see a real one. I would like to go tomorrow, please........"

Annah laughed. "Tell me what you learned and maybe we can go to the zoo soon."

"She said they have bears and wolves and lions and all kinds o' things. I want to go tomorrow, please........."

"Yes, Simon, they do have all kinds of animals but we can't go tomorrow." As Simon crossed his arms and pushed out his bottom lip Annah whispered in his ear. "If you go get the calendar in the kitchen we will plan when we can go. But, you have to stop pouting or you'll trip over your lip on the way."

Simon giggled, "I can't trip on my lip!" as he scooted off the sofa.

While he was in the kitchen getting the calendar Annah turned to Summer and asked, "And how was your day, my dear?"

Summer had been squirming since the moment they sat down, so Annah knew today was a bigger news day than usual. Summer was six and a half and she was in Grade Two. She was a precocious little thing with curly chestnut pigtails, blue velvet eyes, and one deep dimple in her right cheek. She always talked a mile a minute, and every story was a huge drama. Summer was so excited she popped up off the sofa and with hands clasped behind her back, she rocked back and forth.

"We had a practice today for the spring play. You know, the one about the Wizard of Oz, and well, you know Maryjane's family is moving, so Mrs. Wilson asked *me* if I would like to be Dorothy. She asked me.....Mom!!!!" she squealed. By now she was jumping up and down and clapping her hands. She described her costume, including the beautiful sparkly red shoes. She emphasized that she had to learn more lines than *anybody* else. The longer she talked the faster she talked.

As Annah laughed she got up from the sofa. She hugged Summer close and exclaimed, "I am so happy for you, sweetie. I know you will be a wonderful Dorothy. Why don't you go call Grandma and tell her your news while I have a shower? We have to be at Jennifer and Dane's house soon, so I need to hurry. You can tell me more about it when we get in the car. Okay?"

Simon brought the calendar. In two weeks it would be November 11th which happened to fall on a Friday. That gave Annah a three-day weekend. This was the perfect opportunity to take the kids to the Calgary Zoo.

"Please, go get me a red crayon, Simon, and we will mark the day we are going. Starting tomorrow you can cross off the days and count how many days until we go?"

Simon put the calendar on the floor and circled the date.

"What is the date today?" he asked.

"October 28th," Annah replied.

Simon counted out loud until he reached 14 days. "That's two whole weeks," he wailed.

"It will go fast, Honey. Don't forget Halloween is only a few days away now and you didn't think *it* would ever come. Please, put the calendar back and go build me a Lego cougar while I have a shower."

Nanny Bea, thankfully, had given the kids a snack earlier and had them slicked up and ready to go. Annah only had herself to get ready. She showered quickly and jumped into a clean pair of jeans and a forest green cable knit sweater. She towel dried and then added mousse to her hair and left it down to dry in loose curls. While she whisked on a coat of mascara and brushed her teeth both kids joined her in the bathroom. Summer sat on the toilet seat and entertained her with Grandma's response to her good fortune, while Simon galloped and "roared" his way up and down Annah's legs with his newly built Lego cougar. What Simon may have lacked in conversational skills, he certainly made up for with activity as he now tried to crawl through and around Annah's legs. She shooed both of them off to the back door and asked them to start putting on the various layers of winter clothing that all northern mothers cocooned their children in. She scooted into the kitchen to unpack her eagerly awaited "new" winter coat. After unwrapping and unfurling it, she shook it out and laid it flat on the table. With a sigh she lovingly caressed it. It was even more beautiful than the pictures had indicated.

"Hey, that's my mitt!"

"It's mine. Give it back!"

Annah instantly jolted out of her trance and headed for the back door to avert the pending sibling squabble. She propelled Simon down the hall with the whispered bribe of a romp with Jennifer's dogs if he played nicely with his Lego cougar while she helped Summer. And so, the ritual of winter bundling began. First went on the overall ski pants and then the boots. Tie the laces at the top with a bow and then a knot, so that the snow can't get in. Check the coat sleeves for the long gauntlet mitts. Put on the coat, zip the zipper, and snap the snaps. Pull on the mitts up to the elbows and hand Summer her toque to put on. Pull up the hood and tie it. Then last but not least, wind the scarf around the hood and send her out to wait on the front step so that she doesn't keel over from heat exhaustion before Simon is ready. Then start all over again with Simon. When they were finished he waited in the hall while Annah threw on the new coat, Sorel boots, and Thinsulate gloves, and grabbed her purse.

"Pretty," Simon said as he stroked Annah's coat.

"Yes, it is," she agreed. Out the door and into the truck they went. The temperature was only -15° Celsius but the kids always liked to play in the back yard with Jennifer's dogs when they went to visit. Annah made the five minute drive and then settled the kids in the fenced back yard before heading into Jen's house.

"Hey," Annah called out as she let herself in.

"Hey, yourself. Come on in," Jennifer beckoned from the kitchen. "There's a bottle of red wine on the island that needs to breathe. I still get nauseous around alcohol so I couldn't open it. Come open it and pull up a stool."

"It may bother you the whole nine months. I couldn't handle the smell of cooking hamburger with Simon, and I couldn't drink orange juice with Summer," Annah sympathized as she carried in the baguettes and dessert she had brought and set them on the counter.

"Other than that, how are you feeling?"

As Jennifer turned around from the sink she noticed Annah's new coat. It was a deep raspberry, pure virgin wool, Hudson Bay Blanket coat with a white fur lined hood. It had white embroidered Inuktitut symbols of the alphabet framing the zipper, the cuffs, and the hem line, and white wool decals of polar bears stitched on the pockets.

"I feel great. Hey, where did you get that coat? It's absolutely gorgeous," Jennifer exclaimed!

"I found it on EBay about a week ago and got it for a steal. I've always wanted a blanket coat but could never afford one. Someone at school suggested I look on the net. So I did. I can't believe I found it. It's so warm; it's just perfect for working outside."

"It looks great with your fair complexion. You should wear color more often instead of hiding behind black and blue all the time."

"I'm not trying to attract anyone and I don't believe I'm hiding anyway. You know I can't afford a bunch of new clothes. Besides, I'm wearing a green sweater today. So there!" She stuck out her tongue as she walked away to hang up her coat.

"Well, at least you don't have your hair in your habitual pony-tail tonight!" Jennifer exclaimed with a flip of her trendy spiked and streaked locks. "You do look exhausted though. Your face is pale and you're packing some serious baggage under your eyes."

"Thanks, it's always nice to be told you look ravishing or is it ravished and left for dead. It's been a really long week, Jen."

"Girl, you need to get some serious sleep. As soon as Dane gets home we'll eat and you can make an early night of it. You could have called and cancelled."

"I know, but this is the only social life I have. It's good for the kids to get out and I needed to get out as well. I had a bad night again and today was one big humiliation after another. So, I need to share it and have a good laugh. I know I'll feel better after a glass of wine and some chuckles. Honestly, Jen, I don't know what the problem is with my appearance. You've seen me looking worse, and it's not as if Dane or the kids care how I look. What's the big deal?" she asked as she returned to the kitchen.

Then, all of sudden she stopped, crossed her arms and with foot tapping and raised eyebrow she asked suspiciously, "You haven't done anything silly like ask over one of Dane's single friends for supper, have you?"

"*I* would not do that," Jennifer stated indignantly with a sniff. "However, having invited you on Monday, Dane came home late last night with the information that an old friend of his from University was also going to be here for supper. You were already in bed and I couldn't get a hold of you today. So, it's not like I was trying to set up a blind date for you. Besides you've told me numerous times that you have neither the time nor any interest in pursuing any kind of man/woman relationship. I'm not slow, you know. Nevertheless, that doesn't mean you need to go around looking like some old hermit that just climbed down from her mountain."

"My, what a flattering picture you paint of my normal appearance," Annah chuckled, not at all offended by Jennifer's criticism. "So, is the mountain mama going to embarrass you tonight, or am I passable?"

"You actually don't look half-bad except for the bags. Go put on some cover-up, and then tell me your story. Was it another nightmare?"

"Yes. And I don't want to talk about that right now. Maybe you can recommend someone I could see one on one to help me deal with it," Annah requested as she rummaged through her purse for concealer and a mirror. She sat down at the island so she could watch the kids playing outside the French doors while she tried to fix her eyes and entertain Jen with the other events of her day. They both laughed until it brought tears to their eyes. Annah then needed to add even more cover-up to fix the tear tracks.

⌒〜

While the girls were telling stories and laughing Lachlan walked out of the Biology building and searched up and down the street for a shiny black Dodge Cummins Diesel one ton truck with chrome accents. Dane was parked across the street waving for Lachlan to come over.

"This truck is a beaut...I'm going to have to try to talk the bean counters at the station into springing for a couple of these for out in the field. They would have to be white, though. What do you think my chances of success are?" Lachlan chuckled as he swung himself up into the passenger seat.

He extended his hand, "Congratulations, Dane, I couldn't be happier for you and Jennifer. When is the big day?"

"Thanks, I was afraid to hope that we would ever get to this point. The doctors say December 28th. We breathed a huge sigh of relief after her last Doctor's appointment. Jen could have the baby today; it would be a preemie but still survive. The baby is in perfect health and so is Jen. We'll see how close we can get to the due date."

"Well, I'm hoping for a Christmas baby. That just happens to be the date I picked for the baby pool that they have going in your staff lounge. So, what else is new?" Lachlan asked as he settled in for the half-hour commute to Dane's place.

The two old friends chatted comfortably catching up on each other's lives as they hadn't seen each other for several months. Meanwhile they pulled up in front of a corner store and Dane got out saying, "I need to pick up some 2% milk since Jen's friend, Annah, and her two kids are coming for supper. I'll be right back."

Anna! That was the name of the girl Lachlan had been meaning to ask Dane about. He jumped out of the truck and followed Dane into the store.

"Hey, speaking, of Anna. I met a girl today on campus whose name is also Anna and rumor has it she's a widow with two kids. I don't suppose this would be the same girl?" Lachlan inquired.

"Describe her," Dane replied.

"Well, she has blond hair and she's short."

"Oh, come on you can do better than that. The blond hair can be attributed to about half the female students, and as far as being short almost everyone is shorter than you are. Did you see any blond women that were around 6'5" today?" chuckled Dane.

With a sardonic twist of his lips Lachlan saluted Dane. "Touché. All right, she has emerald green eyes that flash with golden lights when she is angry. Her heart-shaped face blushes easily. She looks like she is about twelve but with two kids I'm guessing she must be at least early twenties. She is agile on her feet and quick-witted. Her voice is unexpectedly husky for one so young. When she walks her ponytail bounces, her heart-shaped rear-end wiggles and her voluptuous front-end jiggles. Is that enough detail for you?"

"Well, all that I was really after was estimated age, height, and weight. You seem to have covered all those points and more. I'm pretty sure we're talking about the same girl. How much time did you spend with her today and where did you meet her?" asked Dane.

Lachlan self-consciously cleared his throat. "I literally ran right into her in the hall in the Bio building and then as luck would have it she attended the lecture that I gave this afternoon for Professor Canning. I kind of took her off guard and ended up embarrassing her in front of her class. We definitely got off on the wrong foot. Somehow, I don't think she likes me very much."

"That must put a dent in your ego. Usually women are falling all over you and you need to beat them off with a stick," Dane stated without any animosity. "This should make for a very interesting evening."

"Before we get home what can you tell me about her. I'd really like to avoid committing any more faux pas than I already have today," Lachlan said with a grimace.

"Alright, I'll cut you some slack and make things a little easier for you. Jen and Annah have been friends for about three years. Oh and it's spelled A N N A H for future reference. Just after Annah started University she brought her son in for his six month check-up. Her cousin, Rick, is a partner in Jen's office and he had recommended Jen to Annah. Annah's husband had died about three months before and she was struggling with going to school and being a single parent with two small children. Jen heads up a support group for survivors who have lost loved ones." Dane put the milk on the counter to pay for it.

"Annah was in the car when her husband was killed in the accident. She was trapped and watched him die. It was horrible for her. Both kids were also in the car but unharmed. Through the group they became friends. She is without a doubt one of the strongest women I have ever met and I have nothing but admiration for her. She has been a good friend to Jen, especially encouraging her through her depression from all of our fertility issues. She is in the top of her class both academically as well as in field training. She is also a devoted and loving mother. Please, don't play with her."

Lachlan jerked to a stop as they headed back out to the truck.

"Dane, I'm not a total degenerate. All of the women I've been involved with in the last several years have known up front what my stand is on long term relationships and marriage. I do not get involved with women like Annah. Besides she's not my type at all. You know that. I like 'em tall and willowy with long dark hair and no baggage; not blond, short, and voluptuous with kids. I will be the perfect gentleman tonight. The reason I wanted to ask you about her in the first place was so that I could apologize to her for this afternoon. I didn't mean to embarrass her. You really don't have the highest opinion of my character, do you?" questioned Lachlan with a noticeable hitch in his voice.

"You're my best friend, Lachlan. I love you like you were my brother. You've seen me at my worst and my best, as I have you. I'm being honest with you, unlike the other people in your life that are too afraid to tell you the truth. I know you don't like to hear this but since Amy's death you haven't allowed yourself to become attached to anyone. You're estranged from your father and your twin even though they've both reached out to you to try to repair the rift that was created years ago. Do you even keep in contact with your sister? To my knowledge I am your only friend. I know you have acquaintances and co-workers that you occasionally socialize with but you remain aloof from even your lovers. I want more for you, my friend. You deserve more. Give yourself a break and let people back in. I know it hurts but sometimes if you shut out the pain you also miss the dance and believe me the dance is worth it. Come on, let's go eat. I imagine the kids are starving."

⌒⌒

"So, who is this guy, anyway? I figured all of Dane's friends were married or you would have dragged them out by now."

"Lachlan was married. It is a terribly sad story and you can't let Dane or Lachlan know that I told you. As I said, Dane met Lachlan at University about fifteen years ago. They were both taking a degree in Renewable Resources. Dane's major was Environmental and Conservation Sciences so he could be a conservation officer and Lachlan's major was Forest Business Management. Lachlan's family owns a logging company in B.C. He and his twin brother were to take over the family business. In the summers between university sessions all three boys worked for Lachlan's dad." Jennifer readjusted on her stool.

"The summer between their first and second degrees was when Dane had his accident and was almost killed. Lachlan's old man had been pushing to meet a deadline. A load of logs weren't secured properly and they came rolling off the side of a truck. Dane's leg was crushed, which ended his hope of working out in the field. That was when he decided to become a professor. Lachlan and his dad had a huge blowout over safety precautions and he left the company. His dad cut him off. Lachlan switched gears then and decided to be a conservation officer instead. His brother stayed with the company, which also led to their falling out." Jennifer eased herself off of a stool and into one of the kitchen chairs.

"Meanwhile, Lachlan had gotten a girl pregnant and married her earlier on that summer. When he left the company things went from bad to worse for him personally. Since he was estranged from his family, suddenly Rachael didn't want to be married to a little ol' forest ranger. She wanted the prestige of a logging baron. I never did like her, by the way. I could tell she was a gold digger and I believe she got pregnant just so that Lachlan would marry her. Lachlan had graduated with his second degree and took a posting in Saskatchewan. By now they had been married for about three years. Rachael got a waitress job in the evenings after they moved so they wouldn't have to pay for a babysitter. About six months later when Lachlan was out on a call, even though Amy had a fever Rachael left her with a sitter and went to work. When the young sitter went in to check on Amy and couldn't wake her up, instead of calling someone, she just left her."

The oven timer buzzed so Annah got up and turned it off.

"When Lachlan did get home and he checked, he realized that Amy was burning up and in a coma. They rushed her to the hospital but she died on the way. Lachlan tried to reach Rachael at work on the way to the hospital but he was told she wasn't there. He later discovered she was off with her lover. Lachlan blamed himself for Amy's death. He felt he should have been more attentive to Rachael and then she would have been home with Amy. I don't believe that. I think she wrote him off the second he had his falling out with his Dad and I think she was just waiting for some sugar daddy to come along before she left Lachlan. Needless to say they divorced and went their separate ways. Lachlan transferred to Ontario and now he works up North in Nunavut."

Annah stopped pouring her wine with a jerk, slopping it onto the island. It was just too much of a coincidence that two conservation officers could have followed exactly the same transfer path. What cruel twist of fate was making Annah spend the only free time she had had this week with the one man who had repeatedly seen her humiliated already today.

"Ah, Jen, his name wouldn't be Lachlan *MacGregor*, would it?" Annah inquired as she wiped up the spilled wine. Before Jen could answer the back door opened and male voices could be heard from the hall. Jen looked surprised and made a slicing motion across her throat indicating that their conversation was over. Annah laughed out loud, shaking her head as she wandered over to the window to check on the kids. Oh well, he already thought she was a flake, so she was confident she couldn't possibly make a more memorable impression than she already had. Boy was she wrong.

Dane and Lachlan walked into the kitchen. Dane gave Jennifer a kiss and a hug.

"Look what the cat dragged in," Dane said.

"Jen, it's wonderful to see you. I hope you don't mind the intrusion I understand you already have guests for dinner." Lachlan also gave Jen a hug. "I hear congratulations are in order, as I was told we might have a Christmas baby."

Dane walked over to the window as Annah turned around.

"Annah, although you have not been formally introduced, I understand you have already met my friend, Lachlan."

Annah and Lachlan walked towards each other, hands extended.

"I apologize for everything that I have said and done up to this point to either embarrass or upset you. Truce?" Lachlan sincerely offered.

"Absolutely. Apology accepted. Hi, my name is Annah. May I offer you a glass of Merlot? It is one of my personal favorites," Annah graciously replied.

Just then the back door opened and two rosy cheeked children and two snow encrusted dogs tumbled in. After the children were unbundled and melted snow puddles were mopped up, everyone sat down to a delicious dinner of spaghetti, salad, and garlic baguettes. Supper started out civil enough but when the discussion naturally turned to conservation and the changing roles of officers, things were bound to get heated. Both Lachlan and Annah had very strong ideas that were on very opposite sides of the debate. Dane watched the discussion with relish since he had purposely introduced it, while Jen just rolled her eyes and tried to keep the kids occupied. Annah rose from the table and proceeded to clear away the dishes, as the argument became more intense. Lachlan also got up and helped her. Dane and Jen remained at the table coloring with the kids and watching the drama unfold in front of them. Neither Annah nor Lachlan was conscious of the fact that they continued to work together despite their obvious different points of view.

"Look, I'm not saying that women aren't as intelligent as men because I know that they are. What I am saying is that in order to work effectively and safely out in the field there are certain attributes that men have, that women do not. In my opinion, women should be support staff that remains at the station, while men work out in the field. This arrangement would be in the best interest and safety of all members of the team."

"Oh, please continue, I'm waiting with baited breath to hear what those attributes might be," Annah sarcastically taunted.

"Men are physically stronger than women. Answer me honestly. If you were hanging off of a cliff held only by a rope with one officer on the other end would you want it to be a man or a woman?" Lachlan questioned.

"Actually, I wouldn't care if it were a man or a woman as long as that person had the presence of mind to secure that rope around the base of a tree or something else stationary. Then, I wouldn't only be relying on a single person's strength. Men have the disadvantage of egos, which most women don't. Most men would never believe "they couldn't possibly *not* be strong enough" to pull that person up. That arrogance could ultimately lead to the failure of the rescue. Women know they don't have the physical strength of men, therefore, they have to be smarter and use things like leverage to their advantage. Now, whom would you rather have on the other end of the rope?" Annah challenged.

"Point taken. But as we both know individual men and women can't be stereotyped into definite roles. Some women have egos just as large as some men, or "chips on their shoulders", so to speak because they feel they need to prove they are better than us."

"Absolutely," Annah agreed.

"Furthermore, most men think logically rather than emotionally. When placed in a highly stressful situation their training kicks in and procedures are implemented without emotion clouding their judgment. The cry of a wounded animal or human or the sight of a devastating accident will be handled with the same objectivity or "nerves of steel" that their everyday duties require."

Annah and Lachlan were washing and drying the dishes while their heated exchange continued.

She turned from the sink, scrub pad in hand and exclaimed, "You can't possibly be the head of a station and actually believe that. The level of training be it man or woman, which a person receives can determine the instinctive application of proper procedures in *every* situation. It has nothing to do with gender!"

Understandably, Annah was appalled by his chauvinistic caveman attitude. She made sure that he was left with no doubt as to what her opinion was concerning his narrow-mindedness. Her vehement response to what he thought were logical conclusions on his part took him off guard and before he realized it he was defending his position by using her as an example.

"I disagree and I also believe that men are better capable of maintaining a steady level of concentration no matter the outside influences. You can't possibly deny what happened in class today. You proved this point when I asked you a question that we both know you knew the answer to and yet you failed to respond. Because my presence had disconcerted you, you lost your train of thought. That type of response can put you, other members of your team, civilians, or animals in jeopardy."

Before Annah could explode, Jennifer deliberately tipped a class of milk onto the table, which forced Annah to rush over to mop up the spill. At that point Simon started to whine that he was tired. Annah was saved from telling Lachlan that he was a pompous jackass that should be stripped of his managerial position at his station. With a huff, she rinsed out the sink and hung the dishrag over the tap. She ran outside to start her truck. When she returned she thanked Jen and Dane for the meal and the evening, she coached the kids to say thanks, and then proceeded to herd them to the back door.

"Could you do me a favor and give Lachlan a lift to his hotel on your way home?" Dane whispered as he followed her to the back door. "It's not that far out of your way and I'd really like to give Jen a massage before she goes to bed tonight. She looks really tired and I think it would relax her. Plus, my leg is really achy tonight."

Although Annah would rather have eaten nails that spend one minute more in Lachlan's presence she couldn't possibly turn Dane down. She plastered a sunny smile on her face.

"It would be no trouble at all."

"Lachlan," Dane called. "Annah has offered to drop you at your hotel so that I don't need to head out into the cold. My leg seems to be giving me a bit of grief tonight. I hope you don't mind calling it an early night. Why don't we meet for breakfast tomorrow before you head back?"

"That sounds great. Thank you, for a lovely evening, Jen. Congratulations again and make sure you call as soon as your little bundle of joy arrives." Jen had now joined them at the door and Lachlan gave her a goodbye hug.

With a wave Annah picked up a very tired, very cranky Simon and headed for the truck. Summer and Lachlan followed. When everyone was buckled in Annah headed for the hotel. Simon was asleep before they left the driveway and Summer, not two minutes later. The remainder of the eight-minute drive was tense for Annah. She was still hopping mad, made even more so by the fact that she could tell he was not angry but instead rather amused by her anger. When she pulled to a stop in front of his hotel she turned in her seat to bid him a stilted goodnight. Her words were never spoken as he reached out, cupped her cheek, and looked into her startled emerald eyes. She froze. He leaned across the seat and kissed her slowly, gently brushing her lips with his. Her hands gripped the steering wheel. When his tongue snaked out and lined the crease where her lips met, they instinctively opened. As his tongue slipped in, his other hand came up and held her head. When Annah's sigh escaped, the tempo of the kiss changed from a gentle exploration to a full out assault on all of her senses. She kissed him back with a fierceness she didn't know she had in her. As he moved to pull her closer, sanity finally prevailed and Annah broke contact and pushed him away. Her eyes were wild; his smoldered with controlled passion. Her breath sawed in and out of her chest as she tried to bring herself back under control. With an aura of nonchalance, that belied his inner turmoil, he sat back against his seat. Better able to conceal his emotions than Annah he was stunned by the jolt of awareness he felt when he had kissed her and still marveled at the sensations that he hadn't felt in years. Defensively he chuckled.

"Well, again, my point has been made. Emotional responses made over logical ones tend to put some people in jeopardy. Good luck with your studies. Thank you for a very entertaining day. And thanks for the ride." With that he jumped out of the truck, grabbed his bag from the box, and with a mock salute, turned and sauntered off towards the hotel entrance.

If she was hopping mad before, now her temper was boiling. With an involuntary sob, Annah thumped the steering wheel with her clenched fist and as the tears of exhaustion and humiliation silently coursed down her cheeks she pulled back onto the street and headed home.

CHAPTER 3

HE RAN HIS TONGUE from her earlobe down her neck and feathered her collarbone with butterfly kisses. As his clever mouth drew in her distended nipple and suckled, Annah's back instinctively arched and her pelvis tilted. Clutching the sheets she gasped and tossed her head back and forth impatiently seeking fulfillment. Like the winding up of a spring toy her core tightened with each pull of his mouth. A chilly breeze swirled in from the open window of Annah's bedroom and danced across her T-shirt clad breasts puckering her nipples and sending a flash of pleasure into her subconscious. As another gust swooped over them, imaginary fingers of pleasure plucked at her and caused her to again involuntarily arch into the sensation. In her semi-conscious state she brushed her own hand across her breast further engorging the already aroused nipple. She gently moaned as her core continued to tighten and throb. Allowing her body to give into the pleasure she skimmed her hand down her chest, down her stomach and settled it at the top of her pubis. As the sleet gained strength and changed from a patter on the window to a pounding down-pour she stroked herself with ever increasing pressure and speed. Coincidentally, the resounding crash of her door slamming from the gusting wind covered the groan she unwittingly emitted as she came.

The crash and subsequent orgasm brought her full awake and as she lay gently panting, her body relaxed and flattened back onto the bed. As Annah's breathing and heart rate returned to normal she staggered out of bed, closed the window, opened her door, and crawled back under her sheets. Rolling onto her side she curled into a ball and tucked the duvet around herself as she settled in for a good cry. It was Lachlan's tongue she had fantasized was pleasuring her, not the imaginary lover she had created and used to fulfill past fantasies.

Crying herself to sleep and indulging in a personal pity party was not how Annah had envisioned waking up the next morning. Halloween was only three days away and costumes needed to be finished. There was no time for erotic dreams featuring icy blue-eyed sex gods.

Later that morning Jennifer came over to help finish the costumes. She was anxious to see how things had ended with Lachlan. Annah excluded the part about his mind blowing kiss and her early morning fantasy/nightmare and simply stated that she had dropped him off and continued home. She immediately changed the subject, which led Jen to draw the correct conclusion that more had gone on than Annah was willing to share. The sewing frenzy continued, while across town Dane and Lachlan shared breakfast.

"So, I thought you were going to play nice last night." Dane commented. "What happened to that claim?"

"Dane, I can't explain it but she just brought out the devil in me. I knew I was making her mad last night, but I just couldn't seem to stop myself. We obviously just need to steer clear of each other. This shouldn't be a problem since you and Jen have known both of us separately for years but our paths have never crossed before."

"So, the ride home was uneventful?"

"Yup. Uneventful. Well, if I'm going to make that plane we should really get a move on. I'll get the tab if you go get the truck." Lachlan quickly stood up and quickly went to pay the bill while Dane chuckled to himself and plotted a way to ensure that Lachlan's and Annah's paths would cross again.

After Halloween came the trip to the zoo and then it was almost time for Christmas. This was Annah's favorite time of the year. Since her only income was her husband's insurance, money was always tight. Bills came first, then Nanny Bea's pay, then food and clothing for the kids, and finally the little extras. Christmas was a time to restock their wardrobes with handmade PJs from PJ Elf, who came the night before Christmas Eve, and secondhand clothes from the "Quality New to You Store" around the corner. Annah and Nanny Bea stayed up many nights sewing, crafting, and baking homemade treats to make Christmas morning special. Annah's gifts were always homemade.

Annah's parents sent money every winter which Annah used to buy gas to travel to their home for Christmas and for toys for the kids. There would be two toys for each child, one from Grandma and Grandpa Andersson and one from Santa Claus. Annah traveled back to Saskatchewan every Christmas so that her children could spend it with their aunts, uncles, cousins and grandparents. Annah's husband had been an only child. On Boxing Day she always made the trip to his parent's house so they could spend time with the children as well. The journey back came only once a year. It was something Annah always looked forward to but she was always glad when they were returning home. Although her family loved her they couldn't understand her choice of careers and spent much of their time together trying to get her to move back so they could help her take care of the kids and make her life easier. After three and half years she couldn't seem to get them to understand that even though her life wasn't easy she was happy and so were her children.

Christmas Day had come and gone and so had Boxing Day and Annah still hadn't heard any news from Jen. She started phoning on the 27th and finally got an answer that evening.

"Hello, Knudsen residence." It was the voice that filled Annah's dreams. The one she couldn't get out of her head. It was the voice that made Annah's heart slam into her chest and made her stutter.

"H...Hello, Lachlan. This is Annah. Any news yet?" she pulled herself together.

There was a pause on the other end.

"Hey, Annah. How was Christmas?" Lachlan inquired.

"It was great, thank you! And yours?"

"I worked Christmas Eve, Christmas Day and Boxing Day to give the staff with families those days off. I arrived here today in time to take the anxiously expectant parents to the hospital. Where are you, by the way? Jen tried to call you but said she couldn't reach you."

"I always go to my parents in Saskatoon. My whole family spends Christmas there. It's great for the kids because they don't see their relatives very often. Jen knew where I was and has my cell number but when I checked my cell phone, just now, I realized it was dead. So, is there any news yet?" Annah posed the question again.

"Yes, there is but I'm sure Jen would rather tell you herself. I will tell you this much. Everyone is fine. What number can she reach you at now?"

"I'm leaving early tomorrow morning so tell her I'll come visit her instead as soon as I get back. I'll phone the house and if I don't get an answer I'll assume she's still at the hospital. What room is she in?" Annah asked.

"Her room number is 312. I'm staying at the house to take care of the dogs until they come home. I'm sure that, except to sleep, Dane will be spending every waking minute at the hospital. About what time will you be home tomorrow?

"It should be around four o'clock. I won't be leaving to visit though until after supper since Nanny Bea isn't back to work until the day before New Years, so I'll have to get a sitter."

"I'm at loose ends. I'd be happy to watch the kids while you run up to see Jen. You would only have to repay me with a supper. What do you say?"

The silence on the other end was telling. Lachlan knew she was not comfortable with him but for some reason he felt the need to see her.

"Come on, Annah, you must know your children would be safe with me. Or is it that I intimidate you in some way and make you uncomfortable?"

He knew he had thrown down the gauntlet again. Never say Annah wasn't up for a challenge. Just as expected she didn't disappoint him.

"Don't be ridiculous. You don't intimidate me and I know that you are no threat to my children. We eat at six o'clock. Could you please bring some milk and lettuce? I haven't been home for a week and won't have time to stop at the store. My address is 282A Pine Drive Court. It's the four-plex in the centre of the court."

"See you then," Lachlan disconnected with a smile.

Annah could feel his smile and replaced the receiver a little harder than she had planned. She was very leery after their last encounter. She hoped she would be able to remain unaffected by his presence. But he seemed to keep popping up in her dreams. It was almost always snapshots of them engaged in some heated sexual encounter, which was very disconcerting since she had no control over her dreams. Maybe a good tumble in the hay was all she really needed. It had been over four years. With Lachlan living so far up North and her moving after graduation, chances of ever running into each other again were slim to none. The more she thought about it the more she liked the idea.

Annah had only ever been with her husband, so one night stands were certainly not the norm. But this was 2008. She was a twenty-seven year old widow who was a fulltime mother and student with no time to meet anyone. She also had no interest in a long-term personal relationship right now. This was a man that she instinctively knew she would be safe with. She respected and trusted Dane and if he and Lachlan had been friends for years that certainly said something about Lachlan's character. It couldn't be more perfect. She believed she had felt a response in him when they kissed, so it would simply be a matter of getting up the courage to proposition him. She'd have to give this idea some serious thought on the drive home tomorrow since he'd be leaving again in a couple of days and then her opportunity may be lost.

⌒◡

Annah arrived home in time to pull a casserole from the freezer and pop it in the oven, bath the kids, take a quick shower herself, and throw in a load of laundry. The doorbell rang as she started to set the table. Summer and Simon ran to the door. Annah shooed them away and looked through the peephole. Just the sight of him made her breath catch. It was ridiculous, this affect he had on her. Annah squared her shoulders, took a deep breath, and pulled open the door. Lachlan stood there with his hands full of grocery bags.

"You look like you bought out the store," Annah observed accusingly as she relieved him of some of his burden.

"No. I just know what it's like to come home after being gone for several days. There's no fresh fruit, veggies, eggs, milk, etc. Now you'll be set for a couple of days. I'm sure that grocery shopping with two kids must be an adventure."

"Yes, it is. Thank you. What do I owe you?"

"It's on me. Since you're doing the cooking, it's the least I could do."

Lachlan could feel Annah stiffen up. He knew he had offended her and mentally kicked himself.

"Thanks, Lachlan. But I insist on paying you back. Summer, can you please take Mr. MacGregor's coat and hang it up? Then, please, finish setting the table so we can eat. Simon, can you come and help Mommy put the groceries away?"

Supper went smoothly since Summer kept them entertained with stories about things that she had seen or heard over the Christmas holidays. When Annah looked at the time she realized she needed to get a move on if she was going to make it to the hospital before visiting hours were over. Lachlan assured her that he and the kids could handle the clean up and so she left.

⌒ː

Annah rushed in the door at eight thirty hoping to catch the kids still awake, so that she could give them a goodnight kiss and tell them about Jen and Dane's surprise. Unfortunately, both were sleeping. It had been a busy Christmas and they were both worn out, even though they had napped most of the drive home. Lachlan was sitting in the living room looking through a photo album when she walked in. Although she was considering having sex with him she didn't want him to know any more about her personal life than he already did. She didn't want a relationship with him. She just wanted the sex. Annah's place was small and with Lachlan in the room it somehow made that space seem even smaller. Sometimes his very presence was overpowering. Maybe the sex wasn't such a great idea after all.

"I hope the kids were good. I'm sorry I'm late. I wanted to catch them before they went to sleep," Annah babbled breathlessly as she peeled off her coat.

Lachlan could tell she was on edge now that they were alone. "Everything was fine. They did tell me, however, when we were reading a story, that even though they love Nanny Bea, they wished they could spend more time with you."

Annah was instantly on the defensive. She straightened her spine and scornfully responded, "Unfortunately, if we want to continue to eat, I need to be gainfully employed at some point. In a perfect world I might be able to stay home or at least not be gone quite as much but my world seems to fall a little short of perfect."

"I wasn't criticizing you. I just wanted to share with you what they had told me. I thought as a mother you would appreciate that," Lachlan stated quietly and coolly as he stood and handed the album to her.

Annah blushed. "I apologize for jumping down your throat. I get very defensive regarding my parenting since I do receive a lot of criticism from my family. Apparently if I moved home I could take a nice secretarial course and then my family could help take care of my poor fatherless children. I also wouldn't need as much income since I wouldn't need a nanny." She sighed, closed her eyes, and rubbed her forehead. What was wrong with her? She had just been silently cursing that Lachlan was intruding on her personal life and now she was handing it to him on a silver platter.

"Thank you, for coming and watching the kids so that I could go. It was very generous of you and much appreciated. Please forgive my outburst. It's been a long day."

"Annah, you have beautiful, well-adjusted children. Don't let anyone tell you any differently," Lachlan stated firmly. "Now, what did you think of the surprise?"

"Oh, I'm so glad you didn't tell me. They are absolutely beautiful!" Annah gushed as her eyes shone and she clasped her hands to her chest. "I'm supposed to tell you they finally picked names. They chose Kai and Mikael. Jen and the boys are going to be released tomorrow but you aren't to tell anyone. Dane wants Jen to get some rest that first night home. They have had so much company she's wiped out."

"I'll make sure I've cleared out before they get home then," Lachlan commented as he put his coat on while walking to the back door.

"No!" Annah exclaimed and then blushed again when she realized how forcefully that had come out. "Jen was saying she hoped you would stay and celebrate New Year's Eve with them. They won't be able to go anywhere but she still wanted to have a nice supper and maybe play some games."

Gesturing back towards the kitchen she asked, "Did you want a coffee or something to drink before you leave?"

"Look Annah, I know I make you uncomfortable and tonight you're tired after driving all day. I think it's best if I just say goodnight. I don't want to be accused of taking unfair advantage of you later. I'll think about staying another couple of days. That way we will have another opportunity for some mental sparring. I'm assuming you'll be attending this little bash."

"Yes. Jen asked me and two other couples to come. I volunteered to do supper. Nanny is coming home tomorrow and has been pushing me into finding something to do for New Years. I think we'll fondue."

"I'll probably see you Friday then. Goodnight."

As Lachlan turned and reached for the doorknob Annah stepped forward and placed her hand on his arm. He stopped and looked down at his arm and then back at her questioningly. Annah knew it was now or never.

"Lachlan, will you have sex with me?" Annah blurted out.

Lachlan slowly pivoted his whole body back towards her with a stunned expression on his normally unexpressive face.

"Wh....What did you say?" he stammered. If he lived to be a hundred Annah couldn't possibly have said anything that would have shocked him more. This was so far beyond the expected that he simply stood there speechless.

"Please, come in and sit down so I can explain," Annah requested quietly. Now that the decision had been made and the proposition voiced there was no turning back and she was quite calm. She let her hand fall off his arm and walked back into the kitchen. Lachlan removed the shoes he had just put on and followed her.

"I think I'll have that drink now," he reversed his original decision as he grabbed a chair and sat at the table.

"I only have red wine and scotch," she offered.

"Scotch straight up is fine."

Annah found a single shot glass and a wineglass and poured their drinks. She handed him his and sat down across from him. She took a fortifying sip of wine, then a deep breath, and looked him straight in the eye. She leaned forward in her chair and with steepled fingers under her chin she ploughed forward.

"I haven't been with anyone since Thomas died. Until you kissed me, remembering what it felt like to be a woman with needs was the farthest thing from my mind. Unfortunately, now that I have re-membered I seem to be obsessing over it. I hoped that if you were interested we could spend one evening together and then both go our separate ways. I'm pretty sure that this isn't the way a woman goes about seducing a man but I just don't have the time or inclination to try to figure out how to be coy. Basically, what I'm looking for is a "wham, bam, thank you, Mam" and then goodbye. You'll be going back up North after New Year's Eve and I'll be moving after graduation so we could simply have one night and then go back to our lives."

Lachlan's gaze hadn't wavered during her speech.

"So, what's the advantage for me? I know why you want this, but what do I get?"

Annah blinked and choked on her swallow of wine.

"I don't understand the question. I thought it would be perfectly obvious what you get. You get one night of uncomplicated, no strings, no expectations, and no demands sex." Annah blushed again. "Forget it. I obviously read you wrong. I didn't mean to throw myself at some-one who isn't interested in me. I didn't mean to put you in an awk-ward position. Maybe you should go now." Annah pushed her chair back and stood up.

This time, before she could walk away, Lachlan reached out and clasped her arm in his iron grip. It didn't hurt but it was definitely unbreakable.

"I didn't say I wasn't interested. I just wanted you to explain what you thought the benefit was to me. Some people incorrectly assume that I'm a player and obviously you're one of them."

"Actually, I hadn't analyzed it that deeply. You're a single adult male and as a woman I've been programmed to believe that most guys want no strings sex anytime they can get it. Since I have no real experience in this area I was basing my assumption on comments other women have made about men in general. If I'm wrong, I'm sorry. I didn't mean to offend you."

"I'm actually more stunned than offended by your request. I'm sure I'd be safe in guessing that most men have never found themselves in quite this situation before," he explained. "When and where did you want this event to take place?"

Annah continued to stand although Lachlan had released her. "I thought we could spend the evening with Jen and Dane and then get a hotel room, which I would pay for. You could tell them you preferred to stay at a hotel so you didn't disturb their new family routine. Nanny will be responsible for the kids until I return. I don't want anyone to know about this, including Nanny, Jen, or Dane. I believe this would be nobody else's business. I don't want anyone else involved. Do you understand?"

"Well, you certainly seem to have the whole thing planned out. Do you have any special requests?" he inquired.

"I've only been with Thomas. My tastes are pretty basic and I have no expectations. Sex with a little cuddling after would be nice. What do you need from me?"

"Nothing."

"I'll book the room tomorrow then. Was the hotel you stayed in last time okay? Oh, I'm not on any birth control so if you can handle the condoms, I'll talk to a pharmacist about getting something for me to use as well."

"I think that should cover everything. Except, I'll get the room and pay for it since I'll also be staying there tomorrow night," he replied. Lachlan shot back the remainder of the scotch he'd been sipping, stood up, and again preceded her to the back door.

He put his shoes back on and then stood up and cupping her face with both hands he brushed his lips over hers. She grabbed his forearms but did not pull away. While his look bored into her eyes he kissed the corners of her mouth and when her lips instinctively parted he slipped his tongue inside. The intensity of the kiss went from slow, gentle caressing to deep and drugging. As heat started to coil and then pool in Annah's core her knees started to buckle and her eyes drifted closed. Lachlan moved his hands to her waist and back of her head and maneuvered her against the hall wall.

"Open your eyes," he demanded. "I'll play your little game but I want you always to be aware of who you're with. I won't be some fantasy of someone else for anyone."

With that Annah opened her eyes and was impaled with the passion flaring in his. The rhythm of his tongue made her throb. Tentatively, she stroked his tongue back. Her inexperience surprised but delighted him.

As suddenly as he had begun Lachlan stopped. Annah panted and clutched at his arms as he eased away from her. Her emerald eyes were glazed over and even more luminous than usual. When he was sure she was steady he backed away towards the door and whispered, "That was just a taste, Annah. I promise that after Friday night you'll be good to go for another four years."

With that he quietly pulled the door closed after him. Annah reached over, locked the door, and then slid to the floor. My God. What had she done? What monster had Lachlan unleashed inside her? She had always enjoyed sex and believed that she and Thomas had a good sex life, but she had never felt lust like this before. This could well be the biggest mistake she had ever made. But, there was no turning back now. Not only did she not want to lose face, but also if she was totally honest with herself, she could admit that she wanted this man more than she had ever wanted any other. Reaching up she touched her bruised lips. Oh, she had it bad. Realllllly bad!

CHAPTER 4

ANNAH SPENT ALL OF the next day playing with her children. The temperature was only -5° Celsius so the snow was perfect for making a snow fort in the backyard and a family of snowmen to live in it. The kids chased the cat in and out of the fort while Annah went in to make supper. After supper came baths and stories and bed. Annah had just sat down to make her list for the fondue when she heard Nanny open the back door.

She jumped up from the sofa she had curled herself into and went to help Nanny Bea with her luggage. Then they sat down for a cup of tea to relate their Christmas stories and talk about the new babies. It was nice to be able to sit and visit without Annah having to worry that she should be studying.

"So," Nanny questioned, "what are your plans for tomorrow night?" She fully expected Annah to have none. "And don't tell me you haven't thought about it or haven't had time to make plans with anyone because I warned you that if you didn't have a plan I was goin' have one for you." She straightened up in her armchair and crossed her arms preparing for an argument.

"I'm going over to Jen and Dane's to have a fondue and play games with them, two other couples, and Dane's friend, Lachlan. No kids allowed, except for the babies, of course. Would you classify that as appropriate New Year's Eve activities?" she asked smugly.

"That depends. Who is this old friend of Dane's and is he single?"

"Actually, he is single and he went to University with Dane. I told you about him before. He's that conservation officer who works up in Nunavut. I met him in October when he was down to give a lecture. He's the guy that was at Jen's house the night we went for supper just before Halloween, remember? He came down after Christmas to spend a few days with them. Since he was here and looking after Jen's dogs he offered to watch the kids for me last night so I could go to the hospital. As far as tomorrow night goes, I plan on having a fun evening without the pressure of trying to impress some blind date."

"Alright, I approve. Some nice young single banker or dentist from here would have made me happier but at least you're going out. What are you planning for your fondue?"

Annah and Nanny got down to the business of making a grocery list. Annah could use some of the extra money she had gotten from her parents for Christmas to buy the groceries. It would be the Christmas present she hadn't bought for herself yet. It seemed frivolous to have nothing to show for it when she was done but Jen and Dane were so good to her and the kids it was also a way she could pay them back. Knowing she may have a long day tomorrow, Annah decided to turn in.

⁓

Annah took Summer shopping with her just so they could spend some time alone. They chatted about Summer having playmates over during the remainder of the holiday and planning a skating party. After picking up the groceries and her birth control supplies, there was some money left over. Annah decided to splurge on some new undies for tonight. She also found a discounted pearl necklace that would go perfect with her dress. Every girl deserved a little pick me up now and then. Even though Lachlan would be the only person to see her in her lingerie, she knew that every day she wore it afterwards, she would remember tonight and it would give her a boost.

When Annah and Summer returned home Nanny helped her chop and prepare everything for the supper while the kids played out in their fort. Then Nanny hustled Annah off to bathe, shave, and get dressed, while she freshened up the little black dress Jennifer had talked Annah into buying, after Christmas last year. Annie put her hair up, put on her new underwear, and shimmied into her little black sheath. She finished her toilette by putting on her pearls, and packing her purse. Lastly she kissed the kids and headed out the door. Her stomach fluttered as she thought about the upcoming evening's events.

As soon as Annah pulled up outside of Jen's, Lachlan and Dane came out to the truck to help her haul stuff in. My. ....my........ Lachlan certainly did look dashing tonight; there was that word again, *dashing*, Annah silently acknowledged as she handed him boxes. It was an appropriate description, though. While the guys unpacked Annah slipped off her boots, grabbed her black stilettos, and tiptoed up the stairs to see the babies. Both were sleeping peacefully. Jen came up behind her dressed in her robe.

"They are so beautiful, Jen. I couldn't be happier for you two," Annah quietly enthused as she gave her girlfriend a hug. "How are you feeling?"

"I'm a little sore and, of course, I'm tired but so far the nanny has been great. She's going to take the nights and I'm on days. Even when Dane goes back to work I know I'll be okay. I'm nursing during the day and we're supplementing at night. Mom isn't happy that I won't let her help more, but I told her that we want her to come and enjoy them. I don't want her to come over and feel like she's obligated to care for them when she has already raised her own babies."

"She'll get over it. They say "once a mother, always a mother." She just wants to take care of *her* baby because she knows you need help. Our mothers don't understand why we would use a nanny when they are perfectly willing to help us. What they don't realize is that it's better for everyone, including our children. Hang in there. If she gets really bent out of shape send her my way and I'll try to take some pressure off by using myself as an example. I should go help the guys now, and let you finish getting dressed."

"I'll be down right away. Dane and I want to talk to you and Lachlan before the others get here. By the way, you look like a million bucks. When was the last time you heard me saying that! See what a little effort and some sleep can do. Aren't you glad I made you pick up that dress last winter? Has Lachlan seen you with your coat off yet? His jaded old blue eyes are going to pop right out of his head."

"Jennifer, do you think Lachlan is a player? He certainly looks the type."

"Honestly, Annah, I know that's the image he portrays but I don't believe he is. As far as Dane and I know he leads a pretty solitary life. It's like he doesn't think he deserves to be happy or live a real life since Amy didn't get to live out hers. I think that's why he lives so far north. It's not like there are a lot of single women up there. I wish he would move back down and start living again. Amy's death was not his fault and he does deserve to be with someone nice and to have more children. He really was a good father and given a second chance with the right woman I know he could be a great husband."

"Jen, everyone mourns in their own way in their own time. I imagine both of us have our own form of survivor's guilt. Lachlan will heal and he'll know when he's ready to move on. Speaking of which I had better get a "move on" or we won't be having a fondue tonight."

Annah skipped nimbly down the stairs into the kitchen. Lachlan was taking fondue pots and fuel out of a box and looked up at the sound of her heels clicking across the kitchen tiles. Jen wasn't far off when she had guessed that Lachlan's eyes were going to pop. Annah cleaned up real nice. Lachlan had noticed that she was pretty the first time he bumped into her. The more time he spent with her the more he noticed her individual attributes. Tonight she was a knockout. She sported a classic updo, a little black body stocking that hugged every curve, and four inch stiletto heels.

Without being aware of any reaction she had caused Annah moved over beside Lachlan and began to set up the fondue pots. Furtively, she continued to sneak peeks at the impeccably dressed gentleman that she was lucky enough to be sleeping with later tonight. Knowing that she was going to be secretly indulging in an illicit affair was certainly adding to her sexual tension. She directed Dane and Lachlan to fill the pots with cooking oil and the burners with fuel. Then she set the table, Dane uncorked the wine, and Lachlan laid out the food Annah had prepared. When Jen came downstairs she noticed Lachlan watching Annah and Annah peeking at Lachlan and inwardly smiled.

"May I have your attention, please? Dane and I would like to ask you and Lachlan to be our children's Godparents," she proclaimed.

"I would be honored," Annah choked out as her eyes glistened with tears.

"Likewise," Lachlan responded.

At that moment the doorbell rang announcing the others. So much for never seeing each other again, Annah realized. Now that they were going to be the boys' Godparents they would, at the very least, be together again for the Baptism. Well, there was no turning back now and Annah felt confident that they would still be exposed to each other minimally over the ensuing years.

The evening officially began. After the fondue they all moved to the living room and divided into couples to play Trivial Pursuit. All three teams turned out to be evenly matched and the game continued until after midnight. At twelve thirty Dane and Jennifer emerged victorious. Vehicles were started and the guests departed with well wishes for a "Happy New Year" resounding down the driveway. Annah was the last one to leave.

Once in the truck Annah followed Lachlan to his hotel. She parked, Lachlan opened her door, offered her his hand, and walked with her arm in arm into the hotel as she was still wearing her stilettos and it was slippery. When they arrived at Lachlan's room he opened the door and ushered her in with a flourish. As Annah shrugged out of her coat she surveyed the room with amazement and delight. The lights were dimmed. Lachlan had rented a suite not just a room. Champagne chilled in a bucket on the buffet beside a bowl of strawberries. Steam beckoned from a hot tub out on the deck. Jazz played softly in the background. The room was warm and inviting.

"Thank you, for agreeing to this," she said simply.

"Thank you, for asking me to be your partner," Lachlan returned. He took her coat and his own and hung them in the closet.

"Excuse me please, while I go freshen up." She grabbed her purse and headed towards the washroom. She inserted her dissolving birth control and took a deep breath to try to slow down her racing heart. When she left the washroom she found Lachlan standing by the window with a champagne flute in his hand staring out at the gently falling snow. He felt her presence and so turned back towards her. Annah picked up two strawberries off the buffet on her way over to join Lachlan. She handed him one and took a bite out of hers. He took a bite and offered her his flute. When the glass was empty they put their strawberry stems inside and Lachlan set the glass on the floor.

"May I have this dance?" he gently inquired as he reached out to take her hand.

Annah moved into his arms without uttering a sound. As they swayed to the music wrapped in each other's arms Lachlan feathered butterfly kisses over Annah's face and down her neck. A small moan escaped Annah and she tunneled her fingers through Lachlan's hair at the nape of his neck. He caressed her back and began to peel her little black dress off her shoulders while he continued to kiss her, with slightly more ardor. As he continued to peel her dress down Annah was forced to pull her hands down out of his hair until he had her arms trapped at her sides within her own sleeves. He held her arms at her side and stepped slightly away from her to gaze upon what he had revealed. Black silk straps with black lace demi-cups held Annah's voluptuous, satiny, milk white breasts. The top of the scalloped cups barely covered Annah's straining nipples. Annah's faux black pearl necklace hung nestled in her cleavage. Lachlan bent his head and flicked his tongue across one distended nipple through the lace.

Annah should have felt at least a twinge of trepidation or a fissure of fear. She didn't. Although she would never be able to explain it she knew she was supposed to be with this man. She knew she was safe with him. Annah's breath caught as she unconsciously leaned into him. He continued to lave her first nipple and then turned his attention to her other one. Annah was starting to softly pant as she strained to free her hands.

"Please Lachlan, I need to touch you," she beseeched quietly.

He raised his mouth and replied, "Not yet."

Holding her trapped arms he used his teeth to pull down the first bra strap and then licked and sucked his way down to her elbow. It was a sensation Annah had never experienced. Her fogging brain recognized that she was in for a night of unforeseen pleasures. Lachlan treated the other arm to the same. Grasping the front of her bra at her cleavage with his teeth, and burying his face, he tugged at it just enough to free her straining breasts. Then he suckled at her greedily with no barriers. Annah's head was flung back and Lachlan moved his hands from her wrists to open her clenched hands and entwine his fingers with hers. Annah's legs started to tremble, so Lachlan released her hands and swept her up into his arms to deposit her gently into the middle of the king-sized bed. The movement created a slight breeze that chilled Annah's overheated skin.

Lachlan unclasped Annah's bra and peeled it and that little black dress off her body. Then he stood at the end of the bed worshipping her with his eyes. Her pearls, her black stockings and garter belt, matching lace thong, and her stilettos offered little concealment to her obvious attributes. As she lounged back on her elbows on the bed trying to get her breathing back to normal, Lachlan finally started to remove his own layers. First came off the jet black tailored suit coat. Then the buttons at the wrists of his white dress shirt were undone. One by one the buttons that traveled down the front were opened. He slipped off his socks and shoes and pulled off his belt. As he knelt on the bed he tugged his shirt out of his pants and then flung it to the floor. He reached out and caressed her cheek.

"Remove your pearls and take your hair down," he quietly instructed. She backed herself up against the headboard and pulled off her necklace and slowly removed pins to uncoil the masterpiece. Her hair hung in fat golden curls over her breasts and shoulders. Again he reached out, but this time he used one of her own curls of hair to feather across her nipple. Wrapping his hand around one of her ankles he pulled her back down onto the bed so that she lay completely horizontal. Placing the pearls on the nightstand he produced two silk scarves and loosely bound her hands to the spindles of the headboard. Next he sank down beside her and as he kissed her and licked her from her fingertips to the tops of her nylon hose he continued to caress her with his large work roughened hands. The friction of his hands on her smooth, hose covered skin was in direct contrast to the slick movements of his clever tongue. Annah's hands began to strain at her bindings as she squirmed under his ministrations.

"Please, let me touch you," she requested again.

"Not yet," he whispered as he moved back up her body.

He had touched every part of her except the part that was clenching and lubricating itself. His hands went back to work as he continued to kiss her and lick her. One skillful hand finally tripped over her garter belt and slipped under her thong to cup her mound. Annah almost came with that simple touch, she was so over stimulated. She instinctively arched into his hand as he dipped one finger into her and then stroked upwards. That was all it took. With a gasp Annah tightened her grasp on the spindles and stiffened. Lachlan was far from finished. Knowing he needed to slow things down to build her back up to a more satisfy, shattering conclusion he began to French kiss her with the same tempo he was using to stroke her.

Then without warning he added a second finger and increased the tempo. Annah shifted restlessly and clutched the spindles. He released Annah's right hand from the scarf. Holding it above their heads he entwined his fingers with hers. Lachlan continued to increase the tempo and started stroking in circles as he dropped his head and went back to kissing her neck and suckling at her breasts. Annah could feel herself winding tighter and tighter as he nipped at a nipple and ground his thumb into her clitoris. She arched and exploded into a million little pieces. Wave after wave crashed over her as he continued to stroke at a steady but slower pace. As he smoothed his hand back up her body she slowly sank flat onto the bed and her left hand slid bonelessly off of the spindle. As her insides continued to clench and her labored breathing evened out Lachlan released both her hands and shifted away from her to undo and remove his pants. He pulled off his boxers, and kneeling on the bed proceeded to unclip her garter belt. As he slid off her belt and thong Annah gulped at her first sight of Lachlan's engorged penis. Annah knew this was a night she was never going to forget. He had already given her more than she had ever experienced.

Lachlan removed one stiletto shoe and then peeled the first stocking down her leg. Next he removed the second shoe and stocking. He ran his hands up the insides of Annah's thighs and opened the foil package he had pulled out of his pants pocket and placed it on the bed beside them. After sheathing himself in latex Lachlan knelt between her open legs and placed them over each his shoulders. He bent his head and the assault started all over again. This time Annah grasped the spindles in both hands unconsciously without being prompted or restrained. Still being hyper-sensitized it took only minutes to bring her back to the brink again. As she started to thrash Lachlan slid his body up hers and smoothly entered her, a little more, with each thrust until finally she was impaled on him up to his hilt. He stilled, letting her adjust to the fullness and to slow his own impending orgasm down. As he hovered over her he unclasped her hands from the spindles and again entwined his fingers in hers.

"Open your eyes, Annah," he quietly requested. "I don't want you to have any doubt as to who you are with."

"There was never, nor will there ever be, any doubt that it's you," she smiled up at him with a satisfied promise. Her eyes were glassy and her face flushed and he knew he had never seen a more beautiful sight.

He began to move and with every thrust drew them both closer and closer to the inevitable conclusion. The muscles in his forearms, chest, and neck corded and with a groan he emptied himself into Annah just as Annah arched into him finding her own release again. As he lowered himself onto her, her muscles continued to clench and milk him. He rolled them onto their sides so as not to crush her and wrapped her into his arms. They remained connected and he continued to caress her back until her contractions receded. He hugged her and kissed her forehead gently. As she dozed off he slipped out of her, covered her with a blanket and went to the washroom.

When he came back Annah was up and wrapped in a sheet collecting her various articles of clothing.

"Do you have a curfew?" Lachlan inquired.

"No," Annah giggled.

"Then, my dear, we are not finished yet. You told me we had all night." Lachlan grabbed some water bottles from the fridge and a new condom and reached his hand out to Annah. She dropped her clothes and padded over to him. He pulled her to him, unwound her, and then led her out to the hot tub. He stepped in and helped her ease in beside him. The snow continued to drift down in big fat flakes. Annah raised her face to them, enjoying the sensations of the frosty air on her head and shoulders, the warm water swirling around her naked body, and the cold snowflakes melting on her heated skin. Annah stretched her arms out and laughed for the sheer joy of living. She had experienced more sensations in the last hour than she had her entire married life. Although her husband had been an adequate lover she had had no other experience and assumed that she was one of those women who were non-orgasmic. Lachlan had certainly blown that theory to hell.

Lachlan sat across from her totally enthralled by her. She was inexperienced but very passionate and obviously willing to learn more and to explore her own sexuality. She had no idea what effect she was having on Lachlan and for that he was relieved. The orgasm he had shared with Annah was beyond just sex. With that knowledge she would have power. He had vowed he would never again let someone else hold that kind of power over him. He would teach her more, awaken more of her senses, and then walk away. Lachlan stood, rolled on another condom, sank back down, and then pulled her on to his lap.

While the warm water and steam swirled around them Lachlan rested his hands on Annah's hips. She began drawing herself up and down his shaft. At first her movements were fast and jerky. Kissing her he gently encouraged her and suggested she slow down until she found a rhythm she was comfortable with. Settling down she soon mastered the art of riding. As the snowflakes continued to drift down, Lachlan found a second release as he slid his hand between their bodies and stroked her at the same pace. Grinding herself into his crotch with the onset of her orgasm she pulled him over the edge into his. Sitting wrapped in each other's arms they waited for their heart rates to even out. Lachlan grabbed a water bottle and uncapping it took a long pull before passing it to Annah. After quenching her thirst Annah eased herself off of Lachlan.

"I need to get out, Lachlan. I'm so hot I'm going to pass out, if I don't."

"I'll be right in," he promised as he helped her out. Watching her heart-shaped rear-end wiggle as she returned to the room Lachlan rose and disposed of the used condom. Although he usually liked them long and lean there was definitely something to be said for petite and curvy. Those breasts bobbing in the water were a memory he wasn't soon going to forget.

Lachlan returned to the room and after drying each other off they collapsed on the bed. Exhausted, Annah drifted off. Before Annah's wake-up call came at six o'clock she awoke dreaming that Lachlan had slid into her from behind, stroking her as he pumped her. She realized it wasn't just a dream when Lachlan pulled her leg over top of his to increase his penetration. As she moaned and moved with him Lachlan seemed to jerk awake and realize what he was doing and that he wasn't wearing a condom. Instantly pulling out he rolled away from her, grabbed a condom from the nightstand, and returned to resume. Still half asleep, the implications of Lachlan's actions didn't register with Annah and she welcomed him back to bring them both to completion. Once the aftershocks of her orgasm had faded away Annah glanced at the clock and realized it was time to leave.

"I need to go, Lachlan," she whispered.

He opened his eyes and turned her towards him. He hugged her and kissed her tenderly.

"I know," he released her. She slipped out of bed and got dressed. Annah pulled her hair into a ponytail, brushed her teeth, and washed her face. As she was washing her face the truth hit her. Lachlan had been pumping into her without protection! When she returned Lachlan was up making coffee and wandering around in his boxers. He really did have a magnificent body. Someday he was going to make some woman very happy. He was an incredible lover, both gentle and aggressive, both giving and demanding. He was smart and funny, and he was good with children. Quite a catch if you could put up with the arrogance and chauvinistic attitude and the brooding silences that she just knew must be a part of him.

Lachlan helped her shrug into her coat and as she put on the boots she reached out for the doorknob, turned to Lachlan, and opened her mouth. Before she could utter a sound he pulled her into his arms and kissed her zealously, then drew back and tapped her on the nose.

"We need to talk about the possible consequences of what happened this morning. Although you were protected when I came, there is a slight chance that you may be pregnant. I didn't mean for this to happen and though it's no excuse I was honestly asleep when I started making love to you. If you are pregnant promise me you will not be too proud or stubborn to contact me."

"I promise. Thank you for a night that I won't soon forget." Annah licked her swollen lips and took his hand. She kissed the palm of his hand and folded it closed before she walked out the door.

As Annah made her way out to her truck she wondered, not for the first time, if sleeping with Lachlan was not possibly the biggest mistake she could ever have made. Who could have known how passionate she could be. He had shown her a side of herself that she hadn't known existed and now that it had been revealed she was afraid she was going to want to explore it even more. Oh, Annah, somehow I don't think that last night is going to keep you satisfied for another four years, she said to herself, as she drove home. And good grief, Annah prayed that this morning's slip didn't lead to pregnancy.

Last night had certainly been a pleasant surprise, Lachlan reflected. But, then possibly not as much of a surprise as the night Annah had propositioned him. To the average person she would appear confident but reserved. He should have known that perky little thing would end up being a firecracker in bed after watching her display at their first encounter. It was easy for her to say this was a one-time thing and she might even try to believe that, but Lachlan knew better. What they had shared last night was something special that he had never felt before and he knew she had felt it, too. This was far from over. He had slipped her pearls into his pocket while she was in the bathroom and planned to save them for their next encounter.

"Farewell, for now, sweet Annah," he whispered to the raspberry coated backside of Annah as he watched her climb into her truck and drive away. "This is far from goodbye."

CHAPTER 5

Annah's life went on pretty much the same as it had before the night with Lachlan, with the exception that now her dreams were even more erotic than they had been before. She had four months left of school and then it was on to the real world of working. She buckled down and threw herself full force into studying and training. During the day she had no time to think about him, but occasionally, unbidden, a vision would pop up.

She had sent applications out to all the conservation stations in Western Canada, and had received several responses to them. She did have many points in her favor. She was in the top ten of her class, both academically and on the training field. Also being female was an asset. There was a push on politically to hire more minorities including females, in all sectors of government organizations. And she was able to offer life experience since she was older than most of the other students, and had a family.

So when the secretary from the Nordegg Detachment called Annah and requested she come for an interview, Annah was beside herself. This would definitely be one of her first picks. She had camped in this area as a child with her family and had very fond memories of it. Annah didn't think twice about the fact that Mrs. Larson had asked to speak with Glenn Andersson and then paused when Annah told her she was speaking to her. Although, she hardly ever used her first name, she knew that most people assumed it was a man's name. She was used to their reactions when they discovered it was not. She did wonder, however, why Mrs. Larson had chuckled and then seemed exceptionally eager for Annah to attend the interview. Since Mrs. Larson seemed so friendly Annah decided to ask her about the school situation and housing. It turned out that Nordegg had a school that went from Grade One to Grade Eight. After Grade Eight, students were bussed into Rocky Mountain House, an hour away. For the successful applicant there was the option of renting a staff residence. Being able to rent rather than having to buy a house was a huge drawing card for Annah.

Annah made arrangements to take the kids with her and make a little holiday out of it since the interview was on a Saturday morning. She booked into the Nordegg Lodge for Friday night and asked Nanny to come and babysit during her interview. Then Nanny would have the rest of her weekend off to go see her grown kids in Calgary.

Annah learned through the grapevine at school that the head of this station had recently retired and no one seemed to know who had replaced him. Annah hoped it was someone with progressive thinking; someone without preconceived ideas on what women could and couldn't do. During the week Nanny role-played practice interviews with Annah trying to prepare her for every possible question that might be asked. When Friday night was upon her and she had the kids tucked into their hotel room, she had Nanny open the adjoining door to keep an eye on them while she bundled up and went outside for a walk.

Ice crystals danced in the crisp, clean air with every breath that Annah took. The almost full moon hung like a giant shimmering silver orb over the rugged shadowy snow-covered mountains, plum and amethyst in color. Annah made her way down the main street to the museum. Her Sorel boots crunched through the crust in the ruts on the side of the road. She pulled the fur on her hood closer to her face as she sat down and viewed the vista surrounding her. The village was quiet. There were several trucks parked in front of the village's only pub, which was attached to the hotel where Annah was staying. Except for the sporadic house lights that twinkled beyond in the foothills and the lights from the hotel, the village appeared largely uninhabited. There wasn't another living soul around, not even a dog within sight. Every now and then Annah heard the faint strains of some country honky-tonk coming from the jukebox playing in the pub. The only other sound she heard when a slight breeze came up was the occasional rasp of a tree branch as it scraped across one side of the museum.

This was exactly the place she wanted to raise her children. There was one general store for basic supplies that included a postal outlet and one gas station. There was a school, a museum, a golf course, and a laundry mat. Anything else you might need could be purchased in Rocky Mountain House. There they could catch a show, go swimming, bowling, or to the library. What more could a single mother of two small children ask for? It was fairly isolated but close enough to civilization that a trip to town could certainly be made weekly. Annah believed this was a safe environment for the kids to grow up in and a place where they could learn to truly appreciate nature and the beauty found in simple things. With that thought she stood up, dusted off the ice crystals that had formed around her hood, and made her way back to her room. She was as prepared as she could possibly be for tomorrow. Now all she needed was some sleep and a little luck. Maybe her dreams of a satisfying career and financial security would finally come true.

Lachlan was exhausted as he drove into Nordegg to drop off the company mail on his way home. He had been scanning the road for wildlife as he entered the town limits. His breath caught in his throat when he could have sworn he saw a woman in a bright red coat with a fur trimmed hood wander across the street in front of him and enter the pub. He pulled up outside and strode into the bar to see if she was there or ask the patrons if they had seen where she had gone. The only woman they had seen all night was their waitress and she was definitely not wearing anything that resembled a long red wool coat. Lachlan left the pub shaking his head and thinking to himself that he really needed to get some sleep. Not only was he dreaming about

Annah at night but now he was hallucinating that he saw her when he was awake. He jumped back into his truck and after dropping off the mail headed out to the highway that would lead him home.

Lachlan had arrived at work at five 'clock in the morning to get a jump on the staggering mess of paperwork his predecessor had left behind. Although the previous area manager had physically left only one week ago he had obviously, in reality, retired from working six months previously. On top of the paperwork that needed to be cleaned up Lachlan's bigger challenge was to combat the general feeling of complacency that had settled over most of the staff. The one shining star exempt from his monumental task of staff redirection and motivation was the secretary, Mrs. Larson.

At eight o'clock that morning, Lachlan chaired the first of his weekly staff meetings. He explained his expectations for his fellow officers and made promises in regards to his own conduct and duties. Next he completed several interviews for two new officer positions, reviewed the previous days' reports, and attended to the various miscellaneous duties of an area manager. As his day was winding down, he had two staff call in with the flu and he was forced to remain until replacement staff could be brought in. The station was extremely short staffed at present since he had two officers on sick leave and two officers on holidays. The one officer that was scheduled for tonight was already pulling a double shift so Lachlan worked almost another full shift himself until he was too tired to stay awake. It was now going on midnight and he had more interviews scheduled for the following morning beginning at eight o'clock. Thankfully, even with dropping off the mail, he had less than a five minute drive home.

The last month had absolutely flown by. Two days after his little encounter with Annah, upon returning to Nunavut, Lachlan had received a memo with the new available Western Canadian postings. The Nordegg station was on the list. Lachlan had been keeping an eye out for this one. He knew the area manager was planning on retiring and this location was just the one Lachlan had hoped to transfer to when he returned to "the land of the living", as Jennifer called it. It was isolated, which he preferred, and yet central enough that you were only an hour away from real civilization. His transfer request was almost immediately accepted and within two days he had tendered his own resignation and was packing to relocate. One month later he was waving farewell to the land he had called home for the last five years.

This was his first week at his new post. Every day he had spent ten to twelve hours at the station as he tried to familiarize himself with the staff and its dynamics. Added to this, more funding had finally come through allowing him to hire two more officers. He wanted this done as soon as possible to reduce the work load of the existing officers that would be strained beyond reason once they were organized and had their duties clarified. He wasn't going to be making any friends in the near future but hopefully, he would have a productive, proactive station within a year. Most of his new staff just needed a little leadership to be more effective in their jobs.

On his drive home he acknowledged to himself that the time had finally come to build his home and Nordegg was the perfect location. He had hoped to be able to review the architect's blueprints tonight so that he could approve any final changes to his new log house. Lachlan had kept the originals in storage now for about ten years. He wanted to be breaking ground by the first of May and it was already the beginning of February. Since dry prepared logs needed to be personally handpicked, this process took longer than preparing for a normal stick-built house. He had sent the original blueprints to an architect friend of his right after he'd given his notice. They were down to the wire, time-wise, for maintaining a reasonable building schedule for this year. Because he didn't want to miss anything crucial, the blueprints were just going to have to wait until after the interviews and he'd have to drive down to Calgary later than planned.

As he pulled into his driveway and noticed the big fat snowflakes drifting down, an image of Annah sitting in the hot tub with her face raised to the sky flashed through his mind. The moon was high and full, easing his walk to his back door. As he let himself in he wondered how her classes were going and where she would be applying for jobs. He knew he had been half-heartedly looking for an application from her in the pack but hadn't found one. In fact, he hadn't had a single female apply for either position. In some ways this was a relief since he did have reservations about their ability in the field. His superiors had already indicated that he should try to hire at least one female.

He knew if he received applications from any females he would have to prove they weren't qualified if he decided not to hire any of them. He knew that Dane thought he was only baiting Annah when the subject had come up all those months ago. But, he had been half serious. He had never been in the situation before where he had had to rely on either a woman's physical or mental strength. He wasn't sure he wanted to be.

With a self-deprecating grimace, he acknowledged that he obviously didn't know himself as well as he thought he did. He had truly believed that after he slept with Annah she would be like the others and he would be able to forget her and move on. It wasn't like there had been a lot of women since his divorce. He had made a rule of not sleeping with anyone he worked with and with living in a close-knit community like he had for the last five years, he believed it was best if he didn't sleep with anyone from town either. That left only women that he met on the few occasions when he actually left the North. Those he could count on one hand. Now, a day hadn't gone by that he hadn't thought of Annah at least once. Fate obviously had determined that Lachlan would never find peace. Now that he was healing from Amy's death, he was aching over not having a chance to build a new life. At least he would see Annah in another two weeks since Dane and Jen were having their twins baptized and they both needed to attend. He'd find out then where she had applied and if she was going to be close enough to even consider a long distance relationship.

Jesus, he must be tired he thought, as he mentally shook himself. Annah was the last person he needed to get involved with. He needed someone quiet and demur and willing to stay home and be a housewife and a mother. Annah was the exact opposite of that. She was passionate and vocal, in between the sheets and out. Annah was no shrinking violet and even if she were financially secure and married he knew she would still need to work. Being a conservation officer and contributing to her world was a spiritual thing for Annah. Lachlan could feel it. Annah was so *not* the woman he needed in his life. Lachlan shed his clothes and headed to the shower. Hopefully, that would relax him enough to be able to turn off his racing mind, and sleep.

Annah was up early and had time to stop at the gas station to buy a water bottle and mints before heading to the interview. As she jumped back into the truck she didn't realize that someone had parked a Jeep right behind her. She backed out and bumped into it. She jumped out and checked both vehicles for damage. There was none, but she headed back into the gas station to find the owner anyway. After quickly leaving her own insurance information, she didn't bother looking at what the other driver had written on the paper he had given her. She shoved it back into her purse and ran outside. If she didn't leave now she was going to be late. The driver followed her out of the store and moved the Jeep back so that she could leave.

What a way to start her morning. She wasn't exactly "Miss Calm, Cool, and Collected" anymore. She pulled up into the parking lot of the Conservation Station, turned off the truck, and took a deep breath. She popped in a breath mint and hurried into the office. A lady that looked to be fifty something was sitting at a desk at the entrance.

"May I help you?" she asked as Annah approached the desk.

"Yes, thank you," Annah replied. "I am here for an eight o'clock interview."

The lady's smile broadened into an almost ear-splitting grin. She thrust out her hand.

"Hi. You must be Glenn. I'm Mrs. Larson. I believe we spoke on the phone the other day. Please follow me. Officer MacGregor asked that I bring you in as soon as you arrived." She rose and indicated that Annah follow her.

Annah felt a shiver run up her spine and a sick feeling settled into the pit of her stomach. Instead of following Mrs. Larson she froze at the desk.

"Actually, I go by Annah. I hope you don't mind me asking, but could you tell me what Officer MacGregor's first name is?" she requested in a strangled voice.

"Why, it's Lachlan, my dear. You don't by chance know each other?" she asked as she turned back towards Annah and observed the stricken look on Annah's face.

"Uh, yes, Mrs. Larson, we might have bumped into each other a time or two." They had certainly *bumped* into each other and she had not seen or spoken to him since she let the hotel room.

"Oh, how nice," Mrs. Larson replied. "Lachlan didn't mention that he knew you." By now she was standing outside of Lachlan's door. Annah's feet finally started to work again. As she approached the doorway she watched Mrs. Larson tap on it, open it, and introduce her.

"Officer MacGregor, Glenn Andersson is here for the interview."

Gleefully, she ushered Annah into the office, handed him her resume, and then stood back to watch Lachlan's reaction. She had known since the phone call that Glenn was a woman and had chosen not to pass that info on to Lachlan. Although Mrs. Larson had only worked with him for a week she was a very good judge of character and had enough life experience working in an almost all male environment to figure out his thoughts on female officers. She firmly believed that this station needed a female officer or two and hoped Lachlan could be maneuvered into hiring Annah. Her resume was excellent and her references were from people with integrity. The only fly in the ointment was the fact that they knew each other and obviously there was more to their involvement than simply "bumping into each other." The question was, would this be the push Lachlan needed to hire her or was it the nail in the coffin that was going to end the interview before it even started?

Lachlan glanced down at the resume and then stood; looking up, with his hand extended waiting to shake the hand of Glenn. He faltered, only for a second, then glanced down at the resume again and read Glenn A. Andersson. With a grin and a superior look at Annah he extended his hand even farther forcing her to shake it. She stood before him pale and obviously disconcerted. She hadn't known he was interviewing her any more than he had known who he was interviewing. He just recovered better.

"Please, have a seat, Annah. Can Mrs. Larson get you anything before we start?"

Just a bag to throw up in, flashed through Annah's mind, as she shook her head and slid into a chair.

"Thank you, Mrs. Larson. Please close the door on your way out," he requested as he flashed her with a feral smirk. He suddenly realized that although she hadn't known that Annah and he knew each other she had known all along that Glenn was a woman. He'd have to keep a closer eye on that one. He had already recognized her exemplary qualifications and people skills and watched her manipulate the other staff into doing things she believed needed to be done. This was the first time she had used those skills on him and he would make sure she knew it would be the last.

He turned back to Annah and sat down.

"Annah, I'm not going to pretend that I knew it was you that I was interviewing and I can tell by your reaction that you didn't know I had been transferred. I asked for the interview on the basis of your resume. So let's go back to that. Please tell me about yourself. Give me a brief background excluding your education, since I am already familiar with it. Tell me why you want to work at this station and why you think I should hire you. Following that, I will test your basic knowledge and set up a few scenarios for you to evaluate. If you're ready, please begin."

Since no mention had been made of their personal involvement Annah was able to concentrate on getting herself back under control and on giving the answers she had prepared. She answered the questions with both speed and accuracy. Lachlan challenged her with one situation after another. He was both impressed and surprised by her responses. Her answers were different from everyone else he had interviewed, but they were still all viable solutions. Even though he knew she would classify his final question as a low blow it was a question that needed to be asked and a question that needed to be answered.

"Annah, it's obvious that you won't be able to be indifferent to me, since we have intimate knowledge of each other. How will that affect the performance of your duties if I offer you this job?"

Annah bolted upright in her chair with those emerald eyes flashing golden bolts of fire. As she opened her mouth to deliver her scathing reply, there was a knock at the door.

"Come in," Lachlan commanded in an irritated voice.

An officer walked in and handed Lachlan some keys.

"I'm sorry about interrupting. I'm going to be late for an appointment and Mrs. Larson assured me that it would be okay. Thanks for letting me borrow it. I wanted to get these back to you before I left and tell you that some ditsy broad backed into your Jeep at the gas station this morning. There doesn't seem to be any damage but here's her name and address if I missed something." With that he turned around and looked directly at Annah as he headed for the doorway. He stopped dead in his tracks as he instantly recognized her. A dark red blush crept up his neck and settled in his cheeks.

"The broad's name would be Annah, just in case you need it for future reference."

She stood and turned to Lachlan with her hand extended. "If we are finished here Officer MacGregor, I should really get back to the hotel. Thank you for taking the time to see me. If there was any damage you know how to reach me. Gentlemen," she said as she bowed out of the room and closed the door behind her.

Lachlan chuckled. Her exit was reminiscent of his first encounter with her. She was class all the way. Even when she was at fault she came out on top. Lachlan was well aware that she had used the interruption as an excuse to avoid answering his final question.

Officer Johnson had gone from blushing to flushing with anger at being made to look unprofessional in front of his new boss.

"Who was that?" Matthew inquired stiffly.

"I believe she already answered that," Lachlan commented dryly.

"I know what her name is. But who is she and why was she here?" Matthew asked obviously perturbed.

"Well, she is quite probably one of your new co-workers. You can send in the next applicant on your way out." Lachlan dismissed him and wandered over to the window facing the parking lot. Sure enough Annah was wearing her red blanket coat as she climbed into her truck. She had neither been a figment of his imagination or wishful thinking last night. He really had seen her. With his arms crossed and a pensive look on his face he watched her drive away. She hadn't answered him with words but he knew as well as she did that working together would be a challenge for both of them. She was hands down the most qualified for the position. This station could definitely use an officer with her drive and enthusiasm. The question was would it be the best decision he had ever made or would it destroy one *or* both of them.

CHAPTER 6

Saturday night, two weeks later, Annah and the children were again getting ready for supper at Jennifer and Dane's. The twins, Kai and Mikael, were being baptized after church the next morning. Since there would be many family members there Jennifer thought that Annah and Lachlan might want to spend some time alone with their Godchildren the day before. Annah was looking forward to seeing the boys but nervous about her reaction to seeing Lachlan. Since her interview had been two weeks ago and she had heard nothing she had called Mrs. Larson yesterday to see if he had filled the positions. He hadn't. She had attended three other interviews that week and had been offered one position so far. Because her first pick was Nordegg she needed to know what his intentions were. Annah did not like the feeling of hanging in limbo. She wanted to have a job contract signed so that she could concentrate all of her efforts on her last two months of school rather than on job hunting. Annah normally had a fair reserve of patience but when it came to anything to do with Lachlan she didn't seem to have any. She knew that if he didn't say something first she would be forced to say something before the weekend was over.

Annah hadn't originally told Jen about her interview with Lachlan because they were on holidays when she was interviewed. Since then, because everything was still up in the air, she didn't want Dane to interfere and put pressure on Lachlan to hire her. Both Jen and Dane knew she would prefer a station in central Alberta. She needed a job, but she had enough pride that she wanted to earn the position on her own, not have someone feel coerced into hiring her.

As she got out of the shower she heard the doorbell ringing. She wrapped her head in a towel and flung on a robe. The doorbell rang again as she ran down the stairs to the back entrance. It was obviously someone they knew since strangers wouldn't bother to open the gate into the backyard. Simon met her in the hall running from the back door yelling.

"Mom, Mr. MacGregor is here!"

Annah skidded to a stop and looked up to see him waving at her through the back window. With her stomach doing back flips Annah went and unbolted the back door.

"Is there something I can help you with?" she questioned as she crossed her arms over her obvious nakedness under the robe.

"I need to speak with you and I wanted to do it before we arrived at Dane's. Go get dressed and then we'll talk."

Annah resented his high-handed manner but since she *was* naked she was hardly about to stand there and argue with him.

"Grab yourself a drink. I'll be down in a minute." She turned on her heel and scooted back up the stairs clutching her robe as she ran. So this was it then. He was going to tell her he had found more suitable candidates and let her fall apart in the privacy of her own home. She supposed she should be thankful for his consideration but instead she was boiling mad. She knew she was as qualified as anyone else, but because of his attitude regarding women officers and the fact that he believed she couldn't control herself around him, he was hiring men instead. Annah knew he was not immune to her physically and so she decided to show him what he would never be allowed to touch again. Instead of wearing the blue jeans and sweatshirt she had planned she grabbed a rose colored sweater dress made of angora, which hugged her every curve. She also diffused her hair and left it down. With a spritz of her only good perfume and a whisk of mascara she topped off her look with a little lip-gloss and then tripped lightly back down the stairs.

Annah found Simon and Lachlan lying on the carpet in the living room playing with cars while Summer sat above them coloring a picture. The vision that greeted Annah as she entered the living room was totally domestic and totally unexpected. It actually brought tears to Annah's eyes to envision what the loss of their father meant to her children on a daily basis.

"Would you like to talk in the kitchen?" Annah barked in a voice that sounded harsh even to her ears. Three pairs of eyes looked up as she left the room. Two little sets looked confused since it was a voice they seldom heard. The third set belonging to her nemesis followed her into the kitchen. His eyes flashed with undisguised impatience.

"Annah, I'm not the enemy," Lachlan defended sarcastically. "Playing cars with your son isn't going to scar him for life you know."

"I know that. But the lack of a man in his life might. I wasn't criticizing you. I was questioning my own choices." Annah surprisingly sounded disgusted with herself as she reached for the kettle. She suddenly felt ridiculous dressed as she was. Things tended to take on a different perspective when she put her kids first.

"What is it you need to talk to me about?"

"Come and sit down." Lachlan's dark expression softened as he took her by the arm and led her to a chair. "I know that although you didn't get the opportunity to answer my last question at the interview I need an honest answer to it from you now."

"Lachlan, I want this job. I'll do whatever it takes to perform my duties in a professional manner because working and living in Nordegg is something I need to do for my children and myself. I promise you that if there ever comes a time when I am unable to perform those duties for whatever reason, you will have my resignation," Annah vowed passionately. Her eyes shone with unshed tears and Lachlan melted into a puddle at her feet. Her integrity was unquestionable. This fragile yet strong beauty that sat across from him humbled Lachlan. With a resigned look upon his face Lachlan thrust out his hand.

"Welcome aboard, soon to be Officer Glenn Andersson," Lachlan announced as he shook her hand. "I will leave it up to you to tell Dane and Jennifer."

Let the games begin he thought to himself as he reveled in the feel of her hand in his. He had already shaken up his new staff quite a bit and he knew that with Annah on staff things were going to get even more interesting.

The kettle started to whistle and as Annah got up to make tea Lachlan filled her in on the details of her new job. When Summer wandered into the kitchen looking for a snack Annah looked at the time and realized they needed to be on their way. Since she no longer had time to change again she simply got everyone bundled up and they left for supper. Jennifer was going to wonder if she had fallen on her head when she showed up in a dress but she decided she was going to bluff her way through it by saying she hadn't gotten the laundry done yet. Somehow she didn't think that Jennifer was going to fall for it.

Annah gave the kids granola bars on the way over to Jen's. After their snack the kids were more interested in playing outside with the dogs than waiting for supper in the house. Jen raised a speculative eyebrow when Annah took off her coat and revealed the body hugging sheath under it. Annah automatically plucked a twin out of Jen's arms and went to sit on a stool behind the island. She crossed her legs and balanced her precious bundle on her lap. Lachlan, who had arrived earlier, walked into the kitchen and caught a view luscious enough to make his mouth water, and he wasn't looking at the lasagna that was cooling on the counter. When his look moved upwards he saw something else riveting. It was the expression that Annah had on her face as she gazed adoringly into the eyes of the infant she lovingly held. This was a woman that not only loved her own children but obviously loved all children. If there was anything undesirable about this woman either physically or within her character it had yet to be revealed to Lachlan. He was in deep trouble, really deep trouble.

Supper went off without a hitch and so did the Baptism the following day. Because Annah now knew that her job search was over she could make some definite plans to prepare for finals and relocate her family. The sooner she got started the better. She left right after lunch knowing that Jen had more than enough family around her and that her presence wouldn't be missed. She was wrong. Someone noticed the second she started herding her children to the door. Lachlan followed her out of the church basement and helped her dress Simon while she bundled up Summer.

"Call me or Mrs. Larson when you need the details for moving into the residence. It isn't occupied right now so it needs to be opened up and cleaned. I would also like a heads-up as to when you can start as soon as you know."

"Can I have a week off after exams to move and get settled?" she inquired.

"Of course. I assumed you might want to take a little holiday before you started, since once you do start you won't be able to take any time off for a year."

"Thanks for the offer, but I really can't afford it. Next year I'll take the week of spring break off and spend it with the kids. I'll see you in a couple of months and I promise you, Lachlan, you will not regret hiring me. I will be an asset to your team," she fervently vowed.

CHAPTER 7

Annah and Jennifer met for lunch on Monday. She filled Jen in on the events of the previous two weeks. Understandably Jennifer was hurt that Annah had felt she couldn't confide in her. After Annah explained that it wasn't deliberate but instead initially a matter of timing, and then later a matter of pride, Jen felt much better. Once she put herself in Annah's shoes she knew that she also would have kept things a secret. Because lunch was cut short due to hungry babies, the two friends made plans for supper and a girl's gossip session again on Friday. Dane would be out of town and Jennifer felt confidant she could get Annah to confess to something a little more interesting than the purely professional relationship that both Annah and Lachlan claimed was going on.

If Annah felt like a juggler before, now she definitely felt like a ten-piece, one man's band. Thank goodness for Nanny Bea with both her unflagging words of encouragement and her packing abilities. Jen and Dane also provided oodles of emotional support and practical advice. Dane met Annah for lunch on Wednesday and after congratulating her on her achievements he got down to the bare bones of what he really wanted to discuss with her. Of course, it was Lachlan.

"Annah, I know that your relationship with Lachlan is none of my business but you are my friend as well as Lachlan and therefore, I want both of you to be happy. For that reason I feel it is my responsibility to give you a heads up on a few things. I don't know exactly what Jen has told you about Lachlan's past and I'm not about to break his trust. However, I am comfortable with telling you that although he seems sexist, he wasn't always like that. When we were younger Lachlan was a champion of equal rights. He was passionate about caring for our environment. He had a wicked sense of humor and a zest for life that I thought nothing could ever snuff out. I was wrong."

Annah quietly sipped her tea while Dane continued.

"First came the falling out with his father and then the tragedy of losing his daughter and the simultaneous betrayal of his wife. Now he projects the image of someone who is unapproachable and guarded. He basically hasn't let anyone become close to him since Amy died. I understand that it is purely a survival instinct. The person that I know is generous, kind, loyal, and loving. He's just buried deep down beneath the feelings of betrayal and heartbreak. Please keep that in the back of your mind after you start working for him."

Dane took a bite of his sandwich and then continued uninterrupted as Annah merely listened.

"I've talked to previous staff members who have worked under him and the comments are that he has high expectations but he is fair. He is brilliant but patient, and therefore, you have the opportunity to learn a lot from him. He willingly and enthusiastically will answer any work related question. His extraordinary skills of observation and retention of facts prevent his staff from getting away with inferior performance. These gifts seem to cause his staff to strive to be the best that they can be, if for no other reason than to win his approval and respect. His one great failing is that he appears cold-blooded or detached. He tolerates no personal questions and remains aloof from his staff. Similarly, he asks nothing personally of his staff so he doesn't interfere in their home lives. I'm not asking you to feel sorry for him or to try to fix him. I just want you to remember what I have said when he is being particularly remote and, or, anal. Annah, he is my best friend and it kills me that he is so alone."

"Dane, do you want me to include him in my family's activities?"

"I would never meddle in your personal life like that and Lachlan would be both indignant and offended if he thought I had asked you to do so." Dane clasped Annah's hands in his own. "I'm not asking you to have a personal involvement with him beyond socializing with us and being the boys Godparents. All I'm asking is that at work try to remember that he is a person not just your boss. You have two advantages over the other members on staff. One is that you do know him personally and two is that you are the only female officer Lachlan has ever hired or had to work with. I know that he is slightly unsettled by that."

"Dane, I promise to be kind and to always try to give him the benefit of the doubt. I instinctively know that I can trust him and that he would never intentionally hurt me or my children. However, he does have a way of pushing my buttons. I can't promise that I will always humbly and without question follow his lead. I am truly looking forward to this job, Dane. I'm scared and yet I'm so excited I can't wait to get going. Working with Lachlan is both a relief and a cause for concern. I have very mixed feelings. I can only hope that everything works out for the best. I promised Lachlan that I would try my hardest to be the best officer that I can be. I promise you that I will never be cruel or unjust to him, and I will always watch his back. But I know that our relationship will not be an easy one."

"I couldn't possibly ask for anything more. Thank you."

As Annah finished her tea, she stood and collected their lunch garbage.

"I've got to get going, Dane. Thanks for lunch. Give the boys a kiss for me and tell Jen I'll see her Friday." After throwing away the refuse Annah gave Dane a quick hug and hurried off to class.

As Dane shuffled off to his office he replayed the conversation he had had with Lachlan the previous Saturday night after Annah had left. They discussed that although Lachlan had some reservations he decided to hire her and was optimistic that she would be a valuable asset to his team. He assured Dane that they had come to an understanding regarding their differences in opinion about female officers and that they could work together. Lachlan promised he would never consciously harm Annah or her children.

Dane felt at ease with the developing relationship between his two friends. He hated to see these two people, which he cared about deeply, being so alone. He almost felt guilty that his own life was so full of love and happiness. As he walked into his office and his phone started to ring.

"Hello, Professor Knudsen speaking."

"Dane, it's me. How'd it go with Annah?" inquired Jennifer.

"Everything went fine and although I didn't come right out and ask her about her feelings for Lachlan it is obvious to me that she does have some kind of feelings for him beyond professional ones. I'll tell you all about it when I get home tonight. I've got a student conference in five minutes so I've got to run. Love you, see you tonight."

As Friday evening rolled around again and Annah bundled up the kids she sighed wistfully. There weren't going to be very many Friday evenings left at Jen and Dane's. As things got busier at school and she needed to concentrate on relocating, that only left two Fridays before the big move. She was going to miss Jen and their gossip sessions. Although she knew that they would always remain friends she was also realistic enough to know that things would not be the same. While Jen had watched Simon and Summer grow up, Annah would only see Mikael and Kai about a dozen times a year. That thought was heart wrenching. Life did move on though and Annah was ready for the next stage of hers.

As the kids tumbled out of the truck and ran to play with the dogs, Annah quietly eased herself in the back door so that she wouldn't wake any sleeping babies. The scent of pizzas wafted from the kitchen as she took off her boots and wandered in. Rock and roll blared from Dane's pride and joy audio system. Either the babies could sleep through anything or they were grooving to the tunes in the living room, since no one seemed to occupy the kitchen. Annah found Jen on the floor with her babies singing up a storm. Off key, mind you, but the boys didn't seem to mind as their eyes followed Jen's every movement and they were grinning from ear to ear to ear to ear. Annah stood and watched until Jen realized she was there and with a self-conscious chuckle she stopped singing and rose from her knees.

"Please don't stop on my account," Annah chuckled. "The boys and I were equally enthralled."

"Funny, Andersson, very funny!! Are Summer and Simon in the back yard?"

"Yes, they can't seem to get enough of those dogs. I'm going to have to get them a dog after I move if I can find a place with a fenced yard. The staff residences don't have fences because the people that usually occupy them are single with no kids. Hopefully in a year or so I'll be able to find something a little bit more suitable for raising kids and pets."

Jen made a mental note to ask Lachlan about whether the residence Annah was occupying could have a fence built around the yard for the kids' safety. That way they could get a puppy right away. Somehow she didn't think Lachlan would put up any objections to that suggestion and she knew that Annah would never ask herself. Oh, how she was going to miss Annah and her children and miss watching this burgeoning relationship between Lachlan and Annah. The relationship that neither one of them wanted to admit existed.

"Grab a baby, Annah, and let's get supper over with so we can get down to the business of bathing, feeding, changing, and putting the boys to sleep so I can have a couple of hours of respite."

Since the boys were not identical Annah made a point of picking up the opposite one first each time she saw them. As she embraced Kai, she headed into the kitchen. After settling both boys into their matching swings she went to the back door to call in her kids and the dogs. After supper the kids helped Annah bathe, feed, burp, and change the boys before putting them down. Jen had gone for a nap right after supper so that she could enjoy a visit with Annah after the boys went to bed. By eight o'clock the house had settled down. Simon and Summer were also in their PJs and quietly watching a movie. Annah returned to the kitchen to do up the dishes and put on a pot of tea as Jen wandered down from her bedroom.

"Thanks for all the help. With Dane gone tonight I was a little nervous about getting everything done and still having enough energy to feed the boys when they get up at eleven o'clock."

"Are they still nursing every three hours?" Annah asked.

"During the day it works out to about every three. Thank heavens for the nanny during the day. She has actually turned into more of a house keeper since I primarily take care of the boys while she sees to making the meals and keeping the house decent. Honestly, Annah, I have no idea what I did with all my time before the boys were born. Go sit down and let me do the dishes. You've been busy all day with school etc. and I'm sure you're tired."

"I'm no more tired than you are so let's just do the dishes together as this is going to be one of our last chances to visit for a while."

"How's the packing going?" Jen inquired.

"Fine. Nanny Bea has been doing it during the day while we are at school. I'm driving to Nordegg tomorrow to take a look at the residence. After I know the layout of the house and how much room we have I'll be better able to plan my packing."

"You're staying overnight then," she stated. "You should let Lachlan know you'll be around so that he can show off the culinary skills he's always claiming he has, that to my knowledge, no one yet has witnessed."

"Jennifer. You and I need to talk and then you need to pass the info onto Dane. I know that you and he have grand plans for Lachlan and I setting up house together and eventually living happily ever after."

"Annah, I am appalled that you would think Dane and I would get involved in anything as common as matchmaking."

"I know you well enough to know that both of you would like nothing better than to have the two of us as happy as the two of you. In case you were in doubt, let me fill you in on the reality of the situation. Please sit down, pour the tea, deal the cards, and make yourself comfortable. I'm going to go check on the children and I'll be right back."

Both Summer and Simon were out cold. Annah tucked their blankies around them and turned off the movie. When she returned to the kitchen the cards were dealt and Jen sat there, hands folded, looking expectantly at her.

"Okay. I'm all ears. Please fill me in," Jennifer batted her eyelashes and implored breathlessly.

Annah swatted at her on her way by and sank into the chair across from her.

"As always I see the drama queen is rearing her ugly head. Alright, here goes. Lachlan, as you well know, is an exceptional example of the male members of our species. I am willing to acknowledge that his wavy black hair dusted at the temples with grey, his penetrating ice blue eyes, the rakish scar sported above his right eyebrow, and the bump on the bridge of his aquiline nose creates an arresting countenance. The height and the breadth of the shoulders of his Viking-like body add to his natural aura of arrogance and self-confidence. So, in answer to your unasked question, yes, I find him extremely sexy. However, having said that, we are not going to end up being the perfect little family like you and Dane. At this point we both have unresolved faithfulness issues and to further our relationship would be premature."

"I don't understand, Annah. Your husband never cheated on you."

"Although I have never talked about it to anyone before Jen, actually he had. That was what we were arguing about when we had the accident. I won't ever know for sure if the accident could have been prevented if Thomas had not been yelling at me and was concentrating on driving instead. I'm, quite possibly, the reason that Thomas is dead."

"Oh my God, Annah, I had no idea. You can't blame yourself for that. You weren't the one cheating. What in the world would cause you to believe that you were responsible for Thomas' death?"

"Thomas had confessed to being with another woman two days before we had gone to his parents for supper. I was wrapped up with caring for three month old Simon and three year old Summer. I would never have known except that his girlfriend had called to ask me to grant him a divorce since she was pregnant. She claimed he loved her but that I wouldn't let him go and that I was blackmailing him. Apparently, I swore I would deny him access to his children if he left. After the initial accusations, denials, and eventual confession I hadn't spoken directly to him for days. He had asked me repeatedly what I was going to do. Since he had me trapped in the car with him on the way home he asked me again what my intentions were. I should have left it alone but I couldn't seem to keep my mouth closed," Annah sighed.

"After spending the evening with his parents and him putting on this big show for them that we were the perfect little family, I just couldn't keep it inside any longer. I very calmly and quietly informed him that I was leaving and taking the children with me and that he could have the freedom he was so obviously wanted. He was livid. He started yelling at me and slamming his fist on the steering wheel and then everything slowed down and became surreal. I saw the truck running the red light and I knew it was going to hit us on Thomas' side. I could hear someone screaming. Later, I realized it was me."

"Oh, Annah, I'm so sorry," Jennifer reached across the table and clasped Annah's hand. Her heart ached for her friend. She knew that the accident had been bad but she hadn't known the real toll it had taken on Annah's psyche.

"No one can ever know this, Jen, because I don't ever want the children to find out. They were too young to remember that we were arguing and I want it to stay like that. I watched Thomas bleed to death unable to save him and I won't ever forgive myself for that. I still have nightmares and wake up with the sounds of him begging me to forgive him and to save him, echoing in my mind. I need to stay focused on giving my children the best life they can possibly have without their father. Do you understand what I'm trying to tell you?"

"You don't think that you deserve to be happy?"

"No. What I am trying to explain is that although Lachlan is sexy and smart and will probably be a great life partner for some lucky woman that woman is not going to be me. I don't know if I will ever be able to give my heart again. I was obviously a really poor judge of character the first time around. Plus Lachlan has got baggage of his own. I don't want to be responsible for hurting him, any more than I want to open myself up to being hurt again. I can be his friend, Jen, but nothing more can come of it."

"Annah, I obviously didn't know how much the two of you had in common but I believed before and now I believe even more fervently that the two of you could be good for each other. Lachlan needs someone besides Dane and I to count on and so do you. I won't pretend that I wouldn't love for the two of you to become an item but realistically I just want you to remain open to the suggestion of being his friend. Lachlan is a stand up guy. He can be counted on when you're out in the boonies, on your own with your children. Please remember that. How much of this can I share with Dane?"

"I expected you to tell him everything I've told you but I also expect that it will remain between the three of us. As I told Dane, I will treat Lachlan with respect, and work hard for him. I will give him the benefit of the doubt whenever possible and I promise to watch his back. As far as elevating our relationship to the next level of friendship, that ball is in Lachlan's court. I'm going to be so busy with getting the kids adjusted and trying to do a good job that I honestly won't have the emotional energy to try to develop a more in-depth relationship with anyone. For now, that's all I can promise."

"That's more than enough, Annah. I'm not trying to add to your stress level. I was trying to come up with a solution to relieve it. Dane and I will both back off a little. You know we love you and are only trying to help."

"Of course I do, that's why I told you about Thomas tonight. Rest assured that the kids and I are ready to embark on our next journey and that we are going to be just fine. I think all of these revelations and all of this soul-bearing deserves a piece of cheesecake. What do you think?"

"I couldn't agree more. I'll get the strawberries," Jen announced as she sauntered over to the fridge.

CHAPTER 8

ANNAH AND THE KIDS were up early and on the road by eight o'clock the next morning. She had arranged to meet Mrs. Larson with the key at three o'clock in the afternoon. Actual driving time was about five hours so she had an extra hour for any unforeseen delays along the way. The temperature was unusually low for this time of year but the sun shone down on last night's most recent snowfall making the surrounding landscape glitter. It was a beautiful day for a drive and since the plows had already been out Annah made good time despite the snow. She stopped in Rocky Mountain House to book a hotel room for the night and to let the kids run and play outside for a half hour before ushering them back into the truck for the final leg of their journey. After the fresh air and the exercise both kids were asleep within minutes of returning to the road. Annah enjoyed the scenery as she drove, mentally hugging herself over the thrill of the new job she had wanted so badly and had been lucky enough to obtain. Somehow she just knew that this was where she and her children were meant to be. As she pulled up to the office both kids were still napping. She woke them gently and then ran in to meet Mrs. Larson.

"Good afternoon, Annah. I see you're right on time. I'm going to take you over to the house so that we can make a list of things that need to be done before you move and I can make sure they're done. I had the heat turned on yesterday so I hope it's starting to warm up in there by now. You never know with those old furnaces and that particular house hasn't been used for almost a year. I'll meet you there."

Annah followed Mrs. Larson back out to their vehicles and then followed her down the highway to the small grouping of identical residences about five miles away. There were six units in all. Three appeared to be occupied since Annah could see steam rising from the chimneys of four of them and there were four driveways cleared. Annah's heart skipped a beat as she recognized Lachlan's Jeep parked in front of one. Mrs. Larson stopped at the house that backed up against the mountains which was directly across the road from Lachlan's. Annah parked and unbuckled the kids to let them get out and run.

"You must always stay on this side of the street," Annah instructed the children. "You can play in the snow behind the house. I don't want you ever to go past the front of the house because you could get run over. Do you understand?"

"Yes, Mom," they both responded as they ran around the side of the house.

"Come. Let's have a look around. They'll be fine. All of the officers are either at work or on holidays today, including Officer MacGregor."

"Do you mean he works seven days a week?"

"He has been so far. I don't know how long he plans on keeping that up. I suppose he wouldn't have anything else to do if he took a day off anyway. There is such a backlog of work to get caught up on, he probably figures he might as well be at work. He doesn't' know anyone here and yet he has turned down every invitation that has been offered so far. We all know he is trying to turn this station around but our community is small and if he is going to be effective he is going to have to do some socializing. They are already calling him lobo."

"Lobo. What does that mean?" Annah inquired.

"Around here it means a lone wolf. It's one that doesn't belong to a pack but is strong enough to survive on its own. I would think it would be a very lonely way to spend your life."

So, Dane did have a right to worry about Lachlan, Annah conceded. Obviously she was going to have to become more involved in his life if for no other reason than to make her own job more tolerable.

As Annah and Mrs. Larson made their way from room to room adding to the list of repairs Annah kept an eye out for the children running and playing in the snow. She heard a truck pull up and a door slam. Then she heard the delighted squeals of children and knew that Lachlan had returned. As she peeked out the window she noticed a snowball fight had developed and the children were running and giggling in the front yard. Instead of reining the children in and telling them not to bother Lachlan she decided to let them be. Lachlan obviously needed a few distractions in life and playing with the kids would be good for him. Mrs. Larson watched Annah's reaction and smiled inwardly as she congratulated herself on her correct analysis regarding their relationship being more than just casual. Obviously Annah's children not only knew Lachlan, but were comfortable playing with him.

All of sudden Simon fell over out of the front yard and onto the road in front of the house. Annah watched Summer grab him by the back of his coat and drag him into the yard. Summer's mouth was working a mile a minute and it was obvious she was scolding him for leaving the yard. As he struggled to remove himself from her grasp Lachlan helped him up. She watched him nodding his head in obvious agreement with what Summer was telling him. He chased the kids into the backyard and Annah followed Mrs. Larson downstairs.

While the main floor had been divided into two bedrooms, a kitchen, a bathroom, and a living room the basement was just one big open area with a furnace and plumbing for a washing machine. Mrs. Larson determined that the entire house needed to be painted and the carpets upstairs needed to be replaced. That meant the old carpet could be laid downstairs for the recreation room. The house came with a fridge and a stove but Annah would have to purchase a washer and a dryer. Mrs. Larson promised the house would be ready to move into by the middle of April. That would be two weeks before Annah was actually done school but she could have the big items she needed to purchase delivered before they moved in. She was going to have to dip into her reserves again but hopefully this would be the last time, since she would finally be getting a paycheck at the end of May.

Financially, Annah was starting to see a light at the end of the tunnel. Nanny Bea was only staying with them until the middle of September. Since both kids would be in school full time this year Annah no longer needed a live-in helper. Because officers worked shift work and Annah was going to need time to find a sitter who could stay until midnight when she worked evenings, she had asked Lachlan if she could work straight evenings for the next four months. Then after Nanny left if she still hadn't found anyone to watch the children it would buy her some extra time since she would then be on days for several months. Although she didn't want to ask for special treatment she was realistic enough to know that sometimes you just had to. Lachlan was happy to accommodate her because no one ever seemed to want to work that shift. Since she would be working one on one with each staff member, as there were only two on in the evening with a dispatcher, it would give everyone a chance to get to know each other. It would also make it easier for Lachlan to pick a partner for her.

Annah let Mrs. Larson know that she was looking for part-time late evening sitters. Since the station now had fifteen members Annah would only have to find a sitter for two evenings a month. Mrs. Larson assured her that even if the several retired grandmas in the area were unable to stay with the kids she would be more than happy to do it herself if they were weekend shifts. Annah heaved a sigh of relief. That was one more thing she could check off of her to-do list. Things really seemed to be falling into place, just like this was meant to be.

"Well, dear, I really need to be going. Here's your key. I'll keep one so that I can let the carpenters in. You can pick it up at the office after you move in. Don't be a stranger. If you need anything just give me a call, you hear."

Mrs. Larson's comment brought Annah back to the present. She walked her out and met Lachlan coming up the steps.

"Lachlan, I see you decided to leave early today. We're having a few friends over for supper tonight and we would be more than pleased if you would join us," Mrs. Larson invited.

"Thank you, June, but I already have plans for the evening. Annah and the kids are coming over for supper. Maybe next time," he responded.

"I'm not going to stop inviting you," she threatened. "So sooner or later you're going to have to give in. Around here I'm known as being rather tenacious you know," she chided.

"Oh, June, never let it be said that you are *rather tenacious*," Lachlan chuckled. Although he had been listening to Mrs. Larson his eyes had never left Annah's. He was well aware that she was bristling with anger and if not for politeness and lack of wanting to create a scene, in front of Mrs. Larson, she would have ripped him to shreds by now. He figured it was tit-for-tat. He had specifically requested she let him know when she was coming down and if he had not over-heard Mrs. Larson calling the local handyman to go down and light the Annah's furnace, he would never have known she was coming this weekend.

"You have a lovely evening then. Bye, Annah."

June was well aware of the stiffness in Annah's demeanor after Lachlan's announcement. She would have bet her next paycheck that Annah had no idea until that moment that she was expected for supper. Things were definitely going to be interesting around here after Annah started work. June couldn't wait.

Annah waited until Mrs. Larson waved and drove away. Then she rounded on Lachlan like a badger backed into a corner. Lachlan was prepared for it and so he crossed his arms and propped himself against the single stair rail, grinning smugly.

"Lachlan MacGregor, you can wipe that self-satisfied smirk right off your face this minute. I promised you that I would follow your leadership and be the best officer I could be but that has nothing to do with after hours. Don't you dare assume that because we have slept together you have any claim over me or my free time. If you ever do that to me again be prepared for me to call your bluff and embarrass you. We obviously need to clear the air and get a few things straight. You know that the only reason that night occurred was because we both thought we wouldn't have any further contact. I would never have suggested a liaison if I had known I was going to be seeing you more than once afterwards, let alone be working for you. Using our intimacy against me is beneath you. I am balancing enough right now without adding a daily sparing match, with you, to the mix. Please back off, Lachlan, and let me finish my exams and get myself and my family settled."

Lachlan's smirk was replaced by his usual protective shield of aloofness. He straightened up from the railing.

"You are absolutely right, Annah. I apologize. Please forgive the intrusion. Do you know your exam schedule yet?"

"No, but I should have it by the end of next week."

"Please inform Mrs. Larson of your expected arrival date so that I can add you to the shift schedule. Enjoy the rest of your weekend." Lachlan turned to walk down the steps.

Annah placed her hand on Lachlan's arm arresting his movement. He looked down at her hand and then back up at her with a raised eyebrow, silently requesting that she remove her hand.

"Lachlan, if the offer of supper is still open, the children and I would be pleased to accept."

Lachlan gaped at her and then threw back his head and roared.

It was one of the first times Annah had heard him laugh and it caused a welcome transformation in his countenance.

"Lady, you are something! Do you have any other commitments today or are you at loose ends until supper?"

"Actually I have a meeting with the principal at school in about fifteen minutes. What time is supper and what would you like me to bring?" she asked.

"Supper is whenever you get here and you don't need to bring anything. Do you want me to watch the kids while you go?" Lachlan offered.

"No, thanks, I thought it would relieve some of their stress if they could see their new school. Then the first day won't be quite so scary. I'll see you in a bit then."

"Okay," Lachlan replied.

As he strode back over to his own residence he silently acknowledged her strength of character and admired her for it. If he had thought he would be able to bulldoze his way into her life she had just put him in his place and reminded him that her strength and independence were two of the qualities that he found so attractive in her.

His mother had always told him that hard won battles were always the sweetest. So far she had never been wrong. This one could be his hardest battle yet. And if he won he knew it would have the sweetest reward of any. He just had to convince Annah of that.

My God! It was like a thunderbolt had just hit him. How had he come to the conclusion that Annah was his fate without previously acknowledging that he was in love with her? As far as revelations went this was paramount. Calmness settled over him rather than the expected "fight or flight" instinct caused by panic. She was his fate? She was his fate. Now that he had a goal all he had to do was make a plan and follow it through. He looked forward to the merry chase he knew she would lead him on.

Annah locked up the house, rounded up the children and headed back to the village to meet the principal. When she arrived she let the children wander around the school while she talked with the principal. The school had three classrooms, a lunchroom, a small library, and a gym. Each classroom housed three grades. The school had three teachers as well as a principal who also served as the librarian and the gym teacher. Because there were only fifty five children presently attending the village school, Summer and Simon would have the benefit of small class sizes which allowed for more individual student-teacher interaction. They also would have their own computers to use until they moved on to Rocky for Grade Ten.

The school was able to remain open because of an endowment set up by one of the former employees from the town's closed coal mine. The mine opened in 1909 with the primary purpose of supplying the prairies with fuel for their railways. In 1937 the mine went into briquette production and became Canada's largest briquette producer. These were used as fuel for trains as well as for furnaces for heating homes. Oil became the fuel of choice by 1955 and the Brazeau Collieries Mine was shut down. It was at that point that residents began to move out and the town eventually became a village. For those who wanted to stay the endowment was set up so that the school could remain open. Luckily there was enough money in the fund that the school should be able to continue to remain open for many years to come. Annah was one of those parents who were particularly grateful. This school had made Annah's acceptance of this position viable.

After showing the children what classroom Summer would be in, they trekked back out to the truck to head to Lachlan's. Since there was no kindergarten Simon would not be coming to school until the fall. He appeared put out but was easily mollified by the promise of the waterslides back at the hotel.

Annah returned to Lachlan's and they had a very tasty supper of barbequed hot dogs for the kids and steaks for them. He informed her of the community's various amenities. They then moved on to the staff at the station. He explained the various positions of each member, their years of service, and basic familial situations. He then ran through the routine that each officer followed on a normal day shift and then on a normal evening shift. Annah tried to take mental notes for future reference but she knew she wouldn't remember everything. She figured if she retained half of it she was still farther ahead than if she had walked in cold on her first day of work. They had just finished cleaning up from supper when she realized it was already seven o'clock and if she didn't leave immediately there would be no pool time before bed. Annah and the kids thanked Lachlan for a lovely supper and headed back to Rocky Mountain House.

The kids again fell asleep as soon as Annah turned back onto the highway and so she had a quiet trip into town. She thought about how Lachlan didn't like to relinquish control. It was apparent in everything he did and said. The locals might call him lobo but Annah thought a more accurate description of him was the alpha male. Annah knew that working with Lachlan was going to be the biggest challenge of her life. She hoped she had the fortitude to see it through.

CHAPTER 9

ANNAH FINISHED HER EXAMS on a Wednesday and called Jen for a girls' night out.

"Can Dane watch the kids tonight if we go out on a tear? I haven't been to a bar or gone out dancing in years but tonight I feel like doing something crazy. Are you in?"

"Hell, yah! The boys are totally weaned from me now so I could do with a little hurrah myself. Just let me get things arranged and I'll call you at home in an hour. Let's do supper first and then the clubs. If you don't have anything wild to wear call me back and I'll find something for you," Jennifer signed off and promptly called Dane.

Annah drove home and gave her children extra long hugs. The four long years of sacrifices were finally over. Tearfully, she clutched them until they squirmed to be released. Nanny Bea stood back with tears in her eyes.

"You should go out and celebrate tonight," Nanny gently encouraged.

"Funny you should suggest that. Would you mind watching the kids all evening? Jennifer and I are going out for supper and then dancing."

"You know I don't mind. Go have a bath and make yourself pretty. What do you have to wear?" Nanny quizzed Annah.

"I am just going to wear jeans. I'm not trying to pick anybody up Nanny, I just want to go out and have some fun."

"I know but it doesn't hurt to look nice. I'll go find you something."

Annah headed for the tub. She took candles and a glass of wine with her. She locked the door and loaded the tub with bubbles. As she sank into the fragrant waters she let out a long sigh. After a twenty minute soak the kids started banging on the door and Annah decided it was time to get out and get dressed. Nanny had found a pink knitted tank top that Annah had received as a gift for Christmas but had not yet worn. It had scalloped armholes and a lace inset at the bodice. It was the perfect accompaniment to the jeans and cropped blue jean jacket Nanny knew she would wear. It was casual but feminine. Too often Nanny felt that Annah looked like a tomboy. Annah put hot rollers in and then dug through her bathroom drawer to try and find some make-up to put on. When Jen rolled up in the cab Annah had transformed into one hot mama. Her hair was brushed into big waves that hung down her back. It was held in place with an iridescent abalone clip. She wore matching chandelier earrings and her green eyes accented by dark purple eyeliner and pink shadow gave her an unfamiliar yet appealing exotic look.

"Holy, girl, you are definitely looking for trouble tonight! It's a good thing we are cabbing it. I promise to bring her home in one piece, Bea. Don't wait up," Jen advised.

Annah and Jen went to the only seafood house in town. Shellfish was one of the indulgences that Annah allowed herself for special occasions. After a sumptuous meal of scallops and mussels and another glass of wine the girls headed off to the local watering hole. The music was a combination of rock and country. The clientele was a mishmash of twenty to thirty year olds, both male and female, both blue and white collar. Their apparel was as varied as their personas. This was definitely the place to go if you were looking to dance and blow off a little steam.

"Jen, have you ever been here before? I've heard the girls at school talking about it."

"Dane and I don't come to places like this because he can only slow dance. This is a little too fast paced for him."

"My God, Jen, I'm sorry. I wasn't thinking. Too much wine!"

"Don't apologize. Let's just have fun tonight. Go find a table. I'm going to call Dane and make sure he's doing okay alone with the twins."

Annah didn't miss a dance. This was one instance when all of her physical training for work was paying off personally. In between dances Annah re-hydrated herself with water and the "occasional" Black Russian. She laughed and flirted and generally had a roaring good time. By the time last call rolled around she had been asked for her number at least a half dozen times. Every request was laughed off as she flitted off to the dance floor with another partner. Jen danced some but mostly kept a watchful eye over Annah's antics, making sure she stayed safe and didn't do anything too outrageous. When she spied her necking on the dance floor with some guy she had seen her dance with several times, Jen knew it was time to point Annah in the direction of a cab. That one did manage to get the precious, heavily guarded, phone number and promised to call even after Jen informed him that Annah had two children.

Jen poured Annah into the cab and followed close behind to make sure she got home safely. It was after three in the morning and she knew they would both be paying for their breakaway tomorrow, or rather, later today. She was thankful they both had nannies to care for their children since neither of them would be in any shape to do so in about four hours. Annah stumbled into her house, relocked the door, and awkwardly attempted to tip toe to her room. She pulled off her coat and shoes and managed to undo her pants before she flopped, face down on her bed, and passed out.

Hours later Annah awoke to the phone ringing. She instinctively reached over and answered it before Nanny could.

"Hello?" she croaked.

"Hello, Annah?"

"Speaking," she mumbled.

"Annah, this is Lachlan. Did I wake you up? What's wrong with your voice?"

Annah sat bolt upright in bed and instantly regretted it. Her stomach pitched precariously and as the blood drained from her head she almost passed out.

"Lachlan, I'm sorry but I have to call you back." With that she slammed down the phone and tore off towards her ensuite. Without a second to spare she emptied her stomach and then laid her face against the cool porcelain of the toilet. Sweat beaded her brow and her head pounded with a dull throb. Annah could vaguely hear the sound of the phone ringing again as she lay huddled against the bathroom counter. There was fun and then there was too much fun! Evidently, she should have stuck to water and skipped the Black Russians altogether. She honestly didn't think she had had that many. She knew she had only paid for two. Apparently, by the rolling of her insides and the dizziness caused by every slight movement of her head, including the opening and closing of her eyelids, she had consumed a great deal more than two. Thankfully the ringing of the phone stopped. Moments later a tap on Annah's bedroom door preceded Nanny's entrance.

"So you had some fun, I see," Nanny Bea commented dryly.

"Just shoot me," pleaded Annah.

"I'll get you some aspirin and make you some tea and toast. Get in the shower and meet me in the kitchen in fifteen minutes," Nanny ordered. "You will live. I promise."

Nanny backed out of the bathroom and headed for the kitchen. Annah dragged herself off of the floor and peeled off her clothes. Her stomach continued to pitch and roll but the revitalizing spray from the shower pounding into her flesh felt so good that it kept her upright.

Twenty minutes later Annah was seated at the table clutching her tea mug and trying to force down a piece of toasted rye bread. Nanny brought over several phone messages. One was from Lachlan, one from Jennifer, one from Summer's school, and one from someone named Ben. Annah suddenly had a crystal clear flashback to necking on the dance floor with a tall blond. It's a good thing she didn't drink very often because obviously her natural inhibitions definitely dissipated when she drank. As she cradled her head in her hands, Nanny sat down beside her.

"So are there any stories you want to share?" Nanny inquired enthusiastically.

"We had a wonderful supper at *Louie's*. I had scallops and mussels."

"I was wondering what happened after supper, and you well know that," she scolded good-naturedly.

"Nanny, even though I feel like crap today, I have to tell you I had more fun last night than I have had in years. I danced all night and I laughed and flirted. I felt beautiful. It was excellent!" she exclaimed earnestly but quietly.

"Who is this Ben? He asked if you were feeling okay."

"I danced with him several times last night but I don't really know much about him," she confessed. Except that he was a terrific kisser and he didn't dance too badly either she recalled. She would have to phone Jen back before she phoned him to make sure she hadn't done anything really foolish last night. First things first. She needed to phone the school. Since Summer's last day was going to be tomorrow the teacher had called to confirm that Annah was coming to pick up her transcripts. Next she called Lachlan.

"Good Morning, Officer MacGregor speaking."

"Lachlan, it's Annah. I'm sorry for slamming the phone down in your ear before. I was slightly indisposed."

"Annah, how are you feeling? Bea told me you have the flu. I apologize for waking you up."

"Lachlan, it was self-inflicted. So, please don't apologize and please don't ask. What can I do for you?"

"Celebrating your final exam, were you? I wanted to let you know I have guys lined up to help you unload on Saturday. What time should I tell them to be at the house?"

"That's great. You didn't need to do that, but thank you. The truck should arrive about noon. Anytime after that would be fine. Two of my cousins are helping me. We're loading up and leaving on Friday."

"Where are you staying Friday night?"

"We are hoteling it in Rocky and that way I can get some groceries before we come out on Saturday."

"Don't worry about supper Saturday night. I have it covered, if that's alright? Annah, I have another call so I have to go. See you then."

Annah hung up with a speculative look on her face. He was still behaving highhandedly and making arrangements without consulting her. However, since she had given Lachlan a dressing down the day she looked at the house, he had been the perfect gentleman, more than accommodating, and also thoughtful, as this latest gesture proved. The question was "What was his hidden agenda?" She knew he would have one, because his normal course of action would be not to get involved at all. She feared it might have something to do with seducing her back into the bedroom. That was something that she could absolutely not let happen. Although, it had been the most incredible sexual experience of her life, repeating it and having an affair with her boss would put in jeopardy everything she had worked so hard to achieve for the past four years. Even though she had asked him to back off, now she didn't know if he was just lulling her into a false sense of security or if he actually was backing off. Annah was going to have to stay on top of her game and keep her guard up. Lachlan could not win this one.

Just as she picked up the phone to call Jen it rang.

"Hey. So are you going to live?" joked Jennifer.

"Yes, Jen, and thank you for taking care of me last night. I owe you one. I feel like a Mac truck drove over me and I'm not sure how I got so drunk when I know I only paid for two drinks. How are you feeling?"

"I feel great. Just a little tired. Trust me you had more than two Russians. Drinks just kept appearing on the table and while I kept dumping mine in the plant beside me you kept drinking yours. I didn't figure it would kill you. You seemed to be enjoying yourself and before you get all indignant I did dump a couple of yours as well. Any phone calls this morning."

"Actually, I've had several. Are you asking if Ben called? Because, if you are, the answer is yes. I was going to call you before phoning him back because I wanted to make sure that I didn't make a total fool of myself."

"You didn't. But, you were getting awfully friendly just before we left. Do you remember that?"

"Yes, I remember participating in a very pleasant tongue tango with him and then you coming over and saying it was home time. Thank you. If you hadn't been there I honestly don't know what the conclusion might have been."

"So what do you know about him?"

"Well, I know that he is a lawyer and his practice is in Red Deer. He was staying at his brother's on the way home from a ski trip. He's single and thirty-one years old. He has blond hair and chocolate brown eyes."

"Did you tell him you are moving and that you have kids?"

"I believe you took care of the kid issue," Annah commented sarcastically. "Actually, I had told him both of those things and yet he still wanted my number and he did call. If he wants to see me again I think I'll invite him over. What do you think?"

"I think you would be crazy not to. He was gorgeous and it's not like you're committed to anyone else, are you?"

"Okay. I'm going to call him and I'll fill you in later. I need to get some packing done. Bye for now."

Annah grabbed Ben's note and with a sense of determination she dialed. After the third ring it was picked up.

"Hello."

"Hello. May I speak to Ben, please?" Annah inquired.

"Speaking. Is this Annah?" Ben questioned.

"Yes. I got your message and I have to admit I've certainly felt better most mornings. I don't usually get carried away like that. I hope I didn't embarrass you last night," Annah apologized.

"Of course not. Did you have fun?"

"I had a great time Ben. I haven't been out like that in a really long time and I know I kind of had a runaway."

"What are you doing for supper tonight? I thought maybe we could meet."

"I would love to have supper with you but I can't. Would you like to come for coffee after I put the kids to bed? I need to finish packing tonight since we are loading the truck tomorrow, so I can't really afford the time to go out."

"I would like that. What's your address and what time shall I come?"

"How does nine o'clock sound to you? We live in a four-plex and the street address is 282A Pine Drive Court. Would you like something a little stronger than coffee, because I only have red wine and scotch."

"That sounds great. I love red wine so I'll see you then."

After choking the toast down she felt considerably better. Annah and Simon spent the rest of the day packing.

Promptly at nine o'clock the door bell rang. Annah was straightening up from a box when Ben entered the living room. She threw her braid behind her back and surveyed her ink covered hands. The ink from the newspapers she was using to wrap things with had come off on her hands.

"Hi, there. I'll go get us some wine. I hope you don't mind if I continue to pack while we talk." Annah brushed escaped hair from her braid out of her face leaving a smudge on her cheek. Ben walked up to her and gently wiped the ink off. She instinctively backed up, startled, since she wasn't used to being touched. Blushing she turned around and Ben followed her into the kitchen. Neither commented on her reaction.

Annah washed her hands, opened the wine, poured and handed Ben a glass while he chatted about some of the things they had both witnessed last night. In no time he had her laughing about the remembered antics of some of the other bar patrons. The awkwardness of the initial meeting after last night and his touching her was over. He helped her by taping and labeling the boxes as she finished packing them. It was a very relaxed, enjoyable evening with lots of laughter.

Except for Dane, Annah didn't get the opportunity to socialize with men very often and it was fun. What she had going on with Lachlan was in a different category altogether. She felt no threat from Ben but she also didn't feel that sexual lure towards him either. He seemed more like a brother. Lachlan was both a hazard and an enticement. She knew he was bad for her but she couldn't seem to stop herself from wanting him. Why couldn't she be attracted to Ben like that? He was gorgeous and funny and gainfully employed and didn't even live that far away from where she was going to be. He wasn't her soon to be boss or her best friend's husband's best friend. All of those details were points in his favor. Maybe if she just spent a little more time with Ben and a little less time thinking about Lachlan she would get Lachlan out of her system. The one night stand certainly hadn't helped. In fact it had made things worse. Now she actually knew what she was missing and craved it even more.

As midnight rolled around and Annah started to yawn Ben rose from the floor in the living room and made his way to the back door. After putting on his shoes he reached up to caress Annah's cheek and asked if he could give her a kiss goodnight. She didn't flinch this time and leaned in to let him. He kissed her gently and slowly and enfolded her in his embrace. It was definitely pleasant. He had kissing down to an art but no rockets went off. With a sigh he released her and stood back.

"I would be more than happy to help you load tomorrow and drive the truck down for you. I'm at loose ends until Saturday morning when my brother and I can head to the slopes again. We were planning on going to Lake Louise this time. I could just get Brian to follow me and pick me up in Nordegg. Would you like some help? No strings attached. I know you don't want to get involved with anyone right now and I'm not trying to pressure you. I just like you and I'm in a position where I can help."

"Ben, thanks, that would be perfect. I would love to have the help. My two cousins were going to help me load tomorrow. Four is always better than three. Thank you. How about a supper after I get settled. Thank you for understanding that I don't do casual sex." Boy, who was she trying to kid she silently castigated herself. She revised that thought to, "I don't do casual sex, often."

"I can't do a relationship right now. But, by the way, I like you, too," she whispered softly.

"I'll see you in the morning then. Sweet dreams." Ben let himself out and Annah headed to bed. She was not going to have a problem sleeping tonight she thought as she undressed and crawled in. After the lack of sleep she had gotten over the last week, the stress of the exams, and packing all day, she was exhausted.

The next morning Annah sent the kids off to school for their last day. Her cousins Rick and Wayne showed up around the same time as Ben. By three o'clock in the afternoon the loading was done. Rick and Wayne left for home with the assurance from Annah that she had movers booked in Nordegg for tomorrow. They promised to come out for a visit after she was settled. As Ben left with the truck Annah went and picked up the kids from school. She took them back to the home they had lived in for the past four years so that they could see that they were not leaving anything behind. They waved goodbye to the empty abode and set out for their hotel in Rocky. The kids were excited to get back to the pool and waterslide.

As Annah was approaching Rocky, Ben called from Nordegg to let her know he had made it to her house with the truck and that he was leaving the keys at the ranger station. He said he would stop back on Sunday. Annah thanked him and said she'd see him then.

The next morning, after having breakfast in the hotel restaurant, Annah and the kids picked up basic groceries and frozen food that would tide them over until she could make it back into Rocky to do major shopping. She packed the frozen food into coolers she had in the box of the truck. The sun shone brightly and she didn't want anything thawing out before she could put it in her new freezer which was over an hour away. She also stopped at the liquor store to pick up libations for the movers. Once she arrived in Nordegg, Annah stopped at the conservation station to pick up the keys for the moving truck and the extra key for the house that Mrs. Larson had kept. Lachlan walked out of his office as she was getting the keys.

"I met a friend of yours when he dropped off the keys to the truck last night. Have you known him long?"

Annah was taken aback by his accusing tone.

"I'm sure you know that Ben and I met recently. Do you have some kind of a problem with him helping me out?"

"Absolutely not. Are you ready to start unloading?" he asked tersely.

"I will be in about half an hour," Annah responded defensively. "Should I expect you to show up to help?"

"I'm following you right now," Lachlan announced as he closed the door to his office.

"Fine," Annah stated and nonchalantly turned around to leave. She didn't know what burr had gotten stuck up his butt, but she could bet it had something to do with Ben. Well, that was just too bad. If he was going to get bent out of shape over her having male friends then it was going to make it much easier for her to stop obsessing over him. Thomas had been extremely jealous and basically made it impossible for her to even talk to other men. She now knew it was because he assumed that given an opportunity she would be unfaithful just like he was. Annah had promised herself that she would not get involved with someone like that again. She was also not going to let Lachlan think that she would react to or put up with his pouting.

When they reached the residence and Annah let the kids out to run around, Lachlan came over to the truck and started hauling coolers out of the box. Unfortunately, even though she was mad at him she couldn't help but notice that he looked better than any male should have the right to look. His blue jeans hugged his derriere very attractively and the muscles in his forearms bulged below the short sleeves of his cotton tee shirt as he swung down the coolers and carted them to the house. It was too warm for coats and Annah was also in a tee shirt and blue jeans.

"I hired one of the town teenagers to keep an eye on the kids while we unload because a cougar has been spotted prowling around here several times over the last couple of days and I knew you would be preoccupied. Until we can tranquilize it and transport it away from civilization the kids won't be able to play outside unsupervised. I hope I didn't overstep my bounds by organizing these things for you."

Lachlan seemed to have gotten himself back under control in the five minutes it had taken them to drive from the station.

"I appreciate everything you've done for me and no I'm not offended by you anticipating my needs. I think what you have done so far has quite simply made the move easier for me. Thank you."

Lachlan stood stock still holding a cooler as he tried to absorb the compliment that caught him off guard.

"Uh, you're welcome. I'll take these into the house. Gather up the kids and I'll introduce them to Sarah. She's waiting at my house."

While Annah was getting the kids settled she heard several trucks pull up outside and realized that Lachlan's movers must have arrived.

She and Lachlan returned to the moving truck parked in her drive-way. She was surrounded by several very large men of various ages. Lachlan proceeded to introduce them.

"Annah I would like you to meet your moving crew and fellow officers. This is David Fairbanks, John Stover, Dan Granger, Peter Hamilton, Ken Williams, and I believe you already have met Matthew Johnson. Boys meet Officer Glenn Annah Andersson."

Annah shook all of their hands repeating their individual names in her head as she did so.

"I can't thank all of you enough for helping me move. All of the boxes are labeled. So it should be fairly easy to figure out where to put them. The fridge is full of refreshments and there is also a platter of subs in there if you get hungry. Please help yourself." Annah opened the door to the moving truck and started to pull out the ramp.

"Annah, why don't you go into the house and direct us? I think that would really speed things up. You can tell us where you want the furniture placed in each room so that you don't have to move it again later."

In two hours the truck was totally unloaded and the living room actually looked lived in. Peter and John set up the entertainment cen-tre and hooked up the TV and DVD player and connected it to the satellite system that unknown to Annah, Lachlan had installed. With the furniture all arranged the only things missing were pictures on the walls and knick-knacks on the coffee tables. Dan and Ken were set-ting up the bunk beds in the kids' room while David and Matthew put together Annah's bed. Annah set out the refreshments and the subs and then started to unpack boxes in the kitchen. Lachlan came over and helped her.

"Did Nanny do most of the packing and labeling for you?" Lachlan inquired as he read the writing on the side of the box he was unpacking.

"She did some," Annah replied and turned her back to him. She knew that he didn't recognize the handwriting and was trying to fig-ure out who's it was. She figured she would keep him guessing since it was really none of his business.

Instead of asking the question she assumed he was dying to ask, he left it alone and instead questioned her about the placement of a set of mixing bowls. He knew it was a man's handwriting and he was pretty sure it belonged to the same guy who had dropped off the moving truck the night before. He refused to give her the satisfaction of asking. He might be setting the stage for his game plan, but that didn't mean he had to tip his hand as to what he was doing. Also, by not asking the question he would keep her slightly off balance. Meanwhile four big thirsty men entered the kitchen and within minutes chairs and stools were pulled up to the table and sandwiches and cans of beer were passed around. Annah continued to unpack until Lachlan walked over to her and whispered in her ear.

"You're one of us now. Come and sit down and *be* one of us."

Annah put her packing down. She went and sat at the table and took a beer when it was passed to her.

David raised his can and proposed a toast.

"To a new era! We all welcome the feminine touch we know you're going to bring to the station. I know June will be especially happy. To Annah!!"

The other occupants at the table also raised their glasses in welcome. Annah hoped the rest of the staff members were going to be as open-minded and receptive once she started work. In the meantime talk switched to the upcoming NASCAR race scheduled for tomorrow and the fact that two of their fellow officers were lucky enough to be at the Phoenix International Raceway in Avondale attending the race.

Peter looked at the time and suddenly remembered he had company coming for supper and that he was going to be late if he didn't leave immediately. The whole crew made a move for the door. Annah thanked them all again. She followed them outside and then went with Lachlan to his house. After Annah paid Sarah, he drove Sarah home while Annah made a salad to go with the stew Lachlan had left simmering in the crock pot while they worked. After supper Annah and the kids returned to their own home, made beds, and unpacked PJs. Lachlan stayed home and gave her the space he knew she needed. He would leave her alone for the next week, because after that he would be seeing her every day. She could have her reprieve for now. Come May first the full seduction would begin.

CHAPTER 10

ANNAH'S WEEK OFF FLEW by. Summer started school on Monday which left Simon and Annah to unpack the house and try to get things ready for their new routine. As of May first, Annah's evening shifts would begin. Annah was a little nervous having never worked evenings before and was thankful that Nanny would be staying until September to pick up the slack on those days when Annah may be too sleepy to function.

Tuesday, after Summer caught the bus, Annah and Simon headed into Rocky Mountain House for major groceries and to scout out the kid's programs offered at the library. Annah discovered there was a preschool story and craft program on Wednesday mornings. That could work out very well for both of them because she could get her groceries while Simon attended the program and spent time with other kids. She knew he was going to miss playing with others his own age, after attending kindergarten.

Next they stopped by the pool to enroll both Summer and Simon for swimming lessons on Saturday mornings. Then it was off to the bank to open up new bank accounts and to the post office to set up her change of address. McDonald's Play Land entertained Simon at lunch and then the dreaded grocery shopping began. Annah knew she was going to need plenty of staples so she divided her list in half so that she could get one cart full today and her second cart full tomorrow when she came back for story time. Annah loved to bake as well as cook. Now that she was working a normal eight hour shift she hoped to be able to spend more time in the kitchen creating the treats she used to make before going back to school.

After they arrived home while Annah was unloading the groceries the phone rang.

"Hi Annah, it's June. Are you getting settled okay? Hal and I wondered if you would like to come over for supper tonight. Hal had a hankering for a pot roast and it's too big for the two of us to eat. We'll have leftovers for a week if you don't come."

"Thank you, June. That would be great. What time shall I come and what can I bring?"

"Hal is a great cook but he isn't too good in the dessert department. Have you got some ice-cream you can bring over?"

"Dessert is literally a piece of cake. Are either of you allergic to anything?"

"Annah, does it look like I'm allergic to anything? And Hal is definitely not. How does six thirty sound to you? Is that too late for the kids? Do you remember which road to take to get to our house? It's the second right after you turn north off Highway 11 onto Range Road 445. We have a long driveway and you won't be able to see the house until you're almost on top of it. The yard opens up into a meadow behind the house. You can park in front of the garage. Oh, and don't worry about the dogs. They're very excitable and will be barking and bouncing all around you, but their bark is much worse than their bite. We'll see you then."

June signed off before Annah had a chance to say goodbye, let alone confirm the driving directions. Oh well, Annah always carried her cell phone and with a cell tower in Nordegg she should have no trouble getting service that close to town if she got lost. She looked at the time and figured she had better get a move on if she was going to dazzle June and Hal with a spectacular dessert and still make it in time for supper.

Luckily Annah had picked up all kinds of baking supplies that day and so she had the ingredients to make a "skor cake". It was really fast and simple to make, yet was impressive to look at and tasted heavenly. Summer walked in the door from school as Annah was taking the cake from the oven. While the cake was cooling Summer related the events of her day to Annah. Simon and Summer shared a snack and Annah helped Summer with her homework. Once the cake had cooled sufficiently Annah let Summer put the layers together in a trifle bowl. Simon got to put the cherry on the top. Then Annah bundled up the kids, grabbed the dessert, and headed out into the pleasantly lingering twilight. Although the days were getting longer now, it was still dusk by supper time and fully dark by eight o'clock.

As Annah continued down the highway she passed Lachlan leaving the station. He did a double take and then executed a belated wave as he realized she had passed him and was heading in the opposite direction of their houses. Annah chucked to herself knowing it would be killing him wondering where she was going. Hopefully, his direction of travel indicated that he would not be showing up at June's for supper. Although Annah hadn't had any contact with him for three days now and she was almost missing that, she was relieved to know that she could relax tonight and get to know June and her husband without having to keep her guard up. She knew that June would be a fountain of information regarding the other members on staff and that this was a perfect opportunity for fact gathering. Every tidbit she eked out would ease her arrival and hopefully the transition for those she would be working with. She knew this was going to be a big adjustment for several of the members on staff, particularly some of the seasoned officers.

As Annah rounded the last corner of the driveway the little storey and a half stucco bungalow appeared. She drove around it and was awestruck by the view that unfolded before her. The meadow was flanked on three sides by evergreens and budding aspens that ascended the towering mountains. Annah parked and two huge dogs of indeterminate breed came bounding from the edge of the forest and began to bark and bounce around the truck as June had predicted. Before Annah got out of the truck the back door of the house opened and a very large man hollered at the dogs to sit down. Once they were sitting Annah got out and let the children out. She told the kids to stand still and the large man, that she presumed was Hal, commanded the dogs to stay. Then one at a time she let them approach the dogs. Once the kids and dogs were comfortable with each other, Annah herded them towards the house. With an outstretched hand Hal introduced himself.

"The kids could stay outside and play for awhile but there seems to be a cougar wandering around. They haven't been able to catch and relocate the cat yet so it's not the best idea to let them be outside unsupervised."

"Lachlan mentioned that a couple of days ago so I haven't been letting them play outside alone. I am planning on calling the office tomorrow to find out if it has been trapped yet."

"We'll ask June when she finishes changing."

June entered the kitchen in time to hear Hal's comment.

"Whatever it is you need to know about the people and what's going on in this area I'm pretty sure I'll know the answer and if I don't I'll guarantee you that I can find out," she boasted. "Now what is the question? Oh, kids why don't you go downstairs? We have a play station downstairs for our grandkids. Hal, can you get it going for them and I'll make a salad?" June motioned the kids downstairs and turned back to take Annah's dessert from her. "Now, what was that question?"

"I wondered if that cougar had been caught yet."

"Actually, it was. They're transporting it as we speak. Come now, I'm sure you have a million more questions. So, fire away. If you haven't guessed it yet, I love to talk and I pride myself on my limitless abundance of interesting and useful information. And I make no apologies for what some people see as nosiness. Sit, sit," she commanded. "What can I get you to drink?"

"I'm fine," Annah chuckled as she sank into a chair behind the table. "I guess we could start with you telling me about the staff."

"There are fifteen officers including you. The remainder of the staff consists of Lachlan and I and two other dispatchers/receptionists. The midnight to eight in the morning shift is an on call shift that all three of us cover one week at a time. The calls are rerouted to our homes. We rarely get calls during this time and it doesn't make sense to have someone sitting at the station. Our oldest staffer is Fred Saleski. He's a retired officer whose wife passed away about five years ago and whose kids are all grown up and gone. He traveled for a couple of years and then came back as a dispatcher mostly because he was lonely. He has a wonderful sense of humor and is a fountain of knowledge when it comes to the area. I know you'll like him." June finished the salad and continued to set the table. Annah got up to help her and June carried on with her narrative.

"The other dispatcher is Nicole Lange. She's twenty-four and has conned the remainder of the staff into the false impression that she is frail and not real bright. I know differently. She's a master at manipulation and has an almost alarming ability of retaining everything she reads or hears, quite similar to me in fact. She could be an invaluable ally seeing as how there are only three women working at the station. Just be aware that she is smarter than she appears."

"Thank you, for the warning. I am prepared for some resistance. I have dreamed of this career for many years and I'm not about to roll over at the first sign of adversity. I'm in this for the long haul."

"Good. Let's get supper over with so I can dive into that decadent looking dessert you brought. You call Hal and the kids while I finish putting the food on the table," June instructed.

During supper Hal nodded and grunted at the appropriate times while June filled Annah and the kids in with the details of their own lives. They have two grown children. One is a daughter that is married to Peter Hamilton, who had also helped Annah move in, and the other is a son that lives in Calgary. Peter and his wife Linda have three children. They live on an acreage just outside of Nordegg and their kids go to school with Summer. Linda is the village's resident doctor. Annah made a mental note that she needed to get to know her as soon as possible since she was probably going to be using her services.

As they delved into the dessert that both Hal and June enthused over, Summer made sure everyone knew that she had made it. Simon, determined not to be outdone, stated that he had contributed the most important part, the cherry. While Annah and June cleaned up Hal took the kids and went outside to play with the dogs. June added to her staff descriptions by stating that Matthew and David were good friends. While David would undoubtedly be an ally, due to his gentle easy-going nature, Matthew was extremely arrogant and condescending.

John Stover was the station's other new hire and would be starting the same day as Annah. All June knew about him was that he was straight out of school like Annah and she questioned whether Annah knew him. As luck would have it, she did. June continued on down the list as they set the kitchen to rights and by the time she was finished it was time to usher the kids back into the truck. Summer needed to get to bed since she had school in the morning. Annah and the children thanked June and Hal for a lovely evening and continued on home.

As expected June had proven to be extremely informative, Annah reflected as she tucked herself into bed later that night. Any mention of Lachlan had been noticeably absent from June's commentary. She had obviously figured out that Annah and Lachlan had a history and since she was unsure of the exact dynamics of the relationship was waiting to observe their interaction. Annah would be curious to hear June's take on them after she had a chance to watch them for awhile. Maybe if she figured out what was going on between the two of them she could pass it on to Annah and then Annah would stop obsessing over him. Although Annah appreciated the information she had gotten this evening she was not about to give June any ammunition that she could repeat to her various friends and relatives regarding herself or Lachlan. June would have to draw her conclusions based on her own observations. Annah knew Lachlan wasn't any more likely than she was to divulge any details of their past other than the most basic and obvious ones. On that thought, Annah drifted off to sleep to dream of Lachlan just like every other night.

CHAPTER 11

THE REMAINDER OF THE week was spent unpacking, shopping, and familiarizing themselves with the area. Because this was potentially Annah's last free weekend for a while she decided to take the kids to Edmonton to visit her aunt, uncle, and cousins. Although both boys were married only Wayne had children who luckily were close in age to Annah's children. Every birthday and holiday except Christmas had been spent together since Annah and the kids had moved to Alberta. They, along with Jennifer and Dane, had made Annah's past four years much easier. Uncle Ken was always supportive and full of kind advice. Auntie Doreen had a wonderful sense of humor and treated Annah like the daughter she never had. They would go shopping together and share recipes. Since Annah and her cousins had spent a lot of time together as they were growing up they had common interests. They had camped together frequently and hoped to continue to do so now that they had their own families.

Auntie and Annah went shopping for a few hours and then met the daughter-in-laws for lunch while Wayne took the kids to the Water Park at West Edmonton Mall. Uncle Ken cooked and hosted a family BBQ for the dozen of them on Saturday evening and then they played board games. They were all very curious to know the details of

Annah's new job and how she was going to manage after she started work. Since she was now essentially going to be alone, without family close by, they were concerned that she set up a temporary safe place for the kids to go. That way if something happened to her the kids would be okay until one of the clan could drive down to care for them. Annah assured them that although she had nothing pre-arranged she would do that once she got to know more people in the community and before Nanny left. Since Nanny was staying until September this gave Annah time to implement a back-up plan to satisfy all of them.

She didn't tell them that she knew Lachlan would step in and keep the kids safe until someone else arrived. She didn't want to open herself up to a whole battery of questions. Not only did she not want to answer any questions but also she didn't have the answers to some she knew they would ask. She knew they wanted her to find someone to love and take care of her. All of them had been lucky enough to find spouses that complimented them perfectly. It was part of the reason Annah enjoyed her time spent with them so much. They were all obviously, genuinely happy. They were also wonderful role models for Summer and Simon. It was a very comfortable and pleasant weekend for everyone. Sunday, after a home-cooked brunch, fit for a king, Annah and the kids headed back to Nordegg.

The sun shone brightly as Annah rolled into the driveway just in time to see Nanny pull off the highway and make her way to the house. Annah was happy to have plenty of time to get everything setup for tomorrow morning. Although she was scheduled for evenings for the next four months she would be working both the day shift and the evening shift tomorrow along with John, the other new officer. They would be shown the basic routine of the station together rather than having someone have to repeat the orientation.

Annah tucked the kids into bed and after a visit with Nanny she settled herself into the tub for a soothing soak. She reviewed her mental checklist for tomorrow to make sure she hadn't forgotten any details regarding their new routine. Since Nanny would be using Annah's bedroom until she moved out, Annah's closet was in the basement and she slept on the sofa bed in the living room. It wasn't the perfect arrangement but it was the most practical. Annah set up for breakfast and brushed the imaginary lint off of her brand new uniform as she draped it over a chair in the kitchen. She set her alarm, pulled out her bed, and attempted to shut off her mind long enough to get a few hours of sleep. She knew eight hours of sleep was a pipe dream since she was both too excited and nervous to be able to relax.

~

The alarm went off at six o'clock the next morning. She actually had about six hours sleep and felt refreshed and ready to tackle her day. After showering and getting the kids up Annah sat down to enjoy the breakfast Nanny had prepared. She braided her hair, dressed in her uniform, kissed the kids, and set out. Lachlan's truck had already left when she climbed into hers. Annah pulled up to the station and practically sprinted from the truck into the office. Lachlan watched her from his office window. Her smile was as wide as the Grand Canyon and her barely contained euphoria radiated from her very being. Lachlan smiled to himself and hoped for her sake that this career fulfilled all of her expectations. He vowed to help her achieve her goals.

"Good morning, Annah," Lachlan greeted her as he walked from his office to the coffee machine.

She spun around from looking at the staff pictures on the wall and met him at the machine.

"Coffee?" he inquired as he held the pot out towards her. "I see you are bright-eyed and bushy-tailed this morning. Did your weekend away refresh you?"

Annah held up her hand and shook her head at his offer of coffee.

"Actually, Lachlan, I prefer tea. And you have no idea how rejuvenating my weekend was. Thanks for asking. Do you have a kettle? Oh and how was your weekend?" she inquired.

"No, we don't have a kettle, but I'm sure we can find it in the budget to purchase one. Ask June about it. Here she comes now. My weekend wasn't particularly invigorating or refreshing as it was spent reviewing old reports, but thanks for asking."

"Any time," Annah quipped.

June bustled in and removed her coat. She walked over to the coffee machine and filled her twenty-four ounce coffee mug. She proceeded to make the second pot of coffee and then turned to address Lachlan.

"What is it you need to know?"

"Can we buy a kettle so I can make tea?" Annah replied before Lachlan could respond. "I can bring my own tea bags."

"Of course, we can buy a kettle and you don't have to bring your own tea. Just give me a list of what you need or go purchase it yourself and then give me the receipt and I'll pay you back."

"Thank you, I will."

The office had started to fill as they stood there and talked. Lachlan motioned her over to a vacant desk. She sat down and endured the curious stares of the other officers as they grabbed cups of coffee and then went past her desk to their own. They all greeted her on their way by and most offered a smile. The outside door opened one final time and her fellow rookie, John Stover, walked in. Lachlan greeted him with a hand shake and directed him to the coffee and his new desk.

When all were settled Lachlan walked to the front of the room, stood before his staff, and got their attention.

"As I am sure you have probably already guessed we are joined this morning by our two new officers, both fresh from school. I would like to introduce John Stover and Annah Andersson to all of you. John will be following the normal shift rotation with the rest of you while Annah will be working evenings exclusively for the next four months. With the addition of these two new officers your evening and on-call shifts have already been reduced. Annah will be taking twenty of the sixty evening shifts previously scheduled per month. For now John will be with the partner of the member who is scheduled to work evenings. The new members will be assigned permanent partners in August. For today they will both shadow Peter. Matthew has the evening off so Annah will be working solo with David. I expect all of you to be as helpful and accommodating as possible since their success leads to your own success. Please introduce yourselves to them sometime today."

Lachlan hung up a new schedule on the board behind him.

"Check out the revised evening schedule before you head out today. Attendance at Friday morning's staff meeting is mandatory.

The new summer policies will be reviewed and revised if necessary. Summer holiday requests need to be on my desk no later than three o'clock today. I have a conference in Edmonton from Tuesday until Thursday. That's all for now folks. Have a good week. Drive safely and take care of our forest while I'm gone."

With a nod of his head Lachlan turned away and walked down the hall to his office. Paper shuffling and chatting resumed after Lachlan had left. Peter called John and Annah over to his desk. Officers that Annah hadn't met previously introduced themselves on their way out to their trucks or for coffee refills. So far the environment of the station appeared friendly and upbeat. Annah hoped her presence didn't change all that.

Annah grabbed her backpack, coat, and a chair, and sat down across from Peter. She took out a notepad and pen and waited for Peter to begin. They started off with the basic routine. Each team of two had several designated areas they were responsible to manage but they all needed to be familiar with the area as a whole. With each changing season there were different challenges for the officers. The emergence of spring brought new babies, raised water levels in the creeks, rivers, and lakes, forest fires, and an increased human presence. A conservation officer's duties involved preserving the habitat of all forest animals, the animals themselves, and keeping the human visitors to this habitat safe. They also needed to be trained for rescue in many different situations. In order to accomplish these duties, patrols needed to be conducted by truck, aircraft, boat, quad, mountain sled, on horseback and on foot. Because the area was so vast and the terrain was not only diverse but also seasonally changing, the officer's daily priorities needed to be constantly adjusted. Unpredictable changes in weather often caused problems for both the officers and the public. Responsibilities also included issuing licenses and permits. Complaints of poaching or other violations needed to be investigated and documented. All conservation officers are also Peace Officers and Special Officers. Therefore, they are obligated to enforce all provincial and federal statutes and have the authority to arrest any violators.

The first order of the day was to familiarize Annah and John with the computer system they would use to keep track of everything from fish populations and mortality rates in each creek, to the depth of snow, and the percentage of avalanche probability on certain mountain slopes. Although the members each had a partner they all had their own specialized area of expertise. This particular office employed conservation officers, fish and wildlife officers, environmental officers, and forestry officers. Unfortunately, because of the small number of members versus the large number of hectares of land that this station was responsible for, the jobs had to overlap. All of the computers in the office were networked so that all information entered could be shared. You could work the job for twenty years and no two days would be the same. There were too many variables, too little time, and too few officers. The magnitude of the job could be considered either overwhelming or the challenge of a lifetime.

Annah was trained to be an environmental officer. Therefore, her main focus was wildlife management. There were two other environmental officers already working at the station. They were Matthew and David. Chances were good that she, being as Junior C.O., would end up partnered with one of them since they were both Senior C.Os. Annah hoped it was David since she knew that Matthew definitely wasn't a member of her fan club.

After reviewing the computer program Peter walked them around the station. The supply room was first on the tour. They went through the list of equipment each officer carried with them every day. Each team was responsible for maintaining and replacing necessary equipment daily. The practice this station employed was to pack your teammate's gear. This tended to increase each members diligence since your attentiveness directly affected your partner's safety as well as your own. John packed Annah's gear while Annah packed John's. Each equipment bag had the member's name on it as well as a unique, easily recognizable item attached to it. Each member was to carry their equipment bag in their truck. The duty belt was to be worn at all times while on duty. It contained your gun, handcuffs, knife, baton, pepper spray, compass, and flashlight. If caught out in the field without it a written reprimand was added to your file. Three reprimands and dismissal could be enforced because lack of gear endangered your team. This was something Lachlan would not tolerate.

Next stop was the dispatch desk. This was quite likely the most important job at the station. Mrs. Larson was responsible for monitoring all incoming and outgoing radio traffic and telephone calls. Two-way radios were the devices used for allowing all members to keep in contact with each other. At noon the three took a break and ate their lunch while discussing the afternoon's schedule. A field trip was decided upon. Peter sent Annah to inform Lachlan that they were going to head out into one of his designated areas.

"Officer MacGregor?" Annah inquired as she tapped on his door before entering his office.

"Come in, Annah, and call me Lachlan. We are a small staff that has to work together in an environment where trust in each other is vital. The formality of calling each other "Officer" is only necessary when we are in the presence of the public. At the station please call me and all the other members by their given names. Now what can I do for you?"

"Officer MacGregor, unless you force the issue I would prefer to call you Officer. To me it is a sign of respect and an indicator that you are my superior, at work. When I call you Lachlan I want you to know that I am speaking to you as a woman, not as your subordinate. I need to keep our personal relationship and our professional one separate. This is one obvious way I can do that."

Lachlan sat back in his chair and steepled his fingers. Looking at her with ever increasing admiration, he nodded.

"I respect your request and will honor your wishes, Officer Andersson. What was it that you came in to tell me?"

"Peter has decided to take us out to measure some water levels in the creeks in a couple of his designated areas. He asked me to inform you before we left."

"Are you comfortable working the evening shift after working today or is it becoming too overwhelming for you?"

"There is a lot to absorb but I am fine with working tonight. I should be going. Peter is waiting to go over the supply list for the trucks with both John and I." As Annah turned to exit the office she felt Lachlan stand up.

"Annah, this is my cell number. I want you to call me if you have any problems at all, either at work or at home. I always have it on me and it is always charged. Promise me," he quietly beseeched.

Annah turned back towards him. She straightened herself, looked him directly in the eye, and took the piece of paper from his outstretched hand.

"I promise, Lachlan." Annah was not so proud or independent that she would turn down an offer of support. She may never need to use that number but it was a comfort to know that she had it. "Thank you. Enjoy your conference. I'll see you Friday." With that she folded the piece of paper and tucked it into her pocket before she walked out of the office to join Peter and John at the truck.

After going over the truck supply list and replenishing their supplies, they headed to the gas station in Nordegg. The trucks were not assigned to specific teams and so they were logged out each time they left the station. Trucks were to be refueled before they returned to the station each night. However, if the gas station was closed then the truck was to be filled the next day before going out into the field. They proceeded to the first of the assigned areas and then performed and recorded various measurements. They had time to process three creeks before heading back to the station. The recorded data was then entered into the computer. After Peter and John signed out, Annah grabbed her supper and headed over to David's desk.

The station had basically cleared out. The evening dispatcher, Fred, was on duty now. David was the only other member there besides Annah. He waved her over and patted the seat of the chair he had placed beside his desk for her.

"Come and eat your supper while I finish a report that I started last night. Right now I'm doing a five year study on the beaver population in this region. Once the study is finished I hope to have the results published. So tell me about yourself while I finish up last night's report and then we'll get started. What is your area of expertise?"

"I graduated as an environmental officer," Annah responded. She then gave him a brief rundown of her education and her major area of study. She had graduated with a degree in Environmental and Conservation Sciences. She had worked full time between University sessions in the field of Natural Resources Law Enforcement. This entailed issuing tickets to the public for non-compliance of statutes, regulations and standards set out by the federal and provincial governments. She basically rode along on patrols and did whatever she was told to do. She had worked out of a different station each summer. The first station was in central Alberta, the second in northern B.C., and the third was in southern Saskatchewan. She was employed as a summer student in each of these cases which gave her the required twelve months work experience that she needed to apply for this permanent position. Nanny and the children had followed her to each job which had exposed them to new places and experiences.

David was struck by her enthusiasm. Lachlan had told him that she had graduated at the top of her class. She was not only smart but also physically fit and not afraid of work. A fresh new perspective on things would definitely be welcome. Lachlan's leadership over the past couple of months had revitalized the station. An atmosphere of professionalism was obvious. Things were more organized than they had ever been since David had started. Members were expected to be accountable for their actions. Reports were to be finished in a timely manner.

Lachlan had an image of what he wanted the station to become and he was insuring that the members carried out this dream by motivating them into taking pride in themselves and their accomplishments. Now that David had met Annah he knew that she was a part of Lachlan's vision. He knew he was going to enjoy working with her and he instinctively felt they would become good friends. But the first time he had met her he had been struck by an uncomfortable premonition that she was going to be involved in a life altering experience with him that was going to turn out badly. Although the premonition hadn't reoccurred he did remember it. He shook it off and concentrated on the here and now.

"Basically what you are going to be doing for the next four months, since you won't be going out in the field, is reviewing the reports and entering data collected during the day. You will be combining the information and then adding your conclusions and recommendations for our field work. So essentially you're going to be acting as a consultant for all of us. Although we won't be working together every evening we can email each other from shift to shift and that way stay in contact. How do you feel about this?"

"It sounds good. It will allow me time to study the unique features of this area before I actually work out in the field. Thank you for the opportunity."

"I understand you asked for this shift. Why?"

"My nanny is only staying with me until the middle of September so I need to get in as many evening shifts as possible now because it could take me a while to find someone to replace her for that one week a month that we need to work evenings. I know I can find a place for the children to go during the day but it won't be so easy to hire someone for my evening shifts this fall. I made an arrangement with Officer MacGregor that if I worked straight evenings for four months and then tripled my night on-call shifts for the next two months, I wouldn't have to do another evening shift or on-call shift Until January." Annah then changed the conversation back from personal to business and the night flew by.

When she fell into bed that night although she thought she wouldn't be able to stop thinking about all the new things she had learned and the new people she had met, she was wrong. She was out like a light. She got up the next morning in time to have breakfast with everyone and then spent the next few hours playing with Simon. After lunch she had a nap for a couple of hours and then got up to meet Summer's bus. She and the kids spent the next hour together and then she left for work. Her first few days on the job had worked out fine. This was stacking up to be better than she had anticipated.

CHAPTER 12

Wᴛᴛʜ ᴛʜᴇ ᴇxᴄᴇᴘᴛɪᴏɴ ᴏꜰ Wednesday mornings spent in Rocky grocery shopping while Simon went to the library and Friday morning's staff meeting Annah's routine would be almost a carbon copy every weekday. Annah worked Sunday night to Thursday night. Nanny would start her weekends off as soon as Annah returned from the Friday morning staff meeting. Saturday mornings it was back to Rocky for swimming lessons and incidentals and the occasional matinee at the town's theater. It was a comfortable uncomplicated schedule. Both Annah and the children appeared to be thriving. The only fly in the ointment was that Annah could not seem to get Lachlan out of her dreams. She had very little interaction with him but she did see him and he did speak to her every day. Plus, all she had to do was look out of her front room window and she could watch his comings and goings when she was home.

Lachlan would have told her she was crazy if she had accused him of seducing her with his lackadaisical attitude. However, his indifference was having what she suspected was the desired effect. She was preoccupied with sexual fantasies of him that kept popping up at the most inopportune times. However, before she could feel Lachlan out, she received an unexpected visit from Ben. It was Saturday afternoon and she was leaving Rocky. Her cell phone rang.

"Hey, Annah. It's Ben. I'm on my way out to B.C. for a few days and I wondered if you were going to be home tonight."

"Absolutely! Can you make it out in time for supper?"

"Yah. I'm in Rocky now. I can be out there in an hour."

"That's funny because so am I. I'll meet you at the house. Where are you staying for the night? I don't have an extra bedroom but I have a pullout sofa bed in the living room you could use."

"That would be great. I haven't made a reservation anywhere yet. See you soon."

As Annah was pulling into her driveway Lachlan was walking out of his house.

"Hello, Annah. Spend the day in Rocky?"

"Yes. We did swimming lessons, lunch at McDonalds, and a movie at the theater, and then picked up a few groceries. Back to the office, are you?"

"Actually, I'm off to meet my contractor."

"Contractor? Are you building a house out here?"

"Yes. I've decided that this is as good a place as any to settle down. I had the plans drawn up about ten years ago. I bought an acreage when I moved out here and they are supposed to start building on Monday."

"Really! That's very exciting. Where is it?"

"About ten minutes down the road in Whispering Pines. Would you like to come and see it?"

"I'd love to but I'm expecting someone for the evening." With that statement Ben pulled into the driveway behind her.

"I'll continue on my way then. See you later."

"Would you like to come for supper, Lachlan?" Annah asked before he made his way back across the street to his truck.

He stopped short and turned back towards her. He could either turn her down flat and then torture himself all night wondering what she and "mover boy" were talking about and/or doing, or he could graciously accept and spend the evening with the two of them. Either way it would be a test.

"Thank you, Annah. I would love to come for supper. What time should I be back and what would you like me to bring?"

"We're eating at six o'clock and you don't need to bring anything. By the way, have you met Ben? Ben this is Lachlan MacGregor, he's the Area Manager at my station. Lachlan this is Ben LaCosta, a lawyer from Red Deer."

After the pleasantries were exchanged Lachlan headed back across the street and Ben helped Annah bring the groceries into the house. Ben and Annah made supper while the kids played downstairs. She caught up with the latest events in his life and she filled him in on everything she was doing. Ben had brought a bottle of Merlot that they shared while he entertained her with stories about some of his clients, the lawyers he was up against, and witnesses that were too ridiculous to be believed. He had the tears rolling down her cheeks, she was laughing so hard. Lachlan walked in as she was trying to catch her breath, carrying a similar bottle of Merlot.

The atmosphere in the kitchen was comfortable and inviting. Lachlan felt like an intruder. He surveyed the scene and wondered if Annah deserved that kind of life rather than the life he could offer her. Lachlan was definitely not known for his comedic ability. But he did know that he loved her and believed no one else could love her like he did. This was one challenge he was not walking away from. He knew that with perseverance he would get her to fall in love with him. He realized he should have declined her invite to supper because he was not in competition with Ben for her affections. He already had them. She just didn't realize it. Right after supper he excused himself with the comment that he needed to get some paperwork done. It was time for stage two of the seduction to be implemented starting tomorrow night.

Lachlan's departure was unexpected. If he was trying to keep Annah off kilter he was doing an excellent job of it. After putting the kids to bed, Annah and Ben stayed up and played cards while they chatted about life in general.

"Lachlan is more than your boss, Annah. I can tell by the way you watch each other. I felt the undercurrents as soon as you introduced us."

"Ben, it's complicated. I can't explain it because I don't understand it myself."

"You don't have to explain. I was simply making a comment. If you need to talk I'm a good listener. Speaking of which, can I bounce a few things off of you? I met this girl and I could definitely do with some female advice."

The evening continued with advice being bandied back and forth. By midnight Annah was starting to fade so they opened the sofa bed and she made it up for Ben. Lachlan pulled up as she turned out the lights in her room and went to sleep.

The next morning right after breakfast Ben left. She gave him a hug and a kiss on the cheek as he was leaving and wished him well with his new relationship. He thanked her for a wonderful supper and the advice and told her to stop being so uptight and to live a little. With a smile and a wave Ben was gone. Annah and the kids spent the day digging flowerbeds around the outside of the house. Nanny returned in time for Annah to go to work. And so Annah's week began.

Tonight Annah was working with Matthew. Although they saw each other at the weekly staff meetings this was the first time she had actually talked to him since her interview. She knew she was going to have to be the one to make the first move. Any contact she had observed between Matthew and the other staff was friendly and relaxed. Apparently he only had a problem with her.

"Hey, Matthew," she greeted him, "looks like we're going to be shift sharing for the next few evenings. Is there anything you need me to do before I get started on David's reports?"

"Look, I don't like you anymore than you like me. So, how's about if we just stay out of each other's way? And for the record, the reports you are working on are from the project that both David and I are doing." Matthew turned away, but then turned back. "Oh, and in case someone forgot to fill you in, David has a fiancée that lives in Rocky. She's a lawyer and she's very protective of what belongs to her."

"Well, since we're clearing the air, I don't dislike you. However, I don't like being called "some ditsy broad" just like you probably wouldn't like to be called an "arrogant showoff". I am well aware that the project is both yours and David's. But, at this point the reports I am working on are David's. I know that David is engaged and not only do I not fool around with other women's men I am disturbed by the fact that you assume I would when you don't know anything about me. For the record my husband *died*. He didn't leave me because I was cheating on him. Nowhere is it written that you have to like me but we do need to be able to treat each other with respect and to be professional. Whether you like it or not you are going to have to work with me occasionally. Could we please bury the hatchet and move on? I know I can. Can you?" Annah knew she had issued a challenge. He had no choice other than to agree or else look childish and petty and she would win.

"Fine. I can live with that," he answered curtly.

Annah extended her hand and Matthew reluctantly clasped it and gave it an abrupt but firm handshake. He then turned away and sat down at his desk. Annah also turned around and headed towards the coffee centre. She almost ran headlong into Lachlan who was coming out of his office. Lachlan steadied her with his hand on her forearm. She backed away from him like a scalded cat. But it was still enough contact to cause a shiver to run up her spine.

"Lachlan," she exclaimed breathlessly. "I had no idea you were working tonight. I didn't see your truck when I got to work." Unconsciously she had broken her own rule by calling him by his first name. He smiled inside.

"Well, that would be because it's parked out back. I'm sorry. I didn't mean to startle you. How are you and Matthew getting along?"

"I'm sure we will be just fine."

"That's good to hear since you know my policy on trusting your fellow officers. If there is a problem you need to let me know so that it can be rectified."

"If we can't work it out ourselves I will be sure to involve you. So far things look promising."

"I'm happy to hear that. I'll be sure to let you know before I leave. Could you let me know when the water boils, Officer Andersson? I would also like a cup of tea." With that statement he returned to his office.

Annah started the kettle as Nicole, tonight's dispatcher, joined her at the coffee machine.

"I didn't mean to eavesdrop but I did overhear you having words with Matthew. He is really an okay guy. David and Matthew are best friends. They're pretty much joined at the hip. Matthew, David, and his fiancée, Dabria, all grew up together. And Matthew is right about Dabria being very jealous. They got engaged a few years back and she makes sure every female in the county is aware of it. Her ring is the size of a golf ball."

"Trust me, Nicole. I promise you I am not a threat to David or any of his relationships," Annah stated.

"That's good to know. I'll be sure to pass your comments on."

The phone rang and Nicole returned to her post. When the water boiled Annah made tea for herself and Lachlan. After taking him a cup she returned to her own desk and went back to work. At eleven thirty Annah got up from her computer, stretched and went to make herself another cup of tea. She walked into Lachlan's office to see if he wanted a cup and found him sleeping on the couch. She stood for a while watching him and then went to the supply room to get a fleece blanket. She unfolded it and proceeded to drape it over him. As she bent down to tuck it in around him he opened his eyes and looked up at her. She stopped and stood stock still. He reached up his hand and caressed her cheek. He wrapped his hand around the nape of her neck and gently tugged. She sank to her knees mesmerized by his unwavering gaze. Tenderly cupping the side of her face he urged her mouth to meet his as he raised himself up on one arm. He kissed her slowly and tenderly. She slid her hands up his chest and leaned into him. Lachlan stopped kissing her and held her back.

"I want you. I've wanted you since I bumped into you in the hall at University. Like you, I foolishly believed that if we spent a night together I would get you out of my system. I was obviously wrong," Lachlan said.

Annah sat back on her heels. Lachlan sat up on the sofa and swung his legs down to the floor. He took Annah by the hand. He pulled her up onto the sofa beside him. He continued to hold her hand while he talked to her. She didn't pull away.

"I know you don't want a relationship that entails emotional attachment. What I am proposing is that we become lovers. No commitment to each other beyond exclusivity. It would be on your terms.

We would be on your time schedule and you pick the locations since I know you wouldn't be comfortable at your house while the kids are there."

"Lachlan, I don't know if I can do this. I can't imagine where we could possibly execute this affair since we work opposite shifts and the kids are always with me when I'm not at work."

"Actually, I have a solution for that. After you get off shift you can come to my place. You can park your truck at your place and walk across the street. You can leave anytime you like. I promise not to reveal our affair to anyone. Although you will control the frequency and length of each encounter, as lovers we will be equals. I'm not trying to pressure you. Just think about my proposal. Here is a key to my house. If the range light is on in the kitchen it means I'm home and I'm willing." Lachlan looked into her eyes and tried to lighten the conversation that had become filled with tension. "I should probably invest in GE Electric since I don't foresee the light ever being turned off."

Lachlan felt the tension flow out of Annah. She sighed, dropped her head, and then chuckled. He lifted her chin with his knuckle and looked deeply into her eyes.

"Annah, the ball is in your court. I'm going home now. Oh, FYI, I stocked up on birth control."

With that closing remark Lachlan stood up and pulled Annah with him. He turned her around and gently coaxed her out into the hall. He turned off his lights and bid farewell to Nicole and Matthew. Annah returned to her desk and then realized that she had forgotten her tea. She made her way back to the coffee counter, finished making her tea, and resumed analyzing the report. Matthew and Nicole exchanged looks over Annah's bent head. Rumors had circulated speculating that Lachlan and Annah were involved in a clandestine relationship. Up to this point, however, no one had witnessed anything other than a professional association. Although neither Nicole nor Matthew had observed anything specific tonight they both had a feeling that there was more going on than met the eye. Nicole would be adding her thoughts to the rumor mill in the morning. She couldn't wait.

At twelve fifty-five Nicole came over to Annah and tapped her on the shoulder.

"Hey. I know you're trying to be all dedicated and impress every-one since you just started, but really it's time to go. Pack it in, honey, 'cause I'm out o' here. See you tomorrow."

Annah shut down her computer, stood up and stretched. Matthew was standing by the door waiting for her to lock up. He had been very helpful and with the exception of her conversation with Lachlan, things had gone extremely smoothly tonight. Annah followed Matthew out and drove home. As she pulled into her driveway she looked over at Lachlan's and saw the light on. She turned off the truck and sat with her head resting against the steering wheel. If she went in to her own bed she knew she wouldn't get a wink of sleep and she would probably have to deal with the light being on again tomorrow night. Therefore, her only other option was to go over to Lachlan's and begin an affair that she was terrified would end in her being left emotionally scarred or may eventually cost her her job. If she could remain emotionally detached from Lachlan this could be the perfect solution to filling the only void that she now had in her life. If she had sex on a regular basis that should stop her erotic dreams and allow her to concentrate on the other areas of her life. The question was could she remain indifferent?

As she sat there trying to determine which was the lesser of the two evils Lachlan sat in his house waiting for the sound of her truck door to slam. Five minutes ticked by and unable to stand the sus-pense any longer he stood up and looked out the window. There Annah sat with her head still resting against the steering wheel. He knew she wouldn't come over without serious consideration for the repercussions and that this was not a choice she would make lightly. He hated to watch her struggling with the decision he had forced on her. She had so many pressures in her life, demands on her time, and expectations from not only others but mostly from herself. Lachlan didn't want to add to her stress but he believed that in the long run if he could only get her to realize she was already emotionally involved with him, then, he would ultimately be able to share a life with her and share her responsibilities. She needed to learn for herself that she would always be able to depend on him both physically and emotion-ally for not only herself but also for her children. He knew she was afraid that this was going to be a temporary affair and that she was going to end up hurt. Telling her she was wrong was something she wasn't ready to hear or accept. Annah was going to need to reach that conclusion on her own. Lachlan MacGregor was a permanent part of her life now and nothing was going to make him go away.

Although he wished he could go outside and either tell her he was retracting his offer or entice her into accepting it, he knew that he could do neither. She had to make this decision without any interference from him. He wanted her. He needed her. He loved her. But, she had to come to him willingly.

Lachlan turned from the window and went back to the blueprints he had been looking at on the table. He heard her door slam. He waited, unconsciously holding his breath, while he stood leaning over the table straining for the sound of her boots on his steps. Seemingly endless seconds stretched into a minute. Finally brisk determined footfalls sounded on the front porch. Lachlan released his breath and waited for the door to open.

Quietly Annah turned the doorknob and slipped into the kitchen. She softly closed the door behind her. She gasped when Lachlan stood up straight at the table and she realized he was in the kitchen with her. Without saying a word he stood watching her and waiting for her to make her way to him. Annah took off her boots, unzipped her coat and removed it. She undid her braid and shook out her hair. As she walked towards him she continued to remove articles of clothing. First her shirt was unbuttoned and shrugged off. Then her t-shirt was pulled over her head. Mesmerized, Lachlan leaned against the table. Obviously once she made a decision there was no holding back, no hesitation. Off came her belt and then her socks. She stopped just out of arms reach and unzipped her pants and shimmied them down her hips and let them pool at her bare feet. She took one step forward out of them and then undid the clasp of her bra and let it slide to the floor. The last article of clothing was a scrap of pink lace that barely covered her mound. She skimmed her hands over her hips and pulled down her panties. If Lachlan had experienced problems breathing before, now he had forgotten how to breathe altogether and every ounce of blood that had been pumping through his body was now centered in the bulging anatomy straining behind the zipper of his jeans.

Annah reached out her hand and grasping Lachlan's hand in hers placed it on her naked breast. The last vestige of Lachlan's control snapped and he stepped towards her. Before he could touch her anywhere else she placed her hand on his chest halting his progress forward. Although his body was begging for him to take her right now, on the floor, against the door, or anywhere else she would allow him to, he was coherent enough to realize that she wanted to be the one in control this time. She reversed their positions and backing up to the table moved his papers while he continued to hold onto and caress her breast.

Although the table was old and heavily scarred it had been refinished and was smooth on top and steady. Annah perched one cheek at a time onto the top of it and scooted herself back just enough to position comfortably on it with her arms resting behind, supporting her. She leaned back, wrapping her legs around Lachlan's waist and pulled him towards her. With one hand behind her back to hold her up, she used the other to undo his belt and then tried to unzip his jeans. The material was stretched so tightly over his crotch she was forced to use both hands. After releasing his cock and smoothing on the condom he had thoughtfully pulled out of his pocket, she again leaned back and guided his other hand to her opening. As he slid one finger inside, her back instinctively arched and a moan escaped her parted lips. Although his own body was screaming for him to mate he continued to gently knead one breast and stroke with his other hand. When he lowered his head and began to suckle at her exposed breast Annah began to pant and toss her head back and forth. As her arms started to quiver he increased the tempo of his strokes and added another finger. Within moments her body stiffened and lifting his mouth from her breast he covered her mouth with his own, stifling her scream of release.

He unceasingly manipulated her as the contractions relentlessly continued to convulse through her. As she climaxed again he removed his fingers and drove into her in one smooth stroke. She remained taut and he stood stock still letting her come down and adjust to the fullness. As she started to sag he slowly withdrew and then filled her again. She scooted closer to the edge of the table to take all of him in. He released her mouth and kissed up and down her neck. She locked her arms behind her and let him pump into her with his hands on her hips and his lips and tongue skimming her neck. As the tempo increased she could feel his hands tighten on her hips. She allowed herself to come again so that her contractions would in turn pull him over the edge. He surged into her one final time and grinding his crotch into her softness he jerked spastically as he again sought her mouth to stifle his own release this time. She wrapped her arms around his neck and clung to him. Without breaking their connection Lachlan lifted her off the table and walked with her into his bedroom.

With one hand wrapped around her he pulled off his jeans and boxers and turning around fell onto his bed. He continued to kiss her forehead and stroke her hair as he lay on his back with her astride him. She laid her head on his chest breathing heavily as she trailed a path through his chest hair with one finger.

He held her tenderly and he let his mind drift. No one would ever guess that Miss Proper in Public was little Miss Mountain Lioness in the bedroom. For that Lachlan would be forever grateful. She turned him on like no other woman ever had. Possibly for the sole reason that it was so much more than just physical this time. Not a word had passed between them since she had come in and he was loath to break the silence and possibly shatter the moment.

She took the decision out of his hands by speaking first.

"I can't give you more of me than what I have just given you. So, please don't ask. When we are alone my body is yours to do with as you wish. I want to be your equal. This is all there can ever be, Lachlan. Do you understand?"

"Yes," he breathed into her hair. What she didn't realize was that he knew she had given him all of herself and although he wouldn't reveal that to her now, he had no intention of letting this relationship end. After tonight he would forever be a part of her and she a part of him. When she looked back, she would see that he had always loved her.

"You proved tonight that you are my equal, Annah. It took courage to face your sexual attraction and come to me. I will never purposely hurt you. And if I do by accident, promise you will tell me. I don't mean just physically either. Do you understand?"

"Lachlan, I trust you as I have trusted no other. I'm sure you know that the behavior I exhibit with you is unexplored territory for me. While it seems to come naturally to react like this to you, it is still foreign for me to do so."

"Annah, I am thrilled that you feel comfortable exploring your sexuality with me. I encourage any fantasies in which you want to indulge. Lead me where you will and I will do likewise. Just tell me if what I request makes you feel uncomfortable."

"Although I may seem hesitant at first, so far everything has gone beyond what I can imagine. And so as they say "Let the Games Begin"!"

Annah pushed herself upright continuing to sit astride Lachlan and gave him a dazzling smile. The movement caused Lachlan to spontaneously swell. And so the conversation ended and the games progressed. Lachlan dozed off around three o'clock and Annah slipped from his bed, dressed, and locked herself out. She crept across the street into her own home and bed.

In the morning Nanny Bea made breakfast and the kids tussled with Annah on the sofa bed. After breakfast Summer caught the bus and Simon was doing dishes with Nanny when Annah announced that she was going back to bed for a couple of hours and would be sleeping in Simon's room. Nanny looked up past Simon.

"Will the activities of last night be repeated?" Nanny asked.

"Yes," Annah replied with a blush. "Every night that they can until my shift changes to days and you leave. I hope that this isn't a problem. I can stop if you need me to."

"No," Nanny sighed with a shake of her head. "I think it may be good for both of you. When do you want me to call you?"

"Noon would be great."

"Simon and I will play outside this morning after the dishes. Sweet dreams."

Annah fell into Simon's bed and was snoring softly in a matter of minutes. Since she had been sleep-deprived much of the last four years, she had trained herself to fall asleep almost on demand. As she drifted off to dreamland she hoped she would be able to maintain her appearance of personal indifference to Lachlan at work after last night.

Deep down she knew things were different. She had felt the same connection that Lachlan had and recognized the intensity with which he had "made love" to her. It had progressed from uncontrolled and almost frenzied to achingly tender and slow with every caress seeming to be almost reverent. What they had was not simply sex. She refused to admit that to herself yet, when she was fully conscious. However, it became glaringly obvious and somehow not nearly as frightening as it should have been as she drifted off to sleep.

CHAPTER 13

Annah couldn't envision her life any better than it was right now. She cherished every moment she spent with her children and every moment she spent in Lachlan's arms. Annah knew from personal experience, as well as her career, that life was all about evolution and change. So, although she wasn't about to jump into a relationship with Lachlan, beyond the physical, she did give that aspect of it her all. Similarly with every shift at work she learned more about her duties and more about the environment around her.

Spring slipped into summer and before Annah realized it the kids were out of school and summer holidays had arrived. Annah's shift changed so that she no longer had weekends off but instead took two days off during the week. Because there were more tourists out on the weekends none of the staff had weekends off. Days off were spent hiking and fishing and camping and biking with the kids. Because Annah's extended family also loved the great outdoors almost all of her days off were spent camping with aunts, uncles, and cousins as well as her older brother, Hendrik, and his family.

The children saw Lachlan almost daily but Annah made a point of not including him in her family time. She did not want the kids to become attached to him in a way that they might start to consider him as a part of their family. If Lachlan was outside when any of Annah's relatives were about she would introduce them but invitations for Lachlan to camp with them were never forthcoming. Lachlan knew she was trying to keep their relationship within the boundaries that he had set. He never asked her any questions about her family or where she went on her days off. He often overheard her talking to the other staff and knew that her summer was going well and that she was happy. Their relationship at work remained professional and although the staff speculated that there may be an attraction between the two, no one actually witnessed anything conclusive.

Annah knew that her affair was swiftly coming to its end. The time for Nanny's departure approached and soon Annah would be switched to days. She refused to think about what her life would be like once they were no longer lovers. She simply lived in the now and cherished every second they had together.

Although Annah struggled to keep her life separate from Lachlan he went out of his way to include her in his without making it obvious. After the first night they had made love in his kitchen, surrounded by the blueprints of his home, he left them on the table. Every night thereafter when she came over, if he was making adjustments to them or looking at pamphlets for bathroom fixtures etc., he would ask for her input. He solicited her help by claiming that he didn't have time to research all the little finishing or decorating details. He questioned whether the kitchen island should be rectangular or angular. He questioned whether the countertops should be marble or Corion. Unbeknownst to her almost every suggestion or comment she made was implemented the very next day. Particularly when it came to color schemes he took her advice. Once the shell of his home was completed he talked her and the kids into coming out to see it.

It was everything a log house should be. The logs were stacked one floor high with the second level being post and beam. This meant that the ridge pole of the top floor of the house was log as were the corner posts but the remaining walls were sheetrock. The house at this point was basically three attached boxes with a second story on top of the middle box. A two story river rock fireplace dominating the middle. There were no windows or doors cut into the bottom floor so they couldn't go in to look at the inside. Annah knew from looking at the blueprints that the main level had a master bedroom with ensuite in the first box. The middle box contained a kitchen, a bathroom, and a "great room" which was an eating area and living area all in one. The great room had a cathedral ceiling and stairs leading to the second floor which contained three bedrooms and another bathroom. The third box had an office/library. There was decking around the entire bottom level as well as deck off the back of the second story. The backyard was solid bush, but the front of the lot was cleared and when standing on the deck the view of the mountains and a creek off to the left was breathtaking. There was a circular driveway and a log three car garage to the right of the house.

It was like a postcard and Annah instantly fell in love with the house. Lachlan could see the rapture on her face and was relieved since Annah would be sharing his dream home with him, hopefully, one day soon. Annah made no attempt to contain the enthusiasm with which she viewed his house. A quick glance at her watch revealed that it was time to get the kids back to Nanny and get to work. Lachlan waved them off and then went to show his contractor the flooring Annah had picked out the night before.

As fall drew near her lovemaking to Lachlan became more passionate, even less inhibited, and almost frantic. It was almost as if she was trying to fit a lifetime of loving into the short time they had remaining. The kids had returned to school and Nanny had only two weeks left before she retired.

Lachlan knew the countdown was on and felt it was time to let her know that since their very first time together he had decided to pursue her. Their final night together before Nanny's departure was the perfect time to reintroduce the pearls he had hidden from her on that first night.

Annah had no intention of getting any sleep on their last night together since she would go directly from work to Lachlan's and then back to the station Friday morning for the staff meeting. She would sleep after she returned home from the meeting since both kids were in school and Nanny wasn't leaving until Saturday morning. Lachlan had a nap after he got home from work since he also planned on having little sleep after Annah arrived.

When Annah walked into his house after work, the range light was on but Lachlan was not in the kitchen. She could hear the shower running and since she was chilled from the early frost outside she decided to join him. Dropping clothes as she made her way from the kitchen to the bedroom she entered into the bathroom with only one thing remaining in her hand. Laying a foil packet on the side of the tub she opened the shower curtain and climbed into the shower beside him.

"I slept later than planned and I hoped you would join me when you got here," Lachlan breathed as he pulled her into his arms.

Grabbing a shower scrunchie he applied soap and proceeded to smooth it all over her starting at her neck and working his way down. She let him bathe her as she stood under the warming spray. One thing led to another and before he finished, Annah presented him with the foil packet.

"You are always prepared, aren't you?" Lachlan stated appreciatively.

After Annah rolled the condom on for him, the love play continued to the obvious conclusion against the wall of the shower. Clinging to him with legs wrapped around his waist Annah was removed from the shower and carried into the bedroom. Lachlan had snagged a bath sheet on their way out of the bathroom and wrapped Annah in it before he laid her down on the bed and slid out of her. He grabbed another bath sheet off the bureau and proceeded to pat Annah dry as she laid spread out on his bed like a banquet. After Annah's scare the first night they had spent together regarding the missing condom, she had immediately gone on the pill knowing that although she was not in a relationship it was important for her own protection to be prepared just in case. This allowed her and Lachlan some freedom they couldn't previously afford. Annah's choice of birth control that first night needed to be reinserted every four hours since the effects wore off. The pill was much easier and safer for Annah.

As Lachlan dried her and gently smoothed lotion on her Annah gazed around the room. Although she and Lachlan had used every piece of furniture in the house and she was getting more comfortable with her sexuality, they hadn't used any toys up until this point. Annah noticed her missing pearls sitting on the nightstand where Lachlan had set the lotion.

"You found my pearls," she exclaimed as he smoothed lotion into her inner thighs.

"They were never lost," Lachlan informed her. "I took them."

"Why? Were they another trophy for your bedpost?" Annah asked not displeased. She was feeling far too relaxed and spoiled to be annoyed.

"No. I kept them because I knew that night was not the end. It was a beginning for us. Tonight is also not the end. It is simply a new beginning."

"Lachlan, please don't ruin the moment by making promises I'm not ready to hear."

"I hadn't planned on it. Now lie back down and relax while I work some magic on you."

With that Lachlan picked up the beads and rolling them in his lotion-covered hands he grinned wickedly at her.

"Do you trust me, Annah?"

"You know I do."

"Good, then close your eyes and just enjoy the sensations."

Lachlan proceeded to take the pearls and insert them one bead at a time into Annah. Once he was finished he deliberately removed the strand one pearl at a time by pulling it over her aching swollen clitoris. The movement of each pearl as it rolled over top was unlike any sensation Annah had ever felt before. As he removed the final pearl he immediately dove in and using his mouth sucked her over the edge. Laying spread eagled and panting on the bed Lachlan crawled up beside her, and handed the pearls back to Annah.

"You can have them back now," he whispered as he nibbled at her ear.

"I'm sure we can find other uses for them," she responded with a gleam in her eye. "Roll onto your back. Now it's my turn."

Taking the pearls from him Annah took a deep breath to calm her racing heart and she began to wrap Lachlan's penis with them starting at the base. Then adding lubricant she rolled them up and down his engorged member gently tightening them while she licked and nipped at his distended nipples. Feeling him begin to tense Annah released some of the tension and straddling him she slowly impaled herself on him. Realizing she wasn't finished with him Lachlan bit his lip trying to hold off his impending explosion. Using her own internal muscles clenching and releasing without actually riding him she brought him to a mind shattering orgasm. As his body jerked and the beads rolled inside her, Annah reached down and stroked herself to completion.

After this particularly vigorous and erotic bout of lovemaking, tears slowly tracked down Annah's cheeks.

"Are you hurt?" Lachlan asked alarmed, as he shifted to withdraw.

"No," Annah responded with a sniffle.

She let him slide out of her and removed the beads from him while the tears soundlessly continued to fall. Lachlan pulled her onto his chest as she began to sob. He gently stroked her hair and her back and held her until she had exhausted herself. Mortified and still shaky Annah tried to extricate herself from Lachlan's loose embrace. He tightened his arms around her and whispered.

"Just relax. There is no need for you to run off anywhere. It is still early and you are obviously exhausted. Let's just cuddle for awhile and if you fall asleep I promise to wake you in time to get ready."

Burying her face into his chest, Annah let out a long shuddering sigh. Lachlan continued to comfort her and hold her close. Minutes later her breathing evened out and Lachlan knew she had fallen asleep. As he lay with her sleeping in his arms he pondered how to execute the next step of his plan. He knew she was unprepared emotionally to end their affair, because although she still refused to acknowledge it, she was in love with him. The stress of knowing that she would soon be without Nanny, as well as the changes in her job, on top of the ended affair was wearing her down. He had hoped that by the time Nanny left Annah would be moving in with him. She had definitely put a monkey wrench into his assumption that over the summer she would include him in her family outings and thus enhance their involvement. He knew that the children liked him and enjoyed being with him.

Annah, however, had limited their exposure to him so that when Nanny left and their affair supposedly ended the children wouldn't also have the loss of Lachlan in their daily lives. She had done it to protect them from being hurt. This was not something Lachlan had anticipated, although knowing Annah he should have. His time line for the eventual surrender of Annah was slightly off and he was now going to have to figure out a way of continuing the intimacy they shared as well as step up the pace of finalizing a permanent relationship. He had let her run the affair thus far, dictating the frequency and length of each encounter. Now the ball was back in his court. It was up to him to create more family interaction, since she was obviously avoiding it, and to end the current affair as planned, without giving her any suggestions on how to continue.

Although the loss of her nightly visits was going to affect him as much as her, he at least knew this was not the end but simply a change that their relationship needed in order to progress. He would now woo her like any other suitor by inviting her out on dates and buying things for her. This part of the seduction would be made public. Although he knew she would balk at the onset he was confident that after a few weeks of celibacy she would eventually succumb. The new schedule's conclusion was Christmas in his new home with his new family. He prayed his plan wasn't overly optimistic.

⌒‿

Annah's real challenge was about to begin. Nanny had left on Saturday morning after the kids and Annah had a Going-Away Party for her at breakfast. There were lots of tears and hugs all around with the kids waving on the step and a big sniff from Simon as Nanny drove away. Lachlan walked over and picked up Simon.

"Why don't we head off to the lot and have a picnic?" Lachlan suggested.

Annah couldn't be with Lachlan and act just like friends all day knowing that Thursday night had been their final night together. Taking Simon from Lachlan she herded Summer into the house.

"Thank you, for the offer but we are off to the city for the weekend. The kids need some new school clothes and we've been invited to stay overnight at my Auntie Doreen and Uncle Ken's."

Lachlan knew he was being dismissed and possibly punished for not offering an alternate plan for their ended liaison.

Their affair had ended anti-climactically. Although Annah had known from the onset that this was a temporary situation she had hoped that Lachlan would request an extension of their affair and offer some ideas on how to accomplish that. Instead he had walked her to the door, pulled her into his arms and held her. Then he gave her a kiss on the forehead and ran his hands down her arms to clasp her hands.

"I will always cherish the time we had together Annah, I hope you will too," he handed her the pearls and stared intently into her eyes as if waiting for her to make the next move.

But the next move couldn't be hers. She had nothing to offer him. Now that her shift had changed she wasn't about to pay a babysitter so that she could go and have sex with someone. With both kids in school she didn't need a nanny anymore and her budget didn't allow for one anyway. She had put the some of the life insurance money into trust accounts for the kids if they wanted to go to University and a small amount had gone into a savings account for her to buy a house one day. She couldn't have Lachlan over to her house at night because it wasn't unusual for at least one kid to get up during the night and crawl in with her. She had never sent them back to their own beds because she was usually so tired it was just easier to let them sleep with her and also she figured if they needed that little extra security once it a while it certainly wasn't going to hurt anyone.

Originally she had worried that it would be difficult to work with Lachlan while they were sleeping together. Now she worried if she could work with him when they weren't. With grief stricken eyes, Annah reached up and cupped his face in her hands.

"I will never forget our time together or regret one single second of it. Please be happy. You deserve somebody wonderful and a houseful of kids. I know you've heard this before and don't want to hear it again but life is too short for you to be alone. Thank you for reminding me I'm not only a mother but I'm still a woman, too." With that she kissed her fingers, placed them over his lips, and then walked out of his house without looking back.

"I don't plan on spending the rest of my life alone Miss Annah and neither will you," he whispered to himself as she walked across the yard and into her own house to change for the meeting. He could have stopped her but she wasn't ready to hear him. He wanted to tell her that he loved her. He wanted to tell her that he needed to spend the rest of his life with her and have children with her. But he knew she needed to get into her career and raise her children without Nanny or him and prove to herself that she and her children could survive on their own. He gave her three months and then he was asking her to marry him.

~~

Monday morning was a bit of a challenge but Annah got up early enough that she was able to drop the kids off at Mr. and Mrs. Larson's on her way to work. They would be picked up and dropped off by the school bus at Larson's every day from now on.

Annah was excited to start work today since this was going to be her first opportunity to work out in the field with a partner. After watching her interact with all of the staff Lachlan had decided to partner her with David. David, Matthew, and Ken were responsible for the initial training of new recruits. Since Matthew was already working with John, the other new hire, and Ken's wife was expecting, David was up to bat. Ken would float between John and Annah covering the shifts when David or Matthew were either on days off, on nights, or gone on off-site trainings. David was a good match for Annah. While he had come from a life of privilege, Annah had not. Lachlan believed Annah's inner strength gained from her life experience would be an asset to David and hopefully make him an even better officer. He was an excellent teacher, both knowledgeable and patient, but he tended to be a little arrogant. Lachlan hoped Annah's influence would be humbling.

Annah and David's morning began with him indicating to her the area they were responsible for, the wildlife they were tracking in that area, and the points where the highest concentration of tourists tended to go. After going over the checklist of supplies for the truck, they took their lunches and thermos of coffee and tea, hit the road, and her real education began. With map in hand Annah recorded every road and trail they took and the information she needed to remember for when she was out in the field on her own. The quantity of stuff she needed to know appeared endless and yet so thrilling to her she could hardly contain herself. This was what she had worked so hard for over the last four years.

Annah threw herself in, heart and soul, to learning her new career. Between spending her evenings with the kids and helping them with their school work, making meals, keeping up the house, and doing her own night time research for her job, she fell into bed every night exhausted. The first month she was so overwhelmed by her new life that there was no time to dwell on the ended affair. She was also tired enough that she wasn't even dreaming of Lachlan. That, in itself, was a relief since she knew she couldn't fit one more thing on her plate right now.

She and David developed a very comfortable rapport. He had a wonderful sense of humor and made her slow down and quit taking everything so seriously. He loved her enthusiasm. It was like taking a kid into the forest every day. Her obvious love of nature and awe over a simple rainbow in a waterfall reminded him why he had become a conservation officer in the first place. After almost every shift they would return to the station either laughing or good naturedly debating some point of contention. The other staff, including Lachlan, noticed the obvious infatuation that was developing on David's side.

Because they worked together, but separately from the rest of the staff, and they had a natural affinity for each other David started to confide details of his life to Annah. She soon discovered that all was not rosy in the "land of Dabria." David, Matthew, and Dabria had been virtually inseparable all of their lives. They had attended elementary school and high school together and then had all gone on to University together as well. David had started out in Law with Dabria but switched over to Forestry after spending a summer working with his uncle, who was a conservation officer in British Columbia. Matthew had started off taking a veterinary degree and had also switched when he spent that same summer working with David. David indicated that Matthew was like the brother he never had. They did almost everything together. Annah wondered if their friendship was causing some of the friction between David and Dabria. David asked Annah for some advice regarding his failing relationship with Dabria.

"David, does Dabria resent the time you spend with Matthew? Instead of always spending your days off with Dabria you spend a lot of them with Matthew. Maybe you and Matthew need to distance yourself a little from each other. I'm sure that Matthew is great fun to do all of your extreme sports with but maybe since you and Dabria live apart and you are engaged to her you should make more of an effort to spend time with her. I'm only looking at this from a woman's point of view. If you were my fiancée I would want to be with you every opportunity I had."

"Matthew and I always invite her to come along when we go somewhere."

"David, maybe she wants to do those things alone with you. It looks to me like Matthew comes first and then Dabria. That's not the way to start off a marriage. Dabria should always be first and Matthew second."

"Annah, you just don't understand our history. Dabria doesn't mind my relationship with Matthew. In fact she encourages it. She doesn't like to do the sports that I do and so if Matthew goes with me she's relieved."

"Well, what do you and Dabria like to do together, then?" Annah asked.

"We go to concerts and plays together. We go out for supper and to the movies. We attend family functions together."

"And where is Matthew when you are doing these things?"

"Sometimes he is with us. Actually, I guess, most of the time he is with us. But Annah, it's always been the three of us. We're like the three musketeers. Hey, I know one thing we always do alone," David smiled lasciviously. "We f...."

"Yah, yah," Annah cut David off. "I would hope you were doing that without Matthew, but then again, that's not really any of my business. Is it?"

David chuckled at Annah's obvious discomfort.

"You asked for my advice and I'm simply trying to suggest some things that may be bothering Dabria. Why don't you just ask her what the problem is?"

"I have and she claims there is nothing wrong. But she is so bitchy lately I'm really starting to second guess whether or not we shouldn't postpone the wedding. We've been engaged now for a couple of years and instead of things getting better they're more strained than ever. Dabria pushed for this engagement for years and now that we are engaged she doesn't seem as happy as I am about it."

"Have you set a wedding date?"

"No."

"Maybe that's part of the problem. Do you know where you're going to live with Dabria practicing in Rocky and you working out here?"

"I assume that we will buy an acreage halfway between and both commute. I haven't found a place for us out here because I know she would have to commute an hour each way every day. That's why Matthew and I live together."

"You live with Matthew!" Annah exclaimed.

"Yah, I thought you knew that."

"No, I didn't. Now I really think that Matthew could be part of the problem. Good grief, David. If I was engaged to you and you chose to spend more of your free time with your roommate than me, I would be seriously ticked off. Why can't you see that? Don't you want to spend time alone with Dabria?"

"I guess. But Matthew and I have more fun together."

"Then maybe you shouldn't be marrying Dabria you should be marrying Matthew," Annah suggested sarcastically. "Are you in love with her or are you so comfortable with her that she seems the obvious choice?" Annah asked. "When I'm in love I want to spend every free moment with that person. I can't get enough of their company. Everything I do with that person becomes fun. Don't you see?"

"Are you in love with anyone right now?" David probed.

"I'm not sure," Annah answered cryptically.

"What the heck does that mean?" David drilled her with a look of disgust. "You're the one that just asked me if I was in love or if it was just convenience and now you can't tell me whether you are or not. Do you know what love is?"

"David, it's different for me. You and Dabria have known each other your whole lives. I don't know if you've ever fallen in love with anyone else or if Dabria was your first. My first love was Thomas and that certainly didn't turn out so well. I need to be cautious this time."

"So you're not going to tell me who this mystery man is."

"Of course not!" Annah exclaimed. "That would be extremely premature. Anyway, right now maybe we should actually try to get some work done. I'm going to go measure the water depth like you asked me to and then I'll meet you back at the truck."

When Annah and David headed back to the station at the end of the day Annah put in a final shot.

"David, I think you and Dabria need to sit down and figure out what both of you really want out of life. Marriage is a challenge even when both people are working towards the same goal. Thomas and I started off with the same plan. We loved each other, we wanted to share our lives and have a family together. Somehow, in the end that wasn't enough for Thomas and he decided he wanted someone new. If he hadn't died I don't think we would be together today anyway. Nobody deserves to have to share their partner with a third person. Think about that."

"Are you saying that Thomas had a little "somethin' somethin'" on the side?" David asked incredulously.

"Yes."

"And you don't think that your marriage could have withstood that?"

"I can't say for sure. I'm a different person now, David. I'm much more confidant and I know I can stand on my own two feet. If the same thing happened to me again there is no doubt in my mind that the relationship would be over. I know I deserve better than that. Are you saying that you think it's okay to have an affair and that the little woman should just suck it up and carry on?" Annah interrogated David.

"Whoa, I never said anything like that. I just think that sometimes an affair can be the catalyst to making a relationship better."

"Oh, come off it, you have got to be kidding," Annah scoffed.

"No, I'm not. But since we're back and I have an appointment I need to keep, let's continue this tomorrow, shall we?"

"You can count on it. If you actually believe that crap no wonder Dabria gets all crusty with you." With that Annah jumped out of the truck as it came to a stop beside the station.

David threw Annah the keys to the truck and sauntered off towards his car.

"See you in the morning, spitfire," David mocked with a huge grin. He gave her a backwards salute and then blew her a kiss before climbing into the car and driving away.

CHAPTER 14

ANNAH WAS BUSY UNLOADING both her and David's bags and daydreaming about the view she had just had of Lachlan's rear end. And what a tasty backside view it was. She had been so busy lately she honestly couldn't remember the last time she had admired his physique. When she turned around she walked straight into Matthew. After watching the little bi-play in the parking lot Matthew had followed Annah into the equipment room and decided it was time someone put an end to this flirtation. Dabria was coming out for the town's annual Thanksgiving Supper and if Annah didn't back off he knew there was going to be hell to pay.

"I thought you said you had no interest in other people's men?" Matthew accused.

"Wh....what did you say?" Annah blushed as she thought she had been caught admiring Lachlan.

"You know what I'm talking about. You claimed you were above fooling around with other people's men and yet it is blatantly obvious that you've got the hots for your new leader. You think we can't all see what's going on. Back off or his fiancée will be having you for the main course Saturday night instead of turkey!!" Annah's blush confirmed her guilt in Matthew's eyes. Without a backwards glance, Matthew, stomped out of the equipment room and went out to his truck.

All the blood had drained out of Annah's face. With being so caught up in her new job she had been totally unaware that Lachlan was even seeing anyone let alone engaged. How the hell could she have missed that? And how did he find someone to marry that quickly when their affair had only ended a month ago? Instantly she saw red. She marched into Lachlan's office and carefully closed the door so that she didn't provide any more of a show, for the staff, than she apparently already had.

Lachlan felt her as soon as she walked into his office but didn't turn around until after she spoke.

"I understand congratulations are in order. I wasn't aware until moments ago that you were engaged!" Annah announced very quietly, carefully enunciating each word.

Lachlan slowly turned around and was greeted with Annah, hands on hips with her nails digging in, cheeks flushed, glaring at him like she wanted to rip his throat out. She was magnificent. He had no idea where she had gotten that idea but it apparently had an obviously negative effect on her normally cheerful mood. Privately exalting in her show of jealousy he decided he should probably correct her misconception, but only after torturing her a little.

"Where did you pick up this piece of gossip?" he inquired as he crossed his arms and leaned back against the window. He figured he was safe from dismemberment, at the moment, since his oversize oak desk was between him and the she-devil shooting daggers at him from across the room.

"That is irrelevant. Is it true or not?" she fumed.

"Have you seen me dating or entertaining anyone?"

"Lachlan, no one saw us or knew we were *entertaining* each other either, with the exception of Nanny. That just proves you could easily be involved with someone else without me knowing."

"Annah, you live right across the street from me. Don't you think you might have noticed a strange car at my place on several occasions or me being gone more than usual in the evenings?"

"No, Lachlan, I haven't had time to notice anything beyond my own little life this past month. I've been very busy, and even if I had noticed you being gone in the evenings I would have assumed that you were working on the house. So what are you saying? Is my information wrong?"

Lachlan unfolded his arms and pushed away from the window. He walked towards her and stopping right in front of her, he tipped her chin up with his finger and looked directly into her eyes.

"There is no truth to the rumor that I am engaged. Nor am I seeing anyone at this time. Now would you care to tell me how you came up with that information?"

Annah backed away from his touch as she felt the second blush of the day staining her cheeks.

"One of the staff accused me of entering into a flirtation with my leader who just happened to be engaged. He said the entire staff could see that I had the hots for this person and I should back off since the fiancée would be attending the supper on Saturday."

Lachlan started to chuckle which only made Annah angry all over again. He obviously knew something she did not. Not only did she not like people talking about her behind her back, but she was also offended that anyone would believe she would get involved with someone who was already spoken for.

Suddenly, it hit her like a ton of bricks. The person she had been spending every moment with at work for the last month was David. She was no longer mad; now she was just sad. She could see how her obvious good mood and jovial responses to David's antics could be misconstrued as flirting. She had been blissfully unaware because she was so caught up in the delight of her job. The only person who actually realized that this was so much more than a job for her was Lachlan. Until she had started this career Summer and Simon had been the sole focus of her life. Now she had a purpose to carry on after the kids grew up and left home. Annah's shoulders sagged.

Lachlan had watched the play of emotions cross her face and he knew she had figured out what was going on.

"Look, there is a very simple way of clearing up these rumors without actually acknowledging them or confronting anyone. I'm sure that you have heard there is a family Thanksgiving Dinner and Dance on Saturday evening at the hall. Let me take you and the kids to supper and then let's get a sitter so that you and I can go to the dance. I'm buying. Now, knowing what a catch I am, and knowing that peoples' tongues will definitely be wagging if we show up together, I can't possibly see how you could turn my invitation down."

Annah thought about his suggestion and agreed that this was probably the best way to deal with the situation without any kind of confrontation. Also, she could definitely do with a night off and she couldn't think of anyone she would rather spend her evening with. The thought of being held in Lachlan's arms again and dancing all night long certainly held its own appeal.

"So, is it a date, Ms. Andersson?"

"I would be honored to attend the supper and dance with you Mr. MacGregor." Annah curtsied and Lachlan had a flashback of their first meeting in the University corridor.

"I'll pick you up at six o'clock. Can you arrange a sitter?"

"Absolutely."

"Annah," he called as she turned away to leave his office, "don't change how you are at work. People just need to get used to your natural cheerfulness. The atmosphere in the office has already changed to a happier and more productive workplace. I like it and I know most of the rest of the staff also appreciate it. Some of the older ones, I think, are a mite jealous of your enthusiasm. I'm not one of them. "

"Thank you. As you may have noticed I'm not really good at hiding my feelings. When I'm happy it just sort of oozes out. I'm so glad you decided to take a chance on me Lachlan and hire me. I love my job!" she bubbled as she walked out.

"I know you do, Annah. And I love you," Lachlan murmured under his breath. The next stage of Annah's seduction had just been put into motion without almost any effort on Lachlan's part. The unanticipated flash of Annah's jealousy had definitely been a boost to Lachlan's neglected feelings.   He had honestly thought she would have approached him before the end of the first month requesting some kind of liaison. Again he had underestimated Annah's strength of character and her commitment to honoring her promises and obligations. Lachlan had planned to ask her to the dance anyway and the ever present rumor mill had simply given him the perfect reason. Sometimes there were unexpected benefits to living in a community the size of Nordegg.

Despite the chilly looks directed her way by Matthew, Annah resumed her work the next morning as if Matthew hadn't spoken to her the night before. However, he had obviously made some comments to David because David wasn't quite so entertaining before they left the office the next morning. He returned to his normal jovial self the second they climbed into the truck and headed out for the day. Annah did not comment on his behavior. Rather than resuming the conversation they had started the day before, both agreed to disagree and spent the day carrying out their duties in a relaxed companionable manner. John had asked Annah to the supper before they left that morning and she had been forced to tell him she had already been asked. He made her promise to save him a dance and said he'd see her Saturday. Annah certainly hadn't anticipated any offers so she was somewhat surprised to have received two.

Saturday morning dawned a beautiful Indian summer day. The temperature was higher than usual for this time of year and the valley was full of the colors of fall. The dark purple of the mountains was the perfect backdrop for the multi-colored evergreens that stood out amongst the yellow leafed aspens and the golden-needled tamaracks. There was even the occasional splash of red from the willows. The town couldn't have asked for a more perfect day if they had tried.

Annah, Summer, and Simon spent the day raking leaves into piles and then diving into them. They harvested the rest of the garden which included carrots, potatoes, parsnips, beets, and turnips. Everything above ground had frozen a couple of weeks ago. The ground acted like insulation and so the root vegetables were in perfect shape. While the kids continued to play Annah took pictures and counted her many blessings. At four o'clock Lachlan drove up and he and Ranger, his recently acquired Labrador retriever, came over to investigate the sound of squealing and giggling. Annah was nowhere to be found when he entered the backyard and he watched as the kids scooped more and more leaves into a large pile. Lachlan snuck up behind Summer and snatching her up pretended to throw her in the pile.

"No!" she shrieked. "Mommy is under the pile!"

With that, the pile started to rise and Annah emerged from the centre with a golden shower of leaves raining down her body. Ranger bounced around the pile barking. Annah had a grin the size of a jack-o-lantern. Simon jumped into the pile beside her and rolled around in the crispy crunching mass. Lachlan deposited Summer into the pile on the other side and then picked up Annah's camera. Without Annah or the kids being aware he snapped off several candid shots of the three of them at play with his dog. What a heart-warming sight. He put the camera down and clapping his hands and whistling brought the rambunctious crew to attention.

"There is a turkey shoot, turkey bowling, turkey coloring contest and pin the tail on the turkey going on down at the hall before supper. It starts at five o'clock. So who wants to go?"

"Do they really shoot turkeys and then bowl with them?" Summer asked.

"Not exactly," Lachlan chuckled. "For the turkey shoot you pay a dollar to shoot a target. The person who gets the closest to the center or in the centre wins a frozen turkey. For the turkey bowling they set up pins and you slide frozen turkeys across the floor to knock the pins down. Then the winner gets a frozen turkey. The money they raise from the supper and the turkey games is going to help pay for an in-door skating arena."

"Why would anyone want a frozen turkey?" Simon asked.

"Everyone has turkey for Thanksgiving, Simon. If you win one then you don't have to buy one. Come on. Let's go see if we can win a turkey! I'll race you to the house!" Annah called.

Lachlan called Ranger and the two of them headed home to get ready. Wherever Lachlan was Ranger usually wasn't far behind. Although Ranger slept at the station every night, he was Lachlan's constant companion during the day. Lachlan showered and changed into clean jeans and a black T-shirt. He shrugged into a black leather jacket and headed out the door. Ranger would be staying home to-night and once they brought the kids back with the sitter he would be sleeping at Annah's house until she came home. Although labs weren't traditionally guard dogs they could certainly raise a racket if they needed to protect something.

Lachlan had adopted Ranger about six months ago from a family that discovered they were allergic to him. He was two years old and although trained he was more for company than protection. Ranger slept every night at the station and was considered the resident guard dog. When Lachlan had him at home Ranger spent more time with Summer and Simon than he did with Lachlan. It was obvious he was used to playing with and being around children. It was the perfect arrangement for Annah and Lachlan since Annah didn't have the time or the money for a full time dog, and Ranger gave Lachlan the perfect excuse to be at Anna's.

Lachlan loaded up the kids and took the pies that Annah had baked and placed them in the back of the Jeep. As she ran back to lock up the house, Lachlan opened her car door and waited until she seated herself so that he could close it for her.

"Mommy, why is Lachlan hanging onto your door? Is it because he's afraid you're going to slam it the way we do and break it?"

"I don't think so," Annah said with a giggle. "And don't ask him about it either," she warned. "It might hurt his feelings."

Lachlan swung himself into the seat and off they went to the Annual Town Thanksgiving Supper and Turkey Shoot. The whole town and surrounding area showed up for the event. There were grandmas, grandpas, babies, and everything in between. Lachlan couldn't have picked a better time for arriving. The Larson's and David, Matthew, and the infamous Dabria all pulled up to the hall at the same time. Nicole and two of her girlfriends were standing outside having a smoke and they also saw the arrivals and would be sure to pass on what they saw to whoever walked past them.

When they came to a full stop Annah grabbed Lachlan's hand before he could leave the Jeep and urgently whispered to him.

"Do not do the door thing here, please."

"Don't worry. I plan on carrying in your pies instead. Is that not a chivalrous task to impress both you as well as the masses?" he gently chided.

"I think that will do just fine," Annah acknowledged with a grin.

As they vacated the Jeep David sauntered over with Dabria draped on his arm.

"Dabria, I'd like you to meet my new partner. This is Annah and her two children. This must be Summer and you must be Simon," he stated as he looked down at the two children trying to run off and play with friends they had just spotted. "And, of course , you remember Lachlan. Annah this is my fiancée, Dabria."

Annah thrust her hand out waiting for Dabria to clasp it. When Dabria did not relinquish her hold on David's arm Annah let her hand drop and with a chuckle exclaimed, "What a pleasure to finally meet you Dabria. I've heard so much about you."

"Really," Dabria drawled. "And what was your name again?" she inquired with a glazed look settling over her eyes. An angry flush stained David's cheeks and to avoid causing him any further embarrassment Annah turned away to release the children that had been begging to run and play. When she turned back David had removed Dabria to the entrance of the hall where Nicole and her friends fawned over Dabria's engagement ring.

"Do you know how beautiful you look tonight? Deep purple makes your green eyes shine like emeralds, Ms Andersson," Lachlan whispered into her ear as he passed her a pie to hold while he shut the lift gate.

"Oh, go away with you now. You surely do know how to flatter a little ol' country girl like me, Mr. MacGregor," Annah cooed as she fluttered her eyelashes at him. He took the pie from her and gave her a quick kiss right in front of the entire Nordegg community. That shut her up faster than anything he had ever tried before, and for the third time in as many days he had her blushing again. With nothing left to carry and no kids to herd she had no other choice but to follow him into the hall.

Their arrival had certainly not gone unnoticed. When Lachlan entered the hall with the pies several women rushed over to see what kind they were and to tell him where to put them. Since Lachlan had no idea Annah stepped up and informed them they were Saskatoon and blueberry pies. After the women had whisked away the pies Lachlan reached out, grabbed Annah's hand, and pulled her over to where the turkey bowling competition was just getting underway. He paid their fee and they waited for their turn. Annah perused the comings and goings of everyone in the noisy hall. Several times she caught the eye of someone talking about her as they quickly looked away.

"Was I right? Or was I right? The whole county will have us married off by Monday. You know that, eh?" Lachlan murmured quietly to Annah as he had also seen the speculative glances darting in their direction.

"I forgot what it was like living in a small town. Everybody figures that your business is their business."

"Does it really bother you?"

"There are so many plusses that I won't let a little gossip scare me away. I'm just used to my privacy. I don't like people knowing all of my little secrets. It's rather disconcerting," Annah stated.

"Trust me, Annah, they don't know half of your little secrets and I'm not about to share them," Lachlan pledged with his hand over his heart.

Annah good naturedly punched his arm.

"I would expect nothing less from you, and I promise not to reveal that you aren't really cold and heartless. You are actually hot all over." Annah licked her finger and then touched Lachlan's chest and very discreetly made a sizzling noise. "I'm going to go outside and check on the kids. I'll be right back."

Lachlan released her hand and as soon as Annah walked away the gossips descended. One group sidled up to Lachlan and one group fell into step with Annah. Annah knew he would play it cool, so she did as well.

"Honey, I knew there was something going on right from the morning you came for your interview. Why have you been keeping this a secret? You know we're all happy for you. I heard Lachlan's building a big mansion of a place over at Misty Estates. I heard there are six bedrooms! Six bedrooms! What does a single man need a house with six bedrooms for?" Mrs. Larson inquired.

"I don't know. I guess you'll have to ask him." Annah visually located the kids playing tag with their friends. She realized she didn't actually have to say anything since the women around her were both asking and answering their own questions. It was kind of funny actually. Annah headed back into the hall. The turkey games continued until six o'clock when the dinner bell was rung and supper began. Supper was a pot luck buffet that consisted of a variety of dishes. The turkey, stuffing, potatoes, and gravy were provided by the town hall committee. The families brought salads, side dishes, and desserts. It was a feast fit for a king. Everyone seemed to find a place to sit and the old community hall vibrated with laughter and happy voices. Lachlan and Annah didn't need to circulate at all as various members of the community joined them at their end of the long table and chatted. At seven thirty Annah rounded up the children and the babysitter and left to take them home in Lachlan's Jeep.

Annah returned to the hall just in time to help finish moving tables to create a dance floor in the middle. The DJ was setting up his music on the stage and two bars were set up just inside the main doors. Lachlan snagged Annah's hand and pulled her outside.

"Let's go for a walk before the music gets rolling," he proposed. It was a beautiful night. The air was crisp and clean and there wasn't a breath of wind. Smoke rose straight up from the chimney in the hall. The sounds of laughter and talking and children's giggles drifted across the valley. Annah adjusted the hood of her beloved red blanket coat and they walked hand in hand in comfortable silence from the hall down to the museum and the school. Annah sat on a swing and Lachlan pushed her until she begged him to stop and let her off. They talked about the house building, the kids' school, and Annah's plans for Thanksgiving and Christmas.

"If I cook a turkey and set the table and buy the wine next weekend, will you make the rest of the stuff and come over for supper on Sunday?" Lachlan coaxed.

Annah had admitted to herself that morning that she missed Lachlan and given an opportunity would probably accept any arrangement he proposed. However, as the day and evening had progressed, she had promised herself she wasn't going to accept anything less than a relationship that was public and included her children. She wanted the whole package not just stolen moments here and there but actually a real relationship with the potential of a future together. She didn't want to send Lachlan running for the hills but she figured he deserved the truth about her expectations and desires. Annah pulled Lachlan onto the bench beside her and turning towards him clasped both his hands in hers.

Lachlan held his breath while he waited for Annah to speak. He knew her next words were going to have a profound effect on the rest of his life. At this point he didn't know if it was going to be good or bad.

"I don't know how to start what I need to tell you," Annah stalled.

"Annah, whatever it is, it can't be nearly as bad as what I am imagining, so please just spit it out," Lachlan implored.

"Okay. Here's the deal. Before I met you and we slept together I believed that I could raise my children and have a career and be perfectly happy without a man in my life. Then we slept together and I remembered I'm not only a mother but I'm also a woman. So then I figured I could have my kids, my career, and a little "somethin' somethin'" occasionally on the side and I would be happy. It was great while it lasted but it wasn't real life. The reality of my life, Lachlan, is that I have two kids that take up almost every waking minute of the time when I am not at work. That doesn't leave much time left over for a real man/woman relationship. However, that's what I want and I won't settle for anything less. I want you to be a part of my life and I want to be a part of yours but I can't give you my undivided attention when I'm not working because I have too many other responsibilities. So, are you willing to give this relationship a chance, knowing how little I can actually offer you?"

"Yes," he leaned in and kissed her tenderly. "Annah, you have so much more to offer than you actually realize. Let's just take this one day at a time and see what develops. Okay? The whole town has already labeled us a couple so let's make it a reality. I accept your offer. Now let's go kick up our heels and show 'em how the city folk can dance."

Lachlan pulled her up off the bench and back towards the hall. Annah had surprised him yet again. He had anticipated months of wooing and dragging her kicking and screaming into a relationship, and then out of the blue she asks him to share her life. He knew he wasn't off the hook for the wooing part but at least he wasn't fighting an uphill battle. He couldn't wait to get her back in the hall and wrap his arms around her and show everyone she was his.

CHAPTER 15

NEITHER LACHLAN NOR ANNAH got to sit out a single dance. Every time they tried to take a breather someone else would come along and grab them. Annah had promised John a dance and apparently David and Ken and Mr. Larson and so on. Similarly Lachlan was expected to partner all of the officers' wives and girlfriends as well as the dispatchers.

BY ELEVEN O'CLOCK ANNAH pulled Lachlan onto the dance floor and begged him to take her home before she collapsed. He vowed to do one better than that. Before the dance finished they both headed off the dance floor with a plan to sneak out. Lachlan hit the coat check and met a shivering Annah at the Jeep. They swiftly slipped into the Jeep and drove off while putting on their coats. Instead of turning off at the staff residences Lachlan continued on down the road to his house.

"Are you up for a little midnight rendezvous or are you too exhausted from all the dancing?" Lachlan tempted.

"I could probably be persuaded," Annah responded. "Just let me call the sitter. Is there cell service out at the house?"

"No, but I have a house phone hooked up. The number is 845-5183."

"How clever of you. One might almost think you had planned this little seduction."

"Oh, contraire. I am horrified that you could think I would be so devious."

As they pulled into the clearing in front of the house Annah looked up at the structure silhouetted by the huge orange moon suspended over the roof. A sense of coming home unexpectedly descended over her. She mentally shook herself and forced herself to focus on the reality of the moment rather than the silly fantasy that had just escaped from her subconscious. The reality was that she and Lachlan would have a couple of stolen hours of complete privacy, which may not present itself again for weeks or even God forbid months. She needed to channel all of her energy into these moments since Lachlan had proven himself to be a demanding and exhausting lover.

Lachlan unlocked the door, flicked on the foyer light, and as they walked into the great room Annah couldn't help but be awed by the beauty that surrounded her. The logs gleamed and the massive staircase to the second level beckoned. She was drawn like a magnet to the curved stair rail and was unable to stop herself from caressing the smooth oak. As Lachlan called to her she turned around and stood speechlessly gaping at the two story river rock fireplace that dominated the wall of windows across from the stairs. It was obviously the focal point of the great room. Lachlan stood beside the fireplace offering a cordless phone to Annah. In a daze, she accepted the phone and dialed home to check on the kids.

While the sitter reassured Annah that everything was fine and that she had planned on staying overnight Lachlan set to work laying a fire in the fireplace. Annah gave her the new number and ended the call. She wandered into the kitchen that curved around behind the stairs and discovered a dream straight out of a magazine. The counters on the cupboards and the mammoth sized island were gleaming black marble. The cabinets themselves were a light knotty pine and the contrast of the two was very dramatic. The appliances were industrial in quality but antique replicas of brushed stainless steel and forest green enamel. Although it was dark outside Annah looked out the kitchen windows and was met with a view of a large covered deck surrounded by mood lighting that Lachlan had just turned on.

Although there wasn't so much as a chair to sit on Annah knew that when furnished this house would be a home for Lachlan, not just a house. The attention to lighting and color made the spaces warm and inviting. Lachlan wandered into the kitchen and opened the door to the walk-in pantry. The shelves were bare but for two bottles of merlot, two wine glasses, a cork screw, and a baguette. Lachlan placed the items on the island and then turned to the fridge to retrieve a block of cheddar cheese and a cluster of green grapes. He piled everything on the cutting board and used it as a serving tray. With a tilt of his head, he motioned Annah to follow him back into the great room.

On the floor in front of the fireplace had materialized a padded patchwork sheep skin rug. A bath sheet and bottle of oil sat on the hearth. The foyer lights had been turned off and the glow from the fire was the only illumination in the room. The scene was straight out of a dime store seduction novel. It was perfect. Annah slipped off her coat and sunk onto the rug breathlessly anticipating Lachlan's next move. Lachlan set his tray down beside the rug and sitting on the hearth proceeded to open a bottle of wine. He removed his shoes and socks and then poured them each a glass of wine.

"I know you think that this is corny but I wanted our first night together in this place to be something you would remember for the rest of your life. Even though it is a cliché, have you ever actually made love before on a sheep skin rug in front of a roaring fire?"

"Of course not and I don't think that it's corny. I was just thinking how perfect the ending to this evening, our first *real* date, was actually going to be. Just like our first time together in February you have put in way more effort than I could possibly have anticipated. No one would ever guess that you are, in fact, a true romantic. Your forethought into this evening humbles me. I had hoped we would have some way of making love tonight but I certainly never could have foreseen this."

Lachlan handed Annah a glass of wine and sat down on the rug beside her. He leaned back onto his elbows and from lowered lids viewed the vision seated before him. What she didn't realize was that she was the inspiration responsible for his romantic greatness. Annah sat cross-legged and sipped her wine while she gazed at the room surrounding them. Her face was flushed from the excitement of the moment. The flickering flames cast a glow over Annah's upturned radiant face. Tendrils of wheat-colored hair had escaped the confines of her loose braid and framed her face. It was a softened, relaxed face that turned back to Lachlan and smiled.

"So what do you think of my house so far, Ms. Andersson?"

"I predict that you are going to be very happy in this home, Mr. MacGregor."

"Only time will tell, but I do know I'm happy tonight." With that Lachlan sat up and took Annah's wine glass from her. He set it aside and then coaxed her to kneel in between his sprawled legs. He proceeded to slide his hands under her thick purple sweater and draw it over her head. Wordlessly Annah sat while he undid the braid of her hair and unfurled the waves. He unclasped her bra and let it drift onto the rug. He unbuttoned her jeans and then stood and pulled her up. She shimmied out of her jeans and her thong and slipped off her socks. He spread out the towel and kneeling beside it drew her back down to the now covered rug. She lay on her stomach and waited for his magic hands to begin. Although he had never massaged her before she knew what his hands were capable of and shivered in anticipation.

"Are you cold," he whispered in her ear as he straddled her and swept her hair to the side?

"No," she breathed. "Just wound up."

He dribbled the warmed oil onto her spine from the base of her neck to the hollow just above her tail bone. She heard him remove his own shirt and belt and open the fly of his jeans. She felt him lean forward just before he smoothed the oil from her shoulder blades down to her waist in one firm heart-shaped caress. From there Annah's mind lost all conscious thought. The only senses that she needed now were sound, smell, and touch. She had lost the capacity to see or think. Unconscious muffled moans of pleasure emitted from Annah as Lachlan's hands worked the tension and stress of the last month out of her muscles. It was the biggest turn on Lachlan had ever felt and he was overcome by the lust of needing her to the point that his hands started to shake. Determined to finish the massage she sorely needed he bit his lip and tried to take his mind off of her pliant porcelain skin and his aching engorged cock. Annah was conscious enough to realize that Lachlan was reaching his limit for foreplay. Removing her hands from under her head she rested onto her elbows and glancing behind her, crooked her finger to signal Lachlan to bend down to her lips.

As he leaned over she whispered, "Fuck me, Lachlan. Now!"

Lachlan was so shocked and unsure he had heard her right he sat back on his hunches and stammered, "Wh ....What?"

"You heard me," she said only slightly louder but very clearly. "Do it."

Lachlan jumped off of her, stripped off his jeans, and rolled on protection in record time. As he knelt back down, he smoothed oil over his condom covered penis and drew her derriere up against him. With one forceful thrust he impaled her to his hilt. Although Annah was prepared, his intrusion elicited a gasp as she arched into him, drawing him even deeper. Holding her waist steady he let her adjust before smoothly withdrawing and entering again. Huskily chanting her name, he kept his penetration and retraction rhythmic. Annah gripped the rug in front of her as Lachlan's thrusts became quicker and harder. As she absorbed the friction and her muscles clenched Lachlan reached underneath her and manually stimulated her clitoris. A couple of tweaks were all it took to send Annah over the edge. As her orgasm peaked, it milked Lachlan and plunged him into the same oblivion. With a guttural, primitive howl Lachlan stiffened and clung to Annah until the last shudder hit him. Gently releasing his grip on Annah's hips, Lachlan lowered himself onto her and still connected he rolled onto his back and brought her with him. As she lay spent and panting with her back on his chest and his arms wrapped around her she wondered how each time they came together could possibly be better than the last. She knew he was as wrecked as she was. Could this kind of passion last a lifetime? Or was it simply that they each knew these moments were extra special because they were infrequent?

While Annah wrestled with her thoughts Lachlan forced himself not to flip her over and pour his heart out to her. She had surprised him, yet again. Although he knew she was becoming less inhibited with every sexual encounter they had he could never have predicted tonight's demand. Every moment that Lachlan spent with Annah, whether they were making love, working together, playing with the kids, or arguing was a moment he now couldn't imagine his life without. He needed to tell her his feelings and his plans for their life soon or he was going to end up blurting it out at a really inappropriate time in the very near future. After tonight he figured maybe he could survive two more dates providing there was no sex involved. Since he had already done the dinner and a dance date, he needed a dinner and a show date, and a sports event and a dinner date. Date four would be announce his intentions date. Oh course, so far not all of his best plans had come to fruition. He was behind schedule by at least a month.

Lachlan rolled to his side and continued to spoon Annah as he held her loosely. Annah wiggled out of his grasp and sat up beside him. She handed him the towel and pulling her hair out of the way turned her back to him. He propped himself up on one elbow and proceeded to wipe the remaining oil off of her back. Then he turned her around and handed the towel back to her. She reciprocated by wiping off his chest, arms, and lower body. Before she got things all heated up again Lachlan stole the towel from her and flung it across the room. He pulled her back down onto the soft rug and lying with her cuddled up against his chest he started to talk.

He asked her to catch him up on the events in the kids' lives and the new things she had learned at work. For the first time in over a month they were able to indulge in a little pillow talk. It was comfortable and Annah drifted into sleep. Lachlan held her and listened to her breathe as he casually stroked her arm and hair. Although he wanted to keep her all night he knew she needed to get home. Reluctantly, he eased away from her and dressed while he let her sleep. He watched her sleep as the glow from the flames danced over her flawless skin. She stirred and searched for him in her sleep. He smiled because he knew he was definitely becoming the person she could depend on. He bent down and kissed her awake.

"Annah, it's time to go." Sleepily she opened her eyes and wound her arms around his neck.

"I don't suppose you want to dress me, too?" she asked with a tired sigh.

"That might just start things all over again."

"Better yet, I'll undress you and then we can have Round Two before you take me home. Are you game?"

"Never let it be said that I am a shirker. I wouldn't dream of turning down the request of a beautiful woman."

Annah pulled him back down to her level and began to ravish him.

CHAPTER 16

MONDAY MORNING AT THE office there were very obviously mixed emotions regarding the show that Lachlan and Annah had put on for everyone Saturday evening. The older married officers were relieved that Annah was seeing *anyone* and had made it public. The fact that it was Lachlan just made it better. Since Annah was widowed, attractive, and younger than most of the wives, some of them had felt threatened by her, particularly when she had worked evenings with all of their husbands. Unwittingly, some of these same husbands had made comments about Annah's enthusiasm for her job, her good sense of humor, and the changed atmosphere at the station since her arrival.

"Apparently, looks can be deceiving," was the only comment Matthew made towards Annah on Monday. It left Annah wondering if that was supposed to pass as an apology for his accusation the previous week or if he still believed there was something going on between her and David. After that he returned to his recent attitude of ignoring her. That was easier to deal with than the sullen poutiness prior to their actually working together.

David was another story. His mood Monday morning was that of a bear with a thorn in its paw. In several instances he was abrupt with Annah to the point of rudeness. The easy camaraderie they had enjoyed over the past month was gone. As they headed out to patrol their area David rushed through his equipment check and tried to rush Annah through hers. Since they checked each other's equipment Annah wasn't about to screw this up and end up with a reprimand from Lachlan because David was in a pissy mood. David flung his lunch and supplies into the back seat and impatiently drummed his fingers on the steering wheel of the truck while he waited for Annah to arrange her lunch and his equipment.

The area they were patrolling today was the Ram Falls Recreation Site. It involved a drive down the Forestry Truck Road, which was gravel, but well maintained in the summer. It was plowed weekly in the winter but otherwise it was up to local traffic to basically keep it open by driving on it. It had snowed several times over the course of the last two weeks in this area; however, each snowfall was little more than a few centimeters and at this point there probably wasn't any more than about ten. Yesterday had been warm enough to melt the top layer of snow. It had dropped back down overnight and today it was still below zero and overcast. There was a skin of ice on the ground and the road. This presented no problem for the 4x4 truck that David was driving but it would make for tricky walking on the sloped paths by the falls.

A patrol cabin was stocked with basic first aid supplies, blankets, dry wood, flares, coffee, and freeze-dried food at the entrance to the fall's picnic area and parking lot. The cabin was not only used to store supplies but was also used for sleeping in and living in on overnight patrols for the officers. Today's patrol was to check and replenish any used supplies and to do a census of the herd of Big Horn Sheep that frequently sunned themselves on the gradually inclined shale slopes near the falls. This time of year the hunters were out in full force trying to bag that often elusive record breaking ram. The hunters in this area had tags for mule deer, moose, mountain sheep, mountain goats, and elk. It was a conservation officer's responsibility to stop hunters to check for hunting licenses, the appropriate tags, ATV (quad) licenses, and insurance. They also surveyed the hunters' campsites to ensure that all provincial and federal laws were being observed.

The area in and around Ram Falls was Public Reserve which meant it was owned by the government but could be used by the general public. Most of the area west of Rocky Mountain House was available for free camping and various recreational uses. This included hunting, fishing, ATV riding, horseback riding, hiking, canoeing, and for the brave souls, swimming. Because this was an area that was easily accessible and well used, campers and day trippers were not required to register at the Ranger Station before coming out here. The disadvantage of this practice, for the officers was that they really had no idea how many civilians were out in the area. The disadvantage for the civilians was that if they were incapacitated in some way and unable to use radios to request help, it could take days for a rescue crew to find someone reported missing. The elevation of this area was high enough that temperatures had been dipping below zero at night for over a month and some nights it went into the double digits, -10° Celsius or lower. Although the days were mostly sunny and warm, the nights could kill you.

By noon David and Annah had run across six different groups of hunters and surveyed about a dozen camp sites. So far they had only issued a couple of citations for missing registration papers. Since David's mood had not improved as the day dragged on Annah let him do all of the talking each time they were in contact with the hunters. She spent her time observing and making notes and generally trying to stay out of David's way. He was courteous and professional to everyone they talked with but his usual friendly disposition was definitely missing.

By one o'clock they still hadn't made it as far as the falls but Annah was starving. She asked David if they could please stop and grab a bite to eat. Testily he agreed and they pulled off the road and sat in the ditch while they munched on their sandwiches. Annah wasn't prepared to spend the remainder of her training with David's new attitude. She knew she was the one who was going to have to try to get David's problem out in the open so that they could deal with it and move on. Since they had discussed so many other personal issues in great detail and David had never seemed to have a problem sharing his feelings, she was at a loss as to why he was being so closemouthed today. She figured it had something to do with Saturday night but she wasn't sure if it was her relationship with Lachlan that was bugging him, his fiancée's attitude, or something else entirely.

"David, I don't know what bug crawled up your butt on the weekend but if you can't or won't talk to me about it I suggest you figure out some other way of dealing with it since it's not productive for either of us to try to work like this. If you have some issue with me spit it out. For the life of me, I can't imagine what I've done to you. Did I offend your fiancée on Saturday night?"

"Look, I don't even know where to begin." David opened the door of the truck, jumped out, and stomped off to sit on a tree stump several feet away. With a sigh Annah poured herself a cup of tea and coffee for David. David wasn't known for pouting or sullenness. His usual mood was optimistic and cheerful. Obviously his personal problems had come to a head on the weekend. She jumped out of the truck, grabbed both cups, closed the door with her shoulder, and headed to join David.

"Okay. Let's start at where we left off. Friday evening when I left work everything seemed fine. What happened next?"

David had been sitting with his head cradled in his hands. With Annah's question he raised his head and took the cup she offered. He dusted the snow off the log beside him and Annah sat down.

"Since the first shift that we worked together I felt a kinship with you. I don't know how to explain it but I know we were meant to meet and I believe you have enriched my life. Most things in my life have come pretty easy. I come from an affluent family and was given the opportunity to pursue my dreams. School came easy to me and so did university. I've traveled extensively and people seem to gravitate to me. I've never had to put any work into any relationship I've had. I know what is expected of me both personally and professionally. There have been no real challenges so far. Then you came along. You look to me for guidance like no other trainee ever has. You're full of questions and enthusiasm and you radiate a zest for life. You challenge me on a daily basis. Unknowingly, you have made me question some of the choices and decisions I have made. You have made me strive to be a better officer and a better person. Since we have become partners I know myself better. Even though things come easily to me, deep down, I have always been searching for the one thing or one person that can ultimately make me happy."

"David, I know you are unsettled. That's why you keep tempting fate by participating in the thrill-seeking sports. The average person doesn't need to try sky diving, bungee jumping, heli-skiing, and then scuba diving with sharks. Don't you realize yet that the only person that can make you happy is you? You have to love yourself and be happy when you are all alone. Are you trying to prove something to your family, to yourself, or are you trying to hide something?"

"I don't know, Annah. The only thing that I do know is that I need to make some changes in my life. I know you're going to lose some respect for me after I tell you some of the details of the darker side of my life, but I know I won't be able to move on if I don't. I have always had at least two lovers on the go at the same time. The challenge of keeping them apart and trying to keep everyone happy has always been a thrill. Dabria was my childhood sweetheart. Our fathers grew up together and we grew up together. It was always expected that she and I would join our families' dynasties. I care for Dabria, but I don't love her and I don't think she loves me either. Anyway, after the way she treated you on Saturday night my decision to end the engagement was made so much easier. She's even more self-absorbed than I am. She's a snob and the reality is we have very little in common, definitely not enough to base a marriage on. That's why we left early Saturday. I needed to end something that should have been ended a long time ago."

"How did she take it?" Annah gently inquired.

David took a sip of coffee. It seemed to fortify him for what he needed to say next.

"Not well. I'm afraid she accused me of sleeping with you. I'm not surprised that she figured out I was having an affair, particularly since she's a lawyer. However, it never occurred to me she would assume it was you until Matthew pointed out that you and I seemed to have an obvious rapport. Is that why you went to the dance with Lachlan? I heard there were rumors circulating around the office that you and I were having a fling."

Annah blushed.

"Actually, that is part of the reason why I went with Lachlan. I was accused of chasing after an engaged man. I don't do that sort of thing."

"I know you don't, which is one of the reasons I was drawn to you. Anyway, I was also sleeping with Nicole and I told her things were over last night. She didn't take it too well either since I think she thought I was going to leave Dabria for her. She also accused me of having something on the side with you."

"For heaven's sake can't a man and woman work together and be friends without everyone assuming they're sleeping together?"

"I'm sure they can, but I think I wanted the rest of the staff to think there was something going on between us because I *wanted* there to be something going on between us. I have one more detail I need to see to tonight and then I'm free to move forward with my new life. Things were actually falling into place until I got to work this morning and I overheard comments that you and Lachlan have more than a casual arrangement going on. I'm rearranging my life for you and apparently you have had something going on with Lachlan for a while. I share everything with you and you've been holding out on me."

Annah jumped up and poked him in the chest with her index finger.

"Now, you just hang on one cotton pickin' minute Mr. Is this the reason you've been such a jerk all day? How dare you? You obviously don't share everything with me since I just found out that you're having an affair with Nicole. This, quite frankly, is none of my business. For your information Saturday night was the first time Lachlan and I have been out on a date." She chose not to add that they had been sleeping together for months. "Secondly I wasn't aware that I was supposed to ask your permission to have a personal life."

"Now, Annah," David stood up and reached for Annah's hands. Before he could utter one more word, Annah pulled her hands away from him and stepped back.

"David, you stop right now. I need to explain something to you. I look up to you as my superior. I respect your integrity as a conservation officer. I admire your intelligence and revere your knowledge. I enjoy your quick wit and appreciate the patience you have had with me. I, however, am not in love with you, nor will I ever be. You are my friend as well as my partner but we will never be lovers. I love you like a brother, David. That is all it will ever be. You need to figure out how to be happy without jumping into another new relationship. If you

can't work with me without thinking of being with me, I think maybe
we should request a switch in trainers. Ken's wife has had their baby
now and he's back at work. I'll backup whatever reason you need to
give Lachlan for the switch." Annah grabbed their cups. "We need to
get those sheep counted and head back to the station before it gets
dark."

Annah headed back to the truck. David followed her. After pulling himself into the truck he turned to her before driving back onto
the road.

"This discussion isn't finished yet," he promised. "We'll finish it
tomorrow after I've dealt with my remaining issues."

Annah let that comment slide and promised herself that if David
hadn't asked for a switch by Wednesday she was going to talk to
Lachlan herself. This was one of the reasons that Lachlan didn't want
woman officers working for him. It could lead to the development
of inappropriate and unproductive relationships. Unintentionally
Annah had obviously given David cause to think that their relationship either could or had progressed beyond the point of friendship
and mutual respect for each other. Now she was going to have to cur-
tail this situation before it got out of hand. As they bumped down
the uneven road Annah's thoughts turned to a different developing
relationship. How ironic that she had been so concerned that her
relationship with Lachlan could bring about the loss of her job and
destruction of her reputation when in reality it could actually come
about from a situation that she had never sought out nor encouraged.
Life was definitely strange.

By the time David and Annah restocked the patrol cabin there was
not enough light left to accurately count the sheep. They agreed that
tomorrow would have to be count day. Since they were at the falls
anyway Annah decided to take a stroll over to view them before they
drove back. There was a hunting truck parked in the lot and Annah
had a feeling they should probably check it out as well. David sent her
ahead to the falls and said he would look over the truck.

Annah was always struck by the raw force of thousands of gallons
of water plunging over the edge of a precipice and roaring to a drop
several hundred feet below. Ram Falls was one of the highest falls
in the area making it a most impressive tourist attraction. As Annah

stood on the edge of the cliffs, out of habit, she focused her binoculars on the falls. She followed the water's path from top to bottom and then viewed the river flowing through the canyon. It was then that she saw a flash of orange. Focusing her binoculars she zoomed in and found two hunters near the base of the falls waving frantically at her. One was standing and one was sitting propped up beside a sheep. The pounding force of the water drowned out any sound that the hunters could make. Grabbing her two-way radio Annah called David and requested help. Since he was already walking down the path towards her he started to run. Within seconds he had rounded the last bend of the path. She handed her field glasses to him and waited for his instruction.

"Holy shit, Annah, what are those idiots doing down there?"

"Since there's a sheep lying on the ground beside them I'm guessing they shot it and then slid down the slope to retrieve it. Obviously, they didn't realize that the shale is so loose on that slope and the remaining cliffs so steep that there was no way they were ever going to get back up. The one laying on the ground beside the sheep is hurt. I can make out a splint on his leg."

"Apparently they were also unaware that this is a no hunting zone." As David handed the glasses back to Annah he took a look at the sky.

"We have a problem. There is about an hour left of daylight and I'm sure it's going to snow. There is no way we can leave those guys down there overnight, especially if they're injured. I'll run back and get the truck. You call the station and let them know that we have a situation. Lachlan will expect you to be able to analyze the crisis and give him feedback on a solution. I'll be back in ten." Without a backwards glance David turned and ran for the truck.

Annah waved to the hunters to indicate they were seeking help for them and proceeded to radio base. She changed the frequency of the radio to speak to the station and requested Lachlan. Annah described the plight of the stranded hunters quickly and precisely. Lachlan responded by telling her to survey the area and to determine the best place for a drop. She and David were to fill a rescue basket with survival supplies and lower it down to the hunters so that they would have shelter, food, heat, and a means to communicate with their rescuers.

"Do not; I repeat, DO NOT, attempt this rescue without back-up assistance. I will have STARS air ambulance put on alert and I am heading up a team and leaving as we speak." Assuming Lachlan was done Annah went to switch frequencies back to David. Just before she switched Lachlan clicked on again.

"I just heard that the roads are slick out there. That means the cliff faces are as well. Make sure you and your lines are secured properly before attempting your drop. Annah," his tone softened, "be careful." Annah did an inspection of the area and determined that using the falls viewing platform supports would not only work to secure their ropes but placed them already about a third of the way down the incline. The supports were made of steel drilled into the side of the mountain and the platform, with its steel railing, provided the safety that Lachlan had expressed concern about. As David pulled up with the truck Annah ran over to relay Lachlan's instructions.

"I question Lachlan's request to wait for backup. It will be dark by the time the team gets out here and that puts the lives of those men in jeopardy. If we wait the rescue may not be attempted until morning. We don't know how severe their injuries are. I think we need to send someone down, as well as the supplies. We can lower the supplies first but then I'm calling Lachlan back to discuss sending one of us down as well."

Annah kept her thoughts to herself as she packed the necessities. Lachlan hadn't requested they wait. He had explicitly *ordered* that they wait. She knew that he had more experience in the area of rescues than David. If he wanted them to wait she trusted his judgment and she would wait. David anchored the ropes for the supply drop onto the railings. Annah finished packing up on top of the cliff and waited for David to help her slide the rescue basket down the steep path to the platform. Once the rescue basket was attached to the drop rope David and Annah began to lower the supplies. Annah watched the mobile hunter hurry over to the base of the mountain in anticipation. The one drawback to this drop site was that there were several shelves on the way down and the potential for the basket getting hung up on one of them was very real. For a person rappelling down, the ledges could make the descent easier. Not so, necessarily, for the basket.

Annah adjusted her footing to get a better grip on the rope and reduce the strain on her muscles. The slick platform surface caused her to slip just enough to make the rope jerk and slide through her grasp. Before David's grip could tightened enough to stop the rope it had slipped several inches, which was just enough to hang the basket up on one of those ledges.

"Damn it." David cursed as he tightened his grip and investigated the situation below. "We'll try to rock it off the ledge by pulling back and releasing it again. Are you secure?"

"Yes," Annah replied, without apology. She knew if she had been one of the guys no apology would have been forthcoming nor expected. She had learned during her field training at University that if you wanted to play with the big boys then you needed to know how to act like the big boys. It was hard to respect your partner or place your trust in them if you saw or heard their confidence wavering during a crisis. Although they attempted to swing the basket off the ledge it appeared that some of the elastic nylon webbing used to contain the supplies was snagged on a jagged outcropping of rock. Tying the rope off David turned to Annah.

"You know we don't have a choice. I have to lower you down to the litter so that you can unhook it. Those guys can't be left down there overnight without supplies. You understand that you have to be the one to rappel down because once the basket is unhooked I will have to continue to lower it alone."

Knowing that David offered the only solution, she agreed, appreciating the fact that he hadn't stated what he was obviously thinking. She didn't have the strength to lower the basket herself and it was her fault the thing was hung up in the first place.

"I want you to use my equipment since I know you checked it thoroughly this morning while I did not do the same for you. I'll radio in while you get ready."

Annah carefully made her way back up the slippery walkway to the truck. Once there she made short work of gearing herself up for the descent. Still, by the time she returned to David dusk was starting to settle in. If they were lucky they had about fifteen minutes. The need for speed had now overshadowed the need to wait for backup.

Again David secured ropes onto the railing of the platform and this time he focused all of his concentration on Annah's safety.

Annah swiftly rappelled herself down the rock face. After unhooking the snag, she gave David the thumbs-up sign and waited for his signal to slide the basket off the shelf. At his gesture she slide it off and then moving to the side waited for the it to land on the ground in the canyon floor. One of the rescue basket ropes, which had come from Annah's equipment pack, had a slice in it and the second that section slid through David's hands he knew it didn't have the integrity to stay together and hold up that basket.

"What the fuck!" David shouted.

Lunging after the now falling basket David plunged over the side of the platform. His first security rope also snapped but the second one held him. Unfortunately, the basket was heavy enough that David banged into the face of the cliff hard. He heard, rather than felt, the breaking of at least one rib. Hanging upside down while still gripping the rope from the basket he pulled it up enough to get a better grip of his burden. Annah immediately rappelled down to the bottom of it and with feet braced was able to coax the basket over to rest on a ledge no more than ten feet off the ground. Once David released the rope she would be able to secure it to herself and angle the basket down to the waiting hunter.

"David, let go of the rope. I have the basket secured," she yelled up to him.

Since David could feel the pull of the basket had been released he relaxed his grip on the rope and let it slide through his gloved hands. Drawing his arms up to his chest and cradling his now screaming ribs he assessed his current predicament. He could probably flip himself right-side up with a little maneuvering but he knew there was no way he was going to be able to drag himself back up over the ledge with broken ribs. He decided the best plan of action at this point would be to figure out how to end his upside down position and then try to anchor his body until *he* was now rescued.

As he was working on his maneuvers Annah was able to attach the basket's line to her harness and ease it over the ledge to the waiting arms of the hunter. Once it landed on the ground Annah unhooked it and looked up to see how David was doing. She had seen how hard he hit the wall after his tumble over the railing. If he didn't have broken ribs he would definitely have bruises.

"What the hell happened? Are you okay for a minute?" she called David on her radio.

"The basket rope had a cut in it and I'm guessing so did the security line. I'm good. Finish what you're doing."

He gave her the thumbs-up sign. She lowered herself to the canyon floor, unharnessed herself, and hurried over to the supplies to pull out the radio and show the hunters how to use it. She checked to see how long they had been down there and what kind of injuries they had. After showing the mobile hunter where the food was she grabbed a fleece blanket and a foil blanket and made her way over to the injured hunter. Once she had confirmed that his only obvious injury was a broken leg she laid the foil blanket on the ground with the fleece on top of it. With the help of the other hunter she was able to position the injured one in the middle of the blankets and then carry him over to a more sheltered place by the cliff side. Wrapping him in the blankets and making sure both men had food and water, she radioed Lachlan and apprised him of the latest situation.

"I'm just pulling into the parking lot, now. Attend to the hunters and stay put. Once I've had a chance to inspect David's situation I'll call you back with instructions."

As Annah looked up to check on David's plight she felt the first snowflake land on her nose. With the deepening darkness and the dusting of snowflakes all Annah could make out was the silhouette of David still hanging upside-down. Changing frequencies again she called him.

"David, what's going on up there? I just talked to Lachlan and the troops are minutes away." She lit a can of sterno while she talked and gestured for the hunter to find kindling to start a fire.

"That's good. Busted ribs. Trouble breathing."

"Hang on, I'm coming," encouraged Annah. David's voice sounded garbled. Annah ran back over to the basket and pulled out the tent. She had assessed that the hunter was coherent. Since he had a small fire going already she left him with instructions to build up the fire, set up the tent, and get his injured friend inside. She set his radio and assured him someone would keep in contact with them until they were both rescued. Annah reattached her harness to her rappel lines, strapped on a headlamp, and called Lachlan.

"Lachlan, David is still hanging upside down. He has broken ribs and he just told me has trouble breathing. I need to climb back up and get him upright and I can't wait for backup. I'm not asking your permission. I'm simply telling you what I have to do. The guys on the ground are set up and safe for now. The hunters' radio channel is 1300. I assured them someone would stay in contact with them until they were rescued. Please change your frequency to 700 and tell David I'm coming and that he is going to be okay." She paused for a moment and then clicked back on. "I'm scared for David, Lachlan, he doesn't sound good. See you at the top." Without waiting for a reply she switched her channel back to David's and unclipped her ascending kit from her harness.

"God damn it, Annah, stay where you are!" Lachlan shouted into the radio. Annah never heard him. She had already switched her radio over. Lachlan looked over the side of the platform and could see Annah's headlamp. With the falling snow Lachlan knew his crew needed to get down and rescue David before their lines got slippery. Issuing orders rapidly Lachlan switched back onto David's frequency and continued to assure David that help was on the way. He received no reply.

With both of her hands occupied if Annah stayed on David's frequency she would be able to hear him and Lachlan. They would be able to give her instructions even though she wouldn't be able to reply. Annah had turned around and checked on the hunters. The tent was up and the mobile hunter was in the process of stuffing the injured hunter inside. With a thumbs-up sign Annah pivoted and started to ascend.

As she climbed she could hear Lachlan encouraging David. David wasn't responding. Annah had attached hand ascenders and ascending stirrups to her two rappelling ropes for the climb back up. Placing her feet in the stirrups and her hands in the hand ascenders she basically pulled her way back up the rock face. She simply slid one hand up the rope, which pulled up that foot and then a lock stopped it there. She slid her other hand up which then pulled up the other foot. It looked easy but even if you had a great deal of upper body strength it was still hard work. Once you had a rhythm going you could pull yourself up the canyon walls with relative ease. In a rescue situation where speed was an issue and there was no one at the top to help pull her back up this was definitely Annah's fastest option. She just prayed she was fast enough.

CHAPTER 17

ANNAH COULDN'T CLIMB FAST enough to satisfy the growing panic she felt. She was terrified for David and if it snowed any harder it was going to make her ropes slippery and then she was going to have an even bigger problem. Forcing herself to breathe rhythmically she was able to calm herself down and actually increase her speed. Balancing on a slight outcrop Annah looked up and realized she would be able to reach David in about another two feet. Surveying her surroundings she discovered there was another outcrop about a foot wide just above David's waist. If she could get him flipped around she should be able to prop him against the cliff and hold him there until she got instruction on how to get him back up to the top.

She could see other officers standing behind the railing. The beams of spotlights rained down on either side of Annah. David's arms were no longer clasping his ribs. Instead they hung down. He was obviously unconscious. Annah pulled herself up beside David and crossing her legs to hold herself upright she released her hands to grab onto David to flip him up. Once he was upright she pushed his limp form onto the outcrop and held him there with her body. With one hand she held the radio switch open and called Lachlan.

"Can you see us?"

"Yes."

"Okay. So now what? David is unconscious and bleeding but breathing."

"It's going to get crowded down there. Ken and Peter are coming down with a basket and you're going to hang onto David until they get down there and get him strapped in. We'll pull him back up. STARS Air Ambulance is on its way. Can you hold on?"

"Yes."

With the sound of the radio and being held upright David regained consciousness. Annah shifted on the ledge to give David more breathing room. Unknown to Annah, David's broken rib had punctured his lung. He was bleeding out.

"Hey, how are we doing?" she asked quietly.

David reached up a hand and brushed her cheek.

"I love you," David gurgled out as blood dribbled from his lips. He coughed, spraying blood on Annah's face and clothes. Then David ferociously grabbed Annah close to him. "Don't forget me," he begged.

"David!" Annah cried out. "Hold on! Hold on!!"

David sagged into Annah's supporting arms.

"No!" she shouted. "Don't you dare die on me!"

Oblivious to the tears streaming down her face, the snow falling around them, or the strain on her arms Annah held onto David praying she could miraculously will him back to life. Ken and Peter appeared at her sides. Wordlessly, they slid the basket behind David. They had heard Annah's cry and could see the blood. Peter reached over and felt David's neck for a pulse. There was none.

"Annah, we need to slide David onto the basket. Please help us," Ken coaxed.

"No!" she refused to relinquish her hold on David. She knew if she did she would have to face the reality that David had died in her arms.

Peter's radio had been locked on receive and Lachlan was able to hear everything that was said. Lachlan clicked back onto David's frequency.

"Annah! Let Ken and Peter do their jobs," he forcefully commanded. "Step down and release David immediately. I know you don't want to endanger Peter and Ken's lives. The snow is making the lines slippery and we need to get David out of the canyon so that we can rescue those stranded hunters. Do you understand?"

Without a sound Annah released David to her fellow officers.

"Annah, you need to climb back up ahead of us. We need the room to maneuver the basket" Ken gently instructed.

Wordlessly, Annah swiftly continued her ascent to the platform. She was numb. Lachlan pulled her over the railing and handed her off to John to remove her rigging from her harness.

"I can do it," she insisted pushing John's hands away. "Let me help pull up David," she pleaded to Lachlan.

Without acknowledging Annah's request Lachlan issued orders to John and Dan to anchor themselves and start pulling up the basket. Once David's body was pulled over the railing Lachlan turned to Annah.

"Go with John. I need you to take the basket to the helicopter and turn David over to the EMTs. Have them check you out as well and then get into one of the trucks." With a nod to John, Lachlan turned back to Dan and called Ken on the radio.

As Annah and John slid the basket up the walkway to the helicopter she heard Lachlan giving Ken and Peter instructions to check their lines. If they were comfortable with the shape they were in, they were to continue on down to the hunters and secure the injured one into the basket already in the canyon. They would rescue the injured hunter first and then pull up the other hunter.

Once Annah reached the EMTs she released her grip on the basket line and knelt on the ground beside David. She smoothed the hair on his brow and caressed his cheek as the tears again streamed unheeded down her face mixing with the blood splatters and melting snowflakes. She wiped the blood away from David's mouth. Silently she laid her head on David's chest as she clutched him to her. After rechecking for a pulse the paramedics and John stood back knowing there was nothing that could be done. Confirming that Annah was in good hands John headed back down to the platform to help with the next basket that was being brought up. A blanket was placed over Annah and the EMTs retreated to speak with the R.C.M.P. that had just driven up.

Gently prying Annah's fingers from David's coat one of the paramedics told Annah to come and sit on the tailgate of the truck so that they could check her out and get David ready for transport. With the impending approach of the second basket they needed to insure Annah was okay so that their resources could be used for the injured hunter and his friend.

With one final stroke of David's cheek Annah allowed them to lead her to the truck. Woodenly she sat on the tailgate and let them poke and prod her and wash the blood from her face to confirm that she wasn't bleeding. She answered their questions with one word responses. Wrapping her in a thermal blanket they tried to entice her into drinking hot sugar-laced tea and into getting into one of the trucks. She agreed to drink the tea if they would let her sit outside and watch over David.

The second basket made its way up the path and the EMTs left Annah to deal with their new patient. The R.C.M.P. approached Annah and attempted to ask her questions regarding the situation. She ignored them. Keeping her eyes firmly trained on David's body she blocked out the falling snow, the R.C.M.P.'s questions, the paramedics administering to the hunter, and his responses to them. Annah was oblivious to the fact that the other hunter and her fellow officers had returned up the path. She heard, but paid no attention to Lachlan speaking to the R.C.M.P. It was like white noise. It was as if she were in a trance or some horrific nightmare that she couldn't wake up from. Although it seemed like only moments that she had been watching David it was actually almost an hour. Knowing that there was something important she was supposed to tell Lachlan Annah struggled to remember.

Lachlan turned from the R.C.M.P. and spied Annah sitting on the back of David's truck. With a curse he marched over towards the truck. Annah's view of David became obstructed by Lachlan's body. She jumped off the tailgate and tried to push him out of the way. Lachlan tilted her face up to his and holding her forearms forced her to look into his eyes. Instead of cursing at her for not following his order to sit inside the truck Lachlan felt her anguish and took a different route.

"They will take good care of him, Annah," he said softly. "Let him go."

"No!!!!!" she screeched as she struggled to get around him. Her shriek split the night air like shattered glass. All activity seemed to stop and the officers, hunters, and paramedics held their breath as they witnessed Annah's agony. She pounded on Lachlan's chest and tried to pull away from his embrace.

"Noooooooo!" she wailed as he clutched her to him. Sobbing, thrashing her head from side to side, she continued to resist him until suddenly she went limp and crumpled to the ground. Lachlan scooped her up and leaving the bloodied blanket behind carried her to his truck. John ran ahead and opened the door for them.

Lachlan stripped her out of her damp clothes and enveloped her in her dependable red blanket coat, which he had spontaneously grabbed just before he left the station. He tucked another blanket around her legs and propped her up in the passenger seat. With the truck running and the heater cranked to high, Annah sat shivering and in shock but at least conscious.

"Pour Annah another cup of hot tea from that thermos behind my seat and dump in some sugar packets," Lachlan instructed John as he climbed out of the truck. "Sit in the truck with her and make her drink it. If she seems to become agitated or faints go and get a paramedic or find me immediately. She's in shock. The warmth from the truck and the tea should help. I'll be back when I can."

Lachlan left the truck and returned to direct the rest of his officers. He asked if the R.C.M.P. would follow him back to the station so that the de-briefing could occur there. The chopper started back up again and left for the hospital in Rocky Mountain House. As the sound of the beating blades receded, the clearing took on an unnatural quiet. The remaining officers quickly loaded their gear, jumped into the trucks, and drove back to the station. Lachlan buckled Annah into the middle seat. He sat on the passenger side, tilted her towards him, and held her while John drove his truck. On the way back to the station Lachlan called Mrs. Larson and asked her to keep Annah's kids at her house overnight. He explained that Annah was in shock and was in no shape to be taking care of them.

"Lachlan, Hal will keep an eye on Annah's kids. Linda and I will meet you at Annah's house. I'll stay there with Annah until you come home."

"Thank you, June. I owe you."

"Don't be ridiculous. Are there any other calls you need me to make before I leave?"

"Yes, please call all of the officers' wives and let them know that their husbands are heading back to the station but it could be a couple of hours yet before they get home. Please assure Linda that Peter is fine." Lachlan paused, "June, there was an accident and David was killed. Please don't let this get out yet. The R.C.M.P. is heading over to Dabria's and David's parents, as we speak, to tell them. I should be the one doing it but we are too far out and I don't want to risk them finding out from someone other than myself or the R.C.M.P. Find out where Matthew is. When I was rounding up the rest of the crew I couldn't get in touch with him. I know he was off today but I did see him at the station this morning. Let me know so that I can have someone from the station with him when he is told."

"He's going to be crushed. They have been best friends since they were toddlers. I believe he was heading to Calgary to visit his parents for a couple of days. I'll confirm that and then get back to you."

Mrs. Larson called back with Matthew's parent's address. Lachlan called the R.C.M.P. and requested they send an officer to tell Matthew at his parent's home. At least he would have his family there when he found out.

As John approached Annah's house Lachlan saw Linda waiting in her car. When they pulled up Lachlan told John where the spare key was to Annah's house and had him open the door. Still holding Annah's unresponsive body in his arms he slid from the truck and carried her into the house. Lachlan carried her into her bedroom. While gently laying her down she seemed to regain consciousness. She clutched at his shirt as she realized he was leaving her.

"Annah, Linda is going to check you out and help you into the bath. I have to go back to the station. I promise I will come back to you the second I am finished. Try to get some sleep while I'm gone," he kissed her tenderly. She kissed him back fiercely and then still clutching his shirt she pulled herself up.

"Lachlan, the rope was cut. I remember David telling me that my rope was cut. That's why he was pulled over the railing. How could that be?"

"I don't know. What color was the litter rope?"

"David was using my pink ropes, both for the litter and his security lines."

Striding quickly out the door he left instructions with Linda to call him if Annah's condition changed. Since she had stopped shivering on the way home and now seemed to be aware of her surroundings he was confident she was basically out of shock. He knew he was leaving her in good hands. The sound of the door closing seemed to galvanize Annah into action. Sitting up on the bed she flung off her blanket and stripped out of her remaining clothes. While Linda stood back and watched Annah wrapped herself in a towel and grabbed clean clothes, clothes that weren't stained and spotted with David's blood.

"I'm going to have a shower," Annah announced as she made her way to the bathroom.

"Can you keep the bathroom door open for me?" Linda requested.

"Yes, but I won't faint. I promise. I need to get back to the station and de-brief with the other officers." Linda nodded her head and while Annah showered she took the blood stained clothes and put them in a garbage bag. She then went to the kitchen and made Annah a sandwich and a pot of coffee. She called her mother to tell her not to bother coming over to Annah's since she would be driving Annah back to the station.

"Mom, could you make a platter of sandwiches and take some baking out of the freezer and meet me at the station. Lachlan and the R.C.M.P. will be interviewing all of the officers. That could take several hours. Those guys are all going to be in some form of shock and until they have eaten and drank something I don't want them to head home. The Victim's Services Counsellors may be coming out to talk to them tonight as well."

"All right, I'll meet you there."

Next Linda called Lachlan and told him Annah would be on her way back into the station once she was dressed and had eaten.

"Do you think it is a good idea for Annah to be coming back in tonight?" he asked.

"I think that is exactly what she needs to do. She is an officer just like the rest of you. She is a professional, and part of her job is to de-brief and deal with all types of rescue situations, regardless of the outcome. The way she deals with this will determine her future relationship with her fellow officers," Linda replied. "She needs to do this Lachlan. Let her."

Grudgingly, he accepted that Linda was right and relayed the information to the waiting R.C.M.P. Meanwhile Lachlan told the police what Annah had told him at the house regarding the cut lines. At Lachlan's request, the officers were interviewed one at a time and the interviews were taped by the police. The officers were segregated until after their interview and then as they were released they gathered around David's desk and began to talk. Mrs. Larson showed up with provisions and made pots of coffee and tea. Unaware of the drama that had occurred, since it was her day off, Nicole stopped at the station as she was driving by when she noticed all of the traffic in the parking lot. When she walked in and saw the long faces she knew something bad had happened.

"I forgot my sweater this morning. What's going on?" Nicole asked as she looked over the assembled staff. "Where are Annah and David?"

Peter pulled her aside and told she sit down. He told her that David had died during a rescue. Nicole's face went white as a sheet and for the second time in the same night the officers were shaken by the earsplitting shriek of a female's cry.

"No!" Nicole bawled as she stood up and then promptly fainted. Startled by her unexpectedly dramatic reaction, Peter almost didn't catch her before she fell. Mrs. Larson rushed over and once they were able to revive her she held and rocked the sobbing girl in her arms.

"I loved him," Nicole quietly keened. "I loved him."

Linda drove Annah back to the station and as she walked into the office Nicole sat up, pointed her finger at Annah, and began to screech.

"This is your fault. You did this. He told me about you. You were after him. We all saw it. Didn't we?" she asked the whole staff, waving her arms around frantically. "You're his partner. Why didn't you protect him?" she hysterically howled.

Without knowing the details of the tragedy Nicole decided to blame both David's rejection of her and his death on Annah. Peter picked up Nicole and carried her shrieking into one of the back offices. Linda followed to try to calm Nicole down and possibly administer a sedative.

All eyes were on Annah as she continued into the room. With all of the commotion in the station both R.C.M.P. officers and Lachlan had come out of the offices. When they saw things were back under control the police finished up their interviews and then requested that Annah follow them. Because Annah had been the only officer with David when the accident happened, both of the police officers wanted to be present during her de-briefing. Lachlan also asked to be present. With all of the questions that were bound to arise, he wanted to cover all of his bases to insure the integrity of the investigation.

Starting at the time that they finished restocking the cabin, her walk to the falls, and David's checking of the hunter's truck, Annah relayed the events that occurred. She included every conversation, word for word, that she had had with David, Lachlan, and both of the hunters.

"You seem to be very sure of the conversations that occurred between you and your fellow officers, as well as the hunters. How can you be positive that the exact wording you claim you heard was in fact what was actually said?" questioned one of the police officers.

"One of my best skills is my ability to listen and retain what I hear. Although, you obviously can't question David you can question Lachlan and the hunters regarding what I claim to have heard." Sitting composed and calm in her chair Annah looked from one officer to the next, waiting for the next question. Lachlan pushed himself away from the wall he had been leaning against.

"Can I ask a question?" Lachlan looked at the police.

"Of course," they responded.

"Annah, why was David using your lines instead of his own and when was the last time you checked them?"

"David and I had a routine that we followed each shift. Before we left in the morning I would check his equipment and he would check mine. Every Friday night after my shift I would go through my own equipment to make sure I was familiar with everything I had and where it was located in my bag so that I would be able to find things automatically if a crisis occurred. This was David's suggestion."

"Do you check every length of rope in your equipment every day?" asked one of the R.C.M.P.

"No."

"Did you check them Friday night?"

"Yes."

"Were they all intact then?"

"Yes."

"Who checked them Monday morning?"

"David was supposed to. But he was in a hurry and he admitted later that he hadn't checked the equipment before we left and therefore he was using my lines for himself instead of his."

"Why would he do that?"

"He knew that I had checked his equipment this morning and therefore it was safer for me to use it to rappel than to use lines that hadn't been checked."

"Where is this equipment kept over the weekend and who has access to it?" asked the police officer.

"Everyone's equipment is kept in the equipment room and the door is never locked."

"How do you differentiate between your equipment and someone else's?"

"We each have a specific colored bag. The equipment inside is the same from one bag to the next. My rope color is different because I am the only woman officer and Mrs. Larson ordered me pink ropes to go with my pink bag."

"So everyone working at the station is aware that the pink equipment is specifically yours," the R.C.M.P. stated.

"Yes," Annah responded as a sick feeling settled over her.

"Can you think of any reason why someone would want to sabotage your equipment, Ms. Andersson?"

"I don't know," Annah replied as she looked down at her lap.

"Besides the four of us who else knows that the rope was cut?"

"David," responded Annah. "There was no one else around when David told me."

"Where are all of the lengths of your rope, Annah?"

"All of the equipment at the sight was thrown into bags and brought back to the station. I believe that it is lying on the floor of the equipment room. I'm sure it hasn't been sorted out yet," stated Lachlan.

"I suggest Annah and Constable Rogers go there now and retrieve every bit of pink rope that is in there. Close the door while you are working to prevent other staff from coming in to help. Please conceal it in a black bag and take it out to the car for processing. The rest of the staff doesn't need to know anything about it." Looking at Lachlan he stated, "We can finish your interview while they're gone."

"I believe we are done for now, Ms. Andersson. Please be aware there will be a Coroner's Inquest into David's death. We will have your statement from the tape typed up and a copy delivered to this office sometime in the next couple of days. Please keep the events that you described and that we discussed tonight confidential. Thank you, for your cooperation. We are sorry for your loss." With a handshake to Annah the men rose and Annah and Constable Rogers left the office.

When Annah left Lachlan's office a hush fell over the room as she and Constable Rogers made their way to the equipment room. Conversation resumed once she went in and closed the door. Mrs. Larson and Linda watched from the sidelines waiting to see how Annah's fellow officers were reacting. Within minutes the door re-opened and the R.C.M.P. left the station carrying a black garbage bag obviously filled with something. Annah made her way over to her desk. Peter was the first to stand up. He walked over to Annah and gave her a big hug. His obvious acceptance of her and sympathy for her spurred the remainder of the staff to follow suit and accept Annah back into the fold. One by one the officers hugged her and as tears flowed all around, Linda and Mrs. Larson refreshed everyone's coffee. With the acceptance though, came the questions.

"I'm not allowed to answer any of your questions until the inquest is over," Annah informed them. Although that wasn't what any of them wanted to hear they respected Annah's statement. Instead the conversation turned to the actual rescue of the hunters and speculation regarding what charges they would have laid against them. Someone questioned if Matthew had been contacted and Mrs. Larson informed them that Matthew, Dabria, and David's parents had all been informed.

Annah was exhausted but determined to remain until Lachlan and the R.C.M.P. left the office. Although it seemed like forever, the door finally opened and the remaining police officer made his exit. Lachlan walked to the front of the room and standing, addressed his staff.

"I want to thank everyone for pulling together during this crisis today. I am extremely proud of the performance of each and every one of you. You proved to me that no matter what emergencies are thrown our way this staff will be able to handle them, and that each of you will conduct yourselves in a professional, skilled manner. As I am sure you are all aware there should, and will be, an inquiry into David's death. In twenty years of service this is the first officer I have ever lost and I refuse to lose another. They need to determine that David's death was not due to lack of training, skill, knowledge, or following the chain of command. I promise you if there are any recommendations from the inquest they will be implemented to help ensure our future safety."

Lachlan took a breath and surveyed the room.

"I don't know how to express to you the depth of loss I feel. David's death......" Lachlan faltered. "David will be missed," Lachlan quietly finished.

Mrs. Larson ambled over to Lachlan and hugged him hard. With tears in her eyes she turned away and went to put on her coat and head home. Lachlan went back into his office. It was close to midnight, and although not much sleep would be had, the officers knew it was time to go home. Grief counsellors would be available to the staff in the morning. When the office had cleared out, including a sedated Nicole. Annah stood up and walked to Lachlan's office. She leaned against the door jamb until he motioned her to come and side down. She rested her head against the back of Lachlan's sofa, closed her eyes, and silently waited for him to finish a phone call.

As Annah heard Lachlan sign off and replace the receiver she opened her eyes and sat up. He pushed away from his desk and approached her. Annah stood and walked into his outstretched arms.

They held each other without speaking for a long time. Silently the tears again streamed down Annah's cheeks as she pressed her face into Lachlan's chest. Gently resting his chin on Annah's head he held her and thanked God, not for the first time that day, that she was safe. The ringing of his office phone shattered the intimacy of the moment. Pulling away from Annah he reached behind and answered it.

"Hello," Lachlan listened intently. Annah watched his hand tighten into a fist and his posture straighten. "Yes, sir, I understand. I'd rather not offer an opinion regarding your decision. I will, however, implement your decision effective immediately. Yes, sir, good night."

Lachlan replaced the receiver and turned back to Annah.

"Am I suspended with or without pay pending the conclusion of the inquest?" Annah asked.

"With," Lachlan confirmed.

"Well, that's a relief. I could do with some time off to catch up on a novel I started reading about five years ago," Annah chuckled mirthlessly.

"This is not how I would have proceeded," Lachlan assured her.

"I know that and I appreciate your support. However, maybe it is for the best to have me out of everybody's face until a determination is made."

Annah moved towards the door.

"I need to go lay down, Lachlan, before I fall down. Please keep me apprised of the developments that aren't confidential," Annah requested.

"Annah," Lachlan grabbed her arm and pulled her towards him. "What goes on at work has never had anything to do with our personal relationship, nor have the two ever interfered with each other. The same goes from now on. You will be sleeping at my house tonight, in my arms, and I will be making love to you because I need you just as much as you need me. I will not let this thing jeopardize the personal relationship you and I have."

"Adversity can draw a couple together but it can also pull a couple apart, Lachlan."

"I won't let it," Lachlan vowed. "You have no idea how stubborn or persuasive I can be when I need to be. Come on, let's go home. I need to be back here by seven tomorrow morning and we have some personal business that needs to be attended to before then."

Annah allowed Lachlan to lead her out of the station to his truck. She knew he was right. All she wanted to do right now was prove to herself that she was still alive and making love with Lachlan and then falling asleep in his arms was obviously the natural conclusion to this horrific day.

CHAPTER 18

LACHLAN DECIDED, AS HE lay in bed cradling Annah's sleeping body next to his that he needed to keep her busy so she didn't have time to dwell on David's death, the upcoming inquest, and the possibility that one of her coworkers was out to hurt her. Whoever had cut her lines couldn't possibly have guessed what events would transpire on Monday. Therefore, there were three possibilities for suspects. One was that whoever did it was unaware of David and Annah's routine and they were counting on Annah finding the cut lines herself. That would mean the cuts were there to serve as a warning only. A second possibility was that someone knew their routine, saw Annah checking her lines Friday night, assumed that David would find the cuts Monday morning and that then a reprimand would occur due to her negligence. The final possibility was that someone hoped Annah would have to use her equipment before it was checked again and then get hurt from the failed lines. All three scenarios were abhorrent to Lachlan because it meant that someone in that office was disturbed enough by Annah's presence to want to hurt her either mentally, physically, or both. Lachlan wasn't sure whether he would have suspended her or not if the decision had been his but was relieved that his superior had suspended Annah. Hopefully, it would keep her safe until he figured out who was to blame for those cuts.

The obvious answer to keeping her busy was to have her take over the finishing touches for the house and to decorate and furnish it. His excuse for needing her help was simply that with the loss of two full time officers and the extra hours needed to prepare for the inquest he just didn't have the time to spend on his house. He hoped that, although he knew she would see through his transparent plan, she would still agree to it. Although Lachlan believed in his heart that Annah had not been negligent and that she had reacted responsibly and appropriately during the botched rescue, he had no idea whether or not the inquest's findings would agree with him.

Annah stirred restlessly and suddenly stiffened and cried out.

"Shhhhhh," Lachlan murmured. "I'm right here."

Annah settled and then waking up eased away from Lachlan and sat up. Pulling the blanket to cover up, Annah twisted around to look Lachlan in the eye.

"I promised myself I wouldn't ask you this question but I can't continue what we are doing without an answer. I need to know if you believe I reacted appropriately for the circumstances and if there is anything I could have done to prevent David's death. Please don't sugarcoat it. Tell me the truth. I keep replaying yesterday and I'm going to drive myself crazy, second guessing every move I made unless you can give me some assurance that the way I handled the situation was the only choice I had."

"I have every confidence, Annah, that you handled yourself appropriately. You followed your superior officer's directives and implemented the tasks requested of you successfully. In no way did you endanger the civilians you were trying to rescue or your fellow officers."

Lachlan also sat up and leaning against the headboard turned on his nightstand light.

"You did, however, fail to follow my order to stay in the canyon, when you chose to climb back up to David. You endangered yourself by doing that since the snow was making the lines slick. I can't, in good conscience, reprimand you because David would have died alone if you hadn't gone back up and stayed with him. I would have done exactly the same thing. Unfortunately, however, the inquiry may not feel the same way, since it was a direct order and you specifically told me you were ignoring it. Only time will tell what the outcome of this is going to be. But know that I support you one hundred percent and I stand behind your actions. We will present a united front for the inquest and anyone else that chooses to question yesterday's actions."

Rather than question Annah as to who she thought might want to see harm come to her Lachlan slid out of bed and pulled on a pair of jeans. He decided to do some investigating himself at the office in the morning and let Annah have the day to mull over yesterday's events. He planned on questioning her when he returned from work later today regarding her suspicions of who might be responsible. He headed to the kitchen and poured himself a glass of water. Returning, he sat on the edge of the bed and took Annah's hands into his.

"Since we're both awake anyways, there is something I have been meaning to tell you for a while now and tonight seems to be a fitting time to do it."

Annah sat very still and looked deeply into Lachlan's eyes.

"I love you."

Lachlan cupped her cheek and continued.

"I think I fell in love with you in the hallway the first day we crashed into each other. You are strong and courageous and loyal and honest and so beautiful and loving. I can't imagine my life without you in it. You have brought joy and hope back into my life and given me a reason to dig out my dreams, dust them off, and strive to achieve them. I had hoped to court you with flowers and movies and make you fall in love with me but after today I can't wait. I was so afraid that you were going to be hurt or worse yet, that I might lose you, that I have to tell you how I feel and hope you'll give us a chance. I will not allow you to spend one more night away from me. I want you and the children to either move in with me or for you to marry me. I had wanted us to be a family before Christmas this year anyway, so this just moves up the schedule by a few months."

Annah sat there stunned by Lachlan's proclamation. Not in her wildest dreams did she expect to hear Lachlan say he wanted to get married or for her to move in so soon.

"I don't know what to say," Annah confessed. "I was afraid to allow myself to hope that someday you might want to become a part of my family."

"Answer this one question and then we can deal with the rest later. Do you love me?"

Still holding hands Annah fixed her eyes on Lachlan's and responded solemnly, "Yes, Lachlan I do. You are honorable, ethical, moral, and treat your employees fairly. Although I occasionally question your chauvinistic attitude I have never doubted your integrity. You challenge me like no one else. You frustrate me and make me crazy and yet still make me want you. I have never met another man that makes me thank God that I'm a woman. You make me feel sexy and appealing. Yes, Lachlan, I am definitely in love with you."

With a grin a mile wide Lachlan dove at her and pinned her down. Before he could speak Annah put a hand on his chest and held him off of her.

"I am not ready to get married again yet and I'm not moving in with you without marrying you. We need to get the inquest over with and I need to get back to work, then we can talk about forever. Okay?"

"No. Until we find out who was trying to harm you I refuse to let you live alone with the kids," Lachlan disagreed.

"Lachlan, you are not the boss of me in our personal life. I refuse to believe for one second that someone on our staff wants to get rid of me. With me being suspended I won't be in anyone's face and therefore, I am positive there is no longer any threat to my family or me. I won't be bullied into living with you. Now get off of me."

"Compromise for now. Ranger lives with you for the time being since your cat is hardly a killer security alarm. But this discussion is not over. I want a promise from you that if you hear or see anything unusual, or you feel threatened in any way you are going to tell me immediately. I need to be included in your daily family life. The kids need to get used to the idea that I'm not going anywhere."

"Fine. We can start with supper at my house when you get off work. Now, since it's after six o'clock you might as well get ready for work."

"I'll jump in the shower, but you're coming with me. Let's go."

He pulled her up and swung her into his arms. Carrying her like his new bride through the bathroom door, he deposited her beside the tub and stripped off his jeans while she adjusted the heat in the shower. If he could distract her for another half hour before he left that was one less half hour she would have to berate herself during the day.

Wearing only a white dress shirt of Lachlan's, Annah made him a quick breakfast of fried eggs and country grain toast while Lachlan shaved and dressed for work. After he left, Annah dressed and returned to her home. She changed out of the uniform she had worn last night and into jeans and a sweater. She picked out clean clothes for the kids and made their lunches after calling Mrs. Larson and informing her she would be picking up the kids and taking them to school.

After dropping the kids at school and explaining to them that she would be home for the next month or so and therefore, they wouldn't be taking the bus or going to Mr. and Mrs. Larson's after school, Annah headed into Rocky to get groceries. Annah had made peace with herself regarding her actions of the previous day as she drove, but was unsettled by her recollections of the conversation she had had with David after lunch. Unknown to Lachlan or anyone else Annah was forced to consider that there might actually be three people who wanted her gone from the station. Dabria was the obvious first choice, Nicole was the second, and Matthew was the third. And fourth was the unknown "detail" that David hadn't had a chance to deal with yet. Was it another lover? David had indicated the there was a third person he needed to end a relationship with before he was free to start a new one with her. Was there a third person or not? Was David sleeping with not just two women but actually three? The problem now was that without being at work how was Annah going to be able to investigate her suspicions without including Lachlan? At this point she didn't want to divulge what David had confessed to her.

By the time she finished her errands in Rocky and returned home it was after lunch. Once she had unloaded the truck she sat down and phoned Ben. Luckily Ben was in and could take her call. She explained the events of yesterday and asked Ben to enlighten her as to the process of an inquest. What was the time line for these things?

Did she need to retain her own lawyer? Could she be charged with negligence if the inquest decided that she was in some way responsible for David's death? Could she be fired? Could she loose her certification?

"Slow down Annah," Ben advised. "You're getting way ahead of yourself. You're going to drive yourself crazy with worry if you don't focus on the present and the things that you can control. Officially, what has happened so far?"

"Well, officially, I am suspended with pay until after the inquiry is over. I have given a statement regarding the events of yesterday to the R.C.M.P. They have requested that I not discuss yesterday with anyone."

"At this point, Annah, you don't need a lawyer. All that the inquest will require is that you appear before them and describe the events that occurred. Once the findings have been released, recommendations will be made. Do you believe that you acted within the guidelines of your job? Do you believe that you acted professionally, responsibly, and appropriately for the circumstances? Were you following orders? If you can answer "Yes" to all of those questions then I am sure you have nothing to worry about."

"I figured as much. I just wanted to make sure that I had covered all of the bases that I could. The problem is that I disobeyed a direct order. There were extenuating circumstances, but the inquiry may not care."

"Let's just take this one step at a time. If you could go back and do it over again, knowing what you do now, would you do anything different, or would you still disobey that order?"

"I would have acted exactly the same, and I have no regrets about disobeying Lachlan's order."

"Then I guess you did the right thing and you should be able to live with the consequences of your actions. Right?"

"You know what? You're right. Thanks, that makes me feel better."

"Good. Now, moving on. How are you and Lachlan making out?"

"Personally things are progressing nicely. Professionally I hope that our relationship doesn't jeopardize Lachlan's credibility as a witness or as the Area Manager. Is your love life advancing?"

"Yes, things are going well. Once the skiing starts I'll bring her out to meet you. She' a lawyer and her name is Krista. I think she's the one, Annah. You're going to love her. Oh, I've got to run. My secretary just brought me a note saying my next appointment is here. Let me know when the inquest is starting. I'll try to get some inside info on things for you. Talk to you soon."

Annah hung up and went and picked up the kids. She made homemade spaghetti sauce for supper since she didn't know when Lachlan's day would be done and that way she could feed the kids early. After listening to the events of the day and doing homework, Annah let the kids eat. Bath time and story time came and went. Lachlan didn't actually appear until after eight o'clock. The kids were in bed by then, which was just as well, since Lachlan was obviously exhausted. Annah fed him, took off his shirt, had him lay down on her bed, and gave him a massage. As she had hoped, he fell asleep. She covered him up, turned off the light, and snuck out of the room. Once she had the dishes finished and the kids' stuff ready for the morning she curled up on the couch and read a book. About two o'clock in the morning Annah woke up with a start. She could hear Lachlan getting a glass of water. Padding into the kitchen she wrapped her arms around his waist and snuggled him from behind while he drank.

"I'm sorry I woke you," Lachlan whispered as he turned around and hugged Annah back. "I should go."

"It's cold outside and that will just wake you up more. My bed is warm. Come back and I'll set the alarm. You can sleep for another four hours."

"We need to talk."

"Okay. We can still do that in bed." Annah headed for the bedroom knowing full well that Lachlan would follow.

"I talked to David's parents yesterday and expressed our condolences. The funeral is going to be Friday in Calgary. I'm allowing the whole staff to attend. Rocky Mountain House is sending out replacements for both shifts. Apparently Dabria has specifically requested that you not attend." Lachlan pulled off his pants and climbed into bed waiting for Annah's explosion.

"What! She's barring me from his funeral," she hissed.

"She can't stop you from going but since she made a point of re-questing it, I wouldn't put it past her to create a scene if you do go."

"Do you think I should honor her request?"

"My question is why would she request it in the first place? Annah, is there something that I'm missing that I should maybe know regard-ing David?"

"When David and I had lunch on Monday he told me that he had called off the wedding on Saturday night after the supper, and that he had finally broken it off with Dabria. He said she accused him of hav-ing an affair with me. I have no idea what he told her."

"Well, that could explain it then."

"Do you think I shouldn't go?"

"I think you should do what you want to do. You weren't having an affair with him, so you have nothing to hide or be ashamed of."

"Except that, like you said, it's not beyond the realm of possibility that she will create a scene. I need to think about this before I make a decision." Annah had undressed and pulled on an oversized t-shirt that she used as a nightshirt.

"David's parent's asked me to speak at the funeral."

"You know what, I've thought about it and I'm going. I loved David as a friend and I have every right to be there to say goodbye and stand with my fellow officers. I'll see if Nanny can watch the kids in Calgary during the funeral. She made me promise to come to Calgary at least once a month so that she could see us. I haven't gone yet since she left so this would be the perfect time for her to see us." Annah climbed in beside Lachlan but remained sitting.

"I told the staff about your suspension this morning and that the inquest is scheduled to start three weeks from yesterday. It will be held in the Provincial Building in Rocky Mountain House. I have re-quested approval for hiring two more officers." Lachlan lay with his hands behind his head watching Annah set the alarm and undo her braid.

"Why two?"

"I had planned on hiring another officer in January anyway. So, instead of requesting one now and another one in two months it made sense to hire two now. We know you will be off until at least the mid-dle of November. I could do with an extra set of hands with so many of us having to testify." Yawning, Lachlan reached over and pulled Annah down and snuggled her into his side. This felt so natural and so right.

"There isn't anything else you left out from yesterday is there?" Lachlan wished he could see Annah's expression as she answered. He felt she wasn't telling him everything, even though he knew she would never lie to him.

"David and I talked about several things at lunch yesterday, but at this point I don't think that revealing his secrets is relevant."

"Fine, I'm not going to badger you into telling me. I hope you're right and none of it is relevant. Enough talk for now. We both need some sleep." Lachlan tilted her face up to kiss and then with a gentle squeeze promptly drifted off.

CHAPTER 19

Annah spent the next two days sorting through the kids' clothes, taking out the ones they had outgrown, and making a list of things they would need for the next several months. She was amazed at how much they had grown in the last year. They would need to do some clothes shopping on the weekend, while they were in Calgary. Plus they should definitely go to the zoo again to see if last year's babies had grown up. As she walked back into the kitchen the phone rang.

"Annah?" Lachlan inquired.

"Did you think that someone else was going to answer?" Annah chuckled.

"No. It's just a reflex I guess."

"What can I do for you, Officer MacGregor?"

"I need a really big favor. The painters are heading back over to the house and starting on the upstairs today and I can't get away. Could you please go over and meet them? I'm not really sure of the color I've picked for the bedrooms. I wanted to look at it on the walls before I made a final decision. Could you go take a look? Also, I left some carpet samples there. Could you match them up to the paint and see if it's all going to work together?"

"Lachlan, I would love to. It's a beautiful afternoon for a drive and I've never been inside the house in the daylight. I'd like to see how it looks with the sun shining in all of those incredible windows."

"If it's not too much trouble could you take your camera and take some pictures of the inside? I want to look at furniture this weekend in Calgary and I'd like to be able to have the actual room colors with me to pick things out."

"Did Matthew come back to work today?" Annah asked quietly.

"No, he called first thing this morning and requested a leave of absence for the remainder of the week. He is supposed to return next Monday."

"How did he sound?"

"He was very matter of fact. Very unemotional."

"Lachlan, I don't know if this is something Matthew will ever recover from. Do you think he's strong enough?"

"I don't know if it has anything to do with strength. When Amy died I wanted to curl up beside her little body and never wake up. The anger is what kept me going. Matthew definitely has enough anger to keep him going long enough to grieve and then move on. It will take time but I know that Matthew can do it. We just need to keep you out of his line of fire in the meantime."

"I better let you go. How is the staff managing with three full time officers missing?"

"Rocky Mountain House Station is letting me borrow two officers until next week. Then I'll just have to wait until the new hires start."

"Do you want me to call you back when I'm done?" Annah inquired.

"No, unless the color is horrendous, we can talk at supper tonight."

Annah ended the call, grabbed her digital camera and her coat, and headed out to the truck. Lachlan's holdings were even more breathtaking in the daylight. Annah hadn't been to the house during the day since the windows and doors had been installed. It was like a picture for a brochure selling log homes. The sun glinted off the pristine windows and the newly oiled logs gleamed. All of the decking was unstained leaving the pressure treated green hue to weather naturally. As time went on the deck would turn grey matching the color of the river rocks Lachlan had chosen for the fireplace and give the house a rustic, woodsy look.

Annah let herself into the house and introduced herself to the painters. They were expecting her and waited to see if she would approve the colors. She found the carpet samples and had a painter hold them up to the painted walls. They matched perfectly. Annah wandered around the house snapping pictures and really looking at everything that had been done so far. As she moved from room to room it became obvious to her that Lachlan had implemented almost every suggestion that Annah had made regarding colors of paint, flooring, and counter tops. The proof that this wasn't just her imagination was the unusual light fixture hanging in the dining area. It was a fixture that she had commented on when Lachlan had asked her about a different one for that space.

Plopping down on the fireplace Annah acknowledged to herself that Lachlan had finished this house to suit her in the hopes that she would one day be living here. He had obviously been planning this for a while. A warm feeling of being cherished washed over Annah and she hugged herself, reveling in the good fortune she had had of running into him at the university that fateful day a year ago. Her life had changed so much in that time it was hard to believe. How could she be so lucky to fall in love with someone as wonderful as Lachlan and have him love her back?

As Annah stood up the sun was obscured by a cloud and she had a flashback to a different cloudy day. Instantly sobering, Annah felt a stab of guilt. How dare she feel so happy when David would never feel anything again, and when the lives of all of his family and close friends would never be the same. She couldn't begin to imagine the grief that Matthew must be feeling since she had never had a friendship like theirs. Was Lachlan correct when he assured her that Matthew would recover? She knew he would blame her for David's death. He would need a scapegoat and since he didn't like her, she was the perfect candidate. Even if the inquest findings stated that David's death was accidental and unavoidable, she knew the atmosphere of the station would be changed forever. David was the only officer from that station to ever be seriously injured, let alone die.

The question that Annah couldn't get beyond was how would the other officers feel about her and would any of them be willing to partner with her. Maybe Lachlan had been right all those months ago when he said women should not be out in the field. If Annah had been a man, David would have flipped a coin and whoever won the toss would have climbed down that wall instead of it automatically being Annah. David sent her down because he knew she wasn't strong enough to lower the litter herself. The same could not be said for any other officer on staff.

Annah quietly let herself out of the house and did a walk around Lachlan's clearing. The sun was back out again. Annah decided to take Ben's advice and focus on the here and now. Walking over to the truck she grabbed a pad and pen and jotted down suggestions for the yard for Lachlan. Glancing at her watch an hour later she was surprised to see it was time to head to town to pick up the kids. Running back to the house she called out goodbyes to the painters, ran back to the truck, and left for town.

Lachlan appeared at her door just in time for supper that night. After eating and helping her clean up, he viewed the pictures that she had taken of the house that afternoon while Annah bathed the kids. When she was done they changed places and Lachlan sat with the kids on the sofa and read them a story. Annah cleaned up the bathroom and then bundled her babies off to bed. Returning to the kitchen she found Lachlan printing off the pictures that he wanted to take with him on the weekend.

"I'm leaving for Calgary tomorrow night after work and I was hoping that you, Summer, and Simon would come with me."

"Thank you, for asking me rather than telling me I was traveling with you. I plan to stay for the entire weekend though because I'm taking the kids to the zoo on Saturday and I need to go shopping and add to their winter wardrobes."

"Can I go with you?" Lachlan stopped printing.

"Of course you can. I just didn't think you would want to."

"We're not *going* to be a family, Annah; we *are* a family, whether we sleep together every night or not. Okay?"

"Okay."

"Here's my VISA card. Can you book a suite for us? Something with two bedrooms? Pick a hotel that has water slides. I'm sure the kids would enjoy that."

"Lachlan, I can't afford to pay for half a suite for three nights. I was planning on getting a budget room so that I had more money to spend on winter clothes."

"Annah, for heaven's sake, I don't expect you to pay for things when I invite you to come someplace with me," Lachlan looked at her with exasperation. "We may not be engaged yet but we are seeing each other. Chock this up to a date and please don't fret about it. I can afford it or I wouldn't have suggested it in the first place. Just so that we don't spend all weekend long arguing about money let me clarify things right now. I will be paying for all our meals, our room, and the gas to and from Calgary. If you need to contribute financially you can pay for my admission to the zoo. Agreed? "

"Lachlan, the family rate for the zoo is the same for three as it is for four," she informed him.

"Well, what a bargain for you then," he responded with a big grin. "Come here and give me a kiss and then you can help me pick out the rest of the pictures I should print."

———

Annah spent Thursday packing, ironing her and Lachlan's dress uniform for the funeral, and making a supper for on the road. By the time Lachlan would get off work and they headed out it would be suppertime and the drive was almost three hours.

Once they arrived in Calgary and checked in, they changed into their swim suits and the four of them headed to the pool. By the time the pool closed at ten o'clock the kids were exhausted from swimming and water sliding. Annah helped them into their PJs and they were both asleep almost before she had the lights turned out. Annah sank into the sofa beside Lachlan and curled up.

"Who gets the bed tonight?" she yawned.

"The kids are tired enough that I'm sure we could share the bed and they would never know. We have to be up early anyway so that we can drop them off with Nanny before the funeral."

"You're probably right."

"Come on then. I know we are both too keyed up to sleep right now and tomorrow is going to be a very stressful day. So, let's get at it and try to exhaust ourselves enough so we can sleep," Lachlan suggested seductively as he pulled her up from the sofa and dragged her off to the other bedroom.

"Excellent idea, Officer MacGregor," Annah agreed as she closed and locked their bedroom door. "Oh, Nanny offered to keep the kids for the whole day tomorrow, including overnight. Should I tell her yes?" Annah queried falsely demure.

"I think you already know the answer to that question, missy," Lachlan growled as he swept her up against him and proceeded to reaffirm for Annah that he was the only man she would ever need.

CHAPTER 20

FRIDAY MORNING DAWNED JUST like Annah's mood, overcast and cold. Annah was up early and readied herself first before she dressed and fed the kids room service. Lachlan packed their gear back into the Jeep and they dropped Summer and Simon off at Nanny's new condo. The kids were excited to see Nanny and after a hug they ran in to check out her new talking bird. Nanny gave Annah a long fortifying hug.

"I will meet you at the zoo tomorrow morning at ten o'clock," Nanny instructed. "Now you stand up straight and go say your good-byes." Nanny pushed Annah out the door and as Lachlan turned to follow she grabbed his arm and whispered, "Don't let them hurt her."

"I will do everything I can to protect her," Lachlan reassured.

Lachlan drove to the church and parked in the rapidly filling parking lot. He noticed that several of his officers had already and were standing in group off to the side of the church. Lachlan reached over and squeezed Annah's hand.

"I'm with you all the way, Babe. Let's go."

"If Dabria makes a scene I'll leave for the sake of David's parents, but please don't follow me. You have a job to do today, beyond speaking, and that is to represent our station. Give me the keys to the Jeep just in case and you can call me when you're done so that I can come back and pick you up. You can catch a ride to the cemetery with one of the other officers, okay?"

"Yes," Lachlan leaned over and gave her a kiss. "Did I tell you today that I love you? I am so proud of you."

Annah reached up and stroked his cheek and then turned away to climb out of the Jeep. Silently Annah and Lachlan walked from the parking lot to join the gathered officers. Soberly they were included into the group and as music from the church started to drift outside and the parking lot and grounds cleared they made their way to the entrance. Walking into the church as a group they were lead to two pews that had been reserved behind the family. The church was filled with not only family and friends but also a number of conservation officers from other stations. Some had worked with David in the past and some came merely out of a sense of duty and a show of respect and solidarity. They lined up together and filled the pews at the back of the church.

Annah was flanked by Lachlan and Peter. Peter knew there could be an issue with Annah's attendance and wanted her to know that if Lachlan had her front, he had her back. Lachlan's officers stuck together and would support her until the inquiry findings were released. If they showed that Annah had been negligent, then and only then, would the officers need to individually soul search to determine if they still supported her.

David's family was Catholic, so his funeral was a full Catholic Mass. The service lasted well over an hour. David's open casket sat at the front of the altar. Mourners were expected to view the body as they trailed past when they exited the church. Annah knew that David would have hated this. He had told her during one of their numerous conversations that he wanted to be cremated and have his ashes tossed into the wind from one of his beloved mountains. Either he forgot to tell anyone else or his parents had decided that appearances were more important. Annah figured it was probably the latter. David had confided in her how he struggled with trying to live his life the way he had been raised. His family were devout Catholics and David was definitely not. David's family stood stoically watching as their family friends said their final goodbyes. The procession had started at the back and moved up through the pews. David's fellow officers were the last to file past before the immediate family. As Annah approached the casket she kept her eyes on Lachlan's back rather than looking over at the family. Just before she reached David's feet a shriek of pure outrage shattered the reverence of the moment and out of the corner of her eye she glimpsed a streak of black just before Lachlan stepped between her and Dabria.

"You have no right!" Dabria screamed. "No right to be here!" Poking her finger into Lachlan's chest she demanded, "Make her leave! She's the reason David's dead and I won't have her anywhere near him."

A stunned silence descended upon the church. Matthew swiftly appeared behind Dabria and whispering in her ear he drew her away from Lachlan. Dabria continued to mumble, "She has no right, she has no right," as Matthew herded her back to the family pew. Lachlan had moved back to Annah's side. As she glanced back over his shoulder the look of unadulterated hatred that gleamed from Matthew's eyes made her gasp and take a step back, right into Peter.

"Steady," Peter supported. Neither he nor Lachlan had caught Matthew's glare. Seeing Annah's eyes dart around looking for an escape route, Peter placed his hand on Annah's arm and whispered to her. "You have every right to be here. Don't let her win, Annah. David was your friend. Say goodbye and then we'll walk out of here together. Do this for David."

The procession had come to a halt due to the congestion of the mourners leaving the church. When Annah refocused on her immediate surroundings she realized that she stood right beside David's chest. Turning towards him she had a flashback of him pleading, "Don't you forget me!"

Annah looked up at the stained glass behind the altar and silently vowed, "I won't forget you and I will find out who cut that rope." Straightening up she continued in the procession until they finally exited the sanctuary. Lachlan grabbed Annah's hand and walked with her to the Jeep.

"What did Peter say to convince you to stay? I could feel you tensing up to bolt out of the church and then I felt you relax."

"He told me David would have wanted me there. And I knew he was right. David would have hated this Lachlan. He told me he wanted to be cremated and his ashes sprinkled from a mountain top. I feel so sad. David was not happy and now his life is over and he'll never know what it is to be happy and in love. Do you know how lucky we are? I'm going to find out who cut those ropes, Lachlan, if it is the last thing I do. David deserves at least that and that is one way for me to prove I will never forget him. I'm going to the cemetery with all of you but after that I'm not going back to his parent's house. I will drop you off and you can call me later."

Lachlan spoke at the internment while all of the officers stood guard behind him. As the priest finished David's family laid roses one at a time on the casket before it was lowered into the ground. David's mother quietly sobbed and was held up by David's father on one side and Matthew on the other. Dabria was supported by her parents and stood slightly to the left. Since her outburst at the church she was strangely silent. Annah's eyes were blurry from unshed tears. Lachlan held her hand tightly and turning led the other mourners from the gravesite, giving David's family privacy for their final goodbyes. Reaching the vehicles Peter stopped Lachlan and Annah.

"Lachlan, I know you have to put in an appearance at the house. Annah are you planning on going with him?"

"No."

"In that case, Lachlan, would you mind if I accompanied you. The other officers have chosen not to go. Annah can ride with them and we can meet them later at the lounge in The Palliser Hotel."

"Thank you, Peter," Annah quietly acknowledged.

"You did good today, girl. I'm proud of you," Peter grabbed Annah and gave her a big hug.

"Peter's right, you know. I'll see you in a bit," Lachlan promised as he leaned down and kissed her.

John stood holding the door open for her to slide into his car. With a final glance up the hill Annah sank into the back seat and focused her eyes straight ahead.

~~

The officers and their wives, as well as, Mrs. Larson, her husband, and Nicole all met at the lounge for lunch and a drink. Since Mrs. Larson had been the first person to meet David when he had started at the station she initiated telling stories of some of his and Matthew's exploits over the years. No mention was made of the upcoming inquest or the day David had died. This time was for remembering and rejoicing over David's life.

An hour later Peter and Lachlan joined them and the tribute continued. Around three o'clock the officers that were on duty Saturday got up and started the exodus from the lounge. Annah was glad that it was time to leave. She was exhausted. She and Lachlan went back to the hotel. Once inside the suite she stripped out of her dress uniform and headed for a soak in the bathtub. Lachlan gave her a half hour alone to soak and then went in to entice her into getting dressed and going for a walk with him. Annah's head rested on the back of the two-man jet tub. The jets continued to pulse but she was sound asleep. As Lachlan reached over to turn them off, Annah jolted awake showering Lachlan with warm water. Since he was wet anyways she continued to splash him in earnest hoping that he would join her. Laughing he stripped out of his now sodden clothes and slipped into the tub behind Annah so that she rested against his chest. Wrapping his arms around her he whispered naughty things in her ear and proceeded to demonstrate those very things.

Sometime later they dried off and dressed. This was the first time they had ever gone to a restaurant together and Anna had dressed in more formal attire than she usually wore. She was still in slacks but they were black velvet with a matching bolero jacket and a stark white lace camisole underneath. She had hot-rolled her hair and wore it down in big fat flowing waves. With a hematite pendant and hematite chandeliered earrings this was a look that Lachlan had never seen. She looked exotic and incredibly sexy. Knowing that Annah didn't have a winter dress coat Lachlan presented her with a winter white alpaca wool cape to wrap around herself. Annah was touched by the thoughtfulness of his gift. It was practical and yet beautiful. It was so soft and warm Annah cuddled right into it as they left for their evening out. The sky hadn't cleared and the evening felt wintry. After a brief promenade they picked a restaurant close to the hotel and went in to eat.

Lachlan ordered a glass of merlot for Annah and started off with a scotch for himself. They ordered appetizers and shared them. They did the same with their entrees and topped the meal off with Annah's favorite dessert, a thick slice of New York cheesecake smothered in Saskatoon berry sauce. The restaurant they picked had a small dance floor and a pianist had been serenading the patrons as they dined. As a haunting waltz drifted over them Lachlan rose and extending his hand requested the favor of a dance from Annah. She complied and they glided out onto the floor. Lachlan was an excellent dancer as Annah recalled from the Thanksgiving Supper the previous weekend. As if made for each other they danced several dances despite their solitary existence on the dance floor. Annah would never have felt comfortable doing this before, having all of the other diners watch them, but she loved this man that expertly lead her around the floor. She was oblivious to the appreciative stares of the other diners. As the tempo of the dances increased Lachlan lead her back to their table. The plan was to woo her not to exhaust her. Retrieving their coats they headed back to their hotel.

Lachlan steered Annah into the lounge he had spotted in their hotel which sported oversized leather furniture scattered in intimate pairs around a multi-sided glowing fireplace. Ordering himself another scotch and encouraging Annah to order a Black Russian, Lachlan, reclined in his chair. Annah curled up in hers. She removed her shoes and tucked her feet up underneath her and then leaned towards Lachlan sipping her after dinner drink. As Lachlan allowed an aura of lassitude to descend over him Annah decided this was the perfect time to get him to share some of the personal details of his life that she had deliberately never asked him before. With every probing question Annah asked and Lachlan answered he countered with one of his own questions. They were so involved in each other that the bartender had to interrupt them to offer last call at two in the morning. Annah couldn't believe they had sat there just talking and sipping drinks for almost four hours. The time had flown by. She couldn't remember an evening she had enjoyed more. Lachlan paid the tab and escorted Annah back to their suite.

As they ascended in the elevator Lachlan made Annah promise that she would help him pick out furnishings for his new house after they finished at the zoo. Nanny had volunteered to watch the children at the hotel the following afternoon and evening so that Lachlan and

Annah could go out again. Lachlan figured rather than going out for supper this would be a perfect opportunity to get Annah to furnish what would end up being her home.

Returning to the suite Annah was greeted by turned down bedding and a candlelit bedroom. The scent of vanilla and lavender wafted from the lit candles creating an atmosphere of relaxed intimacy. Slowly Lachlan peeled off the layers of Annah's clothing and proceeded to make love to her with a reverence that brought tears to her eyes. Tonight was a night unlike any other they had spent. This was a night of understood commitment and devotion to one another. Although she had spent many nights with Lachlan over the course of the last several months, this one, while executed more slowly, was a greater turn on than any other night. Annah drifted to sleep confidently wrapped in Lachlan's love for her.

They spent the remainder of the weekend shopping and playing with the kids. It was wonderful to share all of the little daily events with someone that actually cared. Annah reveled in this unexpected turn in her life. Although the reality of the inquest was still looming over her she was reassured by the fact that she wasn't facing it alone and knew that regardless of the outcome her relationship with Lachlan would continue.

CHAPTER 21

In the weeks preceding the inquest Annah spent her time being a stay at home mom for the first time in years. She got caught up on laundry and house cleaning, and was able to indulge in creating meals that weren't feasible when she worked. She arranged the furniture in Lachlan's house that he had purchased in Calgary and spent more time researching on the internet. She had more time to play with the kids on a daily basis before they needed to worry about homework and preparing for the next school day. Although Annah loved her job, she was grateful for this reprieve that had been forced upon her.

Annah's sense of serenity was about to be tested. The first concrete indicator after the funeral that someone still wanted Annah out of the picture was a note left on the seat of her truck. She noticed the scrap of paper on the seat when she went to drive the kids to school on Tuesday morning. Living in the country she had gotten into the habit of not locking the truck doors. Since they were running a little late, due to a lost shoe, she grabbed the scrap and threw it up onto the dash without looking at it. She didn't remember it was even there until she returned from picking them up at the end of the day. The wind caught it as she opened her door and it skittered across the dash onto the floor. Summer grabbed it on the way out of the truck and gave it to her mom as they walked into the house. Annah glanced down at it and noticed it was a typewritten note that looked like it had gone through the washing machine it was so crumpled up. She shoved it into her pocket as she unlocked the doors to the house and ushered the kids inside for a snack.

Later that night after finishing supper, homework, and bedtime stories Lachlan asked her if she wanted him to check her mailbox since he was going to check his. She went to get him the mail key that was attached to her truck keys in her jacket pocket. When she pulled out the keys the note came with them. Lachlan bent down to retrieve the note and handed it back to her. Annah took it from him and read it. She had expected it to be a note from school that the kids had forgotten to give her. She was wrong. She was sure she had just read it wrong the first time. Coming to a complete standstill she reread the note.

"What's wrong?" Lachlan asked as he noticed her sudden stop and heard her indrawn gasp. He noticed the paler of her face and that she had a death grip on the paper. Snatching it back from her he smoothed the scrap of paper out and looked at it. It read:

SOME TIMES THINGS CAN'T BE FORGIVEN
SOME TIMES ACCIDENTS DO HAPPEN
SOME TIMES SOMEONE DISAPPEARS

"Where did this come from and when did you get it?" he demanded.

"It was on the seat of my truck this morning when I went to drive the kids to school. I forgot it in the truck and then I shoved it in my pocket after school without ever actually looking at it. I thought it was a note from school." Annah went to the table and sat down. Lachlan followed her and sat beside her, taking her hands in his.

"When you left last night I don't suppose you glanced inside my truck?" Annah asked.

"No. That means it was left sometime between you returning home yesterday and you leaving again this morning. Did you hear any vehicles last night after I left?"

"No. Right after you left I locked the house doors and then had a bath. I was in the tub for a good half hour with the door closed and music on. The dishwasher was also running. I read until I heard John come home next door at one o'clock, and then went to bed. Ranger scared the daylights out of me about half an hour later when he started barking and trying to go outside. I thought it was just a rabbit or something. Maybe it was more than that."

"I knew I shouldn't have slept over at the new house last night," Lachlan shook his head with disgust as he removed his hands from Annah's and sat back in his chair.

"Who knew at the station that you were going to be sleeping there?"

"I'm sure almost everyone did. Mrs. Larson asked me if the house was finished and if I had moved in yet. I told her it was done but still needed some furnishings and that I wouldn't actually be moving in until the weekend, but that I was staying overnight last night to make a list of things I still needed to purchase. We were standing at the reception desk talking. Anyone around us could hear."

"Were Matthew or Nicole close to you?"

"Nicole was at her desk and Matthew and Dabria walked in while we were talking."

"What was Dabria doing at the station?"

"She came to pick up David's personal things and to talk to me."

"Why couldn't Matthew take them?"

"He had all of the stuff packed up into a box and since she was coming out to see me anyway it probably made sense for him to give it to her."

"So obviously nobody except you, me, and Dabria knows that their engagement was off."

"Dabria isn't acting like it was."

"Do you think it will have to come out at the inquiry? And why did Dabria want to talk to you?"

"I don't know if it will. I guess that depends on what they ask you. Why did you ask me if Nicole was there?" Lachlan questioned. "I think maybe now might be a good time to reveal to me some of those things that David shared with you. Don't you think?"

Annah remained seated at the table and looked out the window past Lachlan obviously struggling with her answer.

"I'm going to get the mail. While I'm gone please decide what you're going to tell me when I get back. Oh, and you can grab me a blanket for the sofa bed as well since you will no longer be sleeping in this house without me." With that he let himself out.

Annah watched him close the door quietly behind him. If Annah could trust Lachlan with her love, her life, and the lives of her children she should obviously be able to trust him with David's secrets. However, he needed to show her that he also trusted her. The first question that was going to get answered was, "What did Dabria want to speak to him about?"

Annah went and changed into her nightshirt and put the kettle on. Instead of pulling the sofa bed out and finding blankets to go on it she made the decision that until the inquest was over and the rope cutter was revealed Lachlan might as well sleep in her bed. Although Annah had proved to herself that she was an independent woman she had two children besides herself that she needed to keep safe. Rather than fighting his proclamation that he would be sleeping at her house every night on the sofa she would surprise him with the offer of her bed and see how he reacted.

Checking on the children, Annah turned out all the lights except for the bedroom and waited for Lachlan to return while she sipped her tea and replayed the conversation she had had with David that day. The lights from Lachlan's truck swung across her walls as he parked in the driveway behind her truck. He locked the front door after coming in and placing her mail on the table. After shrugging out of his coat he ventured to the doorway of her bedroom.

"Where's my blankets, Annah?" he carefully enunciated as he leaned against the door frame, obviously geared up for a fight.

"Lachlan, I refuse to allow you to sleep on the couch for the next three weeks. You need your sleep and that sofa bed is terribly uncomfortable. I also refuse to sleep on it one more night myself. The four months it was my bed when Nanny was here are still fresh in my mind." Raising her hand to stop Lachlan from launching his attack, Annah slid off the bed and walked towards him. Placing her hand on his arm she drew him to the bed and pushed him down onto it. Wordlessly, he sat down and waited for her to continue.

"I want you to understand that I'm not easily scared off and if it weren't for the children I would force you to return to your home tonight. However, I am not so proud that I would refuse protection for them when it is offered. Obviously someone wants me gone. I am not going to turn tail and run for the hills but I'm also not going to ignore the fact that if something happens to me, my children will be orphans. I can't do that to them." As Annah talked she undid Lachlan's shirt and pulled it off him. "Therefore, until the inquest is over and we find out who is behind this latest threat I would appreciate you staying with us at night. I love you and it would just be silly for you to be out on the couch when there is no need. If the kids wake up and ask why you're here I guess we'll just have to tell them we're having a sleepover."

Lachlan shook his head and stared at Annah. She continued to surprise him. Every time he was sure she was going to oppose him she did the complete opposite. Life with her was not going to be dull.

"I accept your offer and now let's get back to what we were discussing before I left." Again he anticipated either a refusal to answer or an argument.

Again he was wrong.

"I thought about what you said and I will tell you what David and I discussed. Trust goes both ways though, Lachlan. Unless you can't tell me what Dabria came to talk to you about, because it is official, I expect you to share that with me as well."

"Fair enough. It was not official and I was planning on telling you before I left tonight. Dabria plans on filing a case of negligence against the station regardless of the inquest's findings and she indicated that I should "get my ducks in a row." She also suggested that since you and I are an item she planned on telling the investigators at the inquiry that she was sure a cover-up of your conduct was a distinct possibility."

"Lachlan, maybe I do need to leave. I can't let your integrity be questioned nor have the station's safety procedures and professionalism doubted," she declared.

"Yes, you can. I stand behind the policies and procedures we have in place. Having my leadership questioned comes with the job. I am confident that you and I will be exonerated. Annah, you just have to trust me."

"Lachlan, you know I trust you. But someone connected to the station wants me gone."

"Okay, so let's hear it. What did David confide in you?"

"He told me that he had called it quits with Dabria on Saturday night and then done the same with his mistress on Sunday night."

"Let me guess. It was Nicole."

"Yes, but he also said he had one more loose end to tie up on Monday night. He didn't tell me what or who that loose end might be. He did, however, tell me that he had always had at least one mistress while he was dating Dabria. He said it was a challenge to juggle at least two lovers at one time."

"Why, all of a sudden, was he cleaning house?" Lachlan asked guardedly.

Annah was untwining her braid. With her face averted she didn't respond immediately.

"Annah?"

Annah shifted back to face him.

"He was freeing himself up because he claimed he felt a connection to me that went beyond friendship. Until Saturday night he didn't know there was anything going on between you and me and since we had just started dating he figured I would be willing to further a relationship with him. As I told you before, apparently when he broke it off with Dabria she accused him of having an affair with me. What she didn't know was that the affair was with Nicole."

Lachlan lay motionless against the headboard as he listened calmly to Annah's report.

"I know that you think I am hopelessly naïve because you saw what the others did regarding my behavior with David. The only reason you didn't think there was something going on between David and I was because you knew we had something going on. Anyway, David claimed he didn't see it either until Nicole also accused him of having a little "somethin' somethin'" on the side with me when he broke up with her. And he claimed Matthew confirmed that the rest of the staff was talking about David and I behind our backs."

"There was some speculation as to whether or not David was getting something on the side because I think most of the staff knew that he wasn't particularly faithful to Dabria," Lachlan informed her.

"And so because David was promiscuous and we obviously enjoyed each other so much that meant I must be too? Why didn't you say something to me if you could see what was going on?" Annah challenged.

"I didn't know for sure that the gossip mill had concluded it was you. But, even Nicole suspected you were having an affair with David, didn't she? That would explain her unprovoked attack on you the night of the accident."

"Yes, this makes her suspect number two. Matthew's obvious dislike of me makes him suspect number three and if you put any stock into David's comments regarding one more piece of unfinished business there could be suspect number four."

"Okay, so tomorrow you're going to drive that note into the R.C.M.P. in Rocky. We are not going to tell anyone here that you found it. I'm sure they won't be able to do much with it. Fingerprints are out since the note was deliberately scrunched up and you, I, and Summer have all played with it. I just want a record of the fact that besides the cut rope someone is still trying to terrorize you."

"Lachlan, I'm tired. Can we talk about this some more tomorrow?"

"Oh course. Just promise me you will lock your truck all the time from now on and you will do a walk around before you drive it. No long walks by yourself or going out to the house by yourself anymore. Okay? And the next time Ranger starts barking please assume that there is something other than a rabbit attracting his attention."

"I promise. Goodnight." Annah lay down and pulled Lachlan with her. She snuggled into his side and promptly started to softly snore.

CHAPTER 22

ANNAH DROVE TO ROCKY the next morning and gave the note to the officer in charge of the case. Although the note was obviously a death threat the station unfortunately did not employ enough members to provide Annah with much protection. The best that they could promise was to check in with her every time they drove by Nordegg. Annah had not expected any more. She finished her errands and returned home in time to put a roast in the oven for supper.

Nanny came back to Nordegg to babysit the kids during the coroner's inquest. No one could predict how many days it would take the inquiry to finish. Annah didn't know when she would be testifying or how long they would require her. As it turned out, she was one of the last to testify. Since no one knew the order of the witnesses all officers had to be in attendance every day. As the week progressed and the officers testified less of them were required to make the journey each morning.

The inquest lasted a week. Lachlan was advised that the findings would not be released for at least two weeks. Because was Nanny was at the house Lachlan had returned to his new home to sleep. Once the inquiry was finished she returned to Calgary and Lachlan worked on persuading Annah to move herself and the kids in with him. The final incident to push the scales into Lachlan's favor occurred the night that Lachlan was forced to work late to cover an evening shift. Once Annah had the kids in bed, and after cleaning up and preparing for morning, she went and had her nightly bath. While she lay relaxing in the bubbles Simon woke up screaming. Ranger was barking and scratching at the back door to get out. Annah leapt from the tub, grabbed a towel to wrap up in, and hurried into Simon and Summer's room. Summer was also awake. Telling Summer to go back to sleep, she picked up Simon and carried him into her room. They sat down on the bed and Annah rocked him and soothed him so that he could stop crying enough to tell her what was wrong.

"Th....there was s...s....s....something looking in the w...w...window at us," Simon stammered. "I saw it, Mommy. I saw it!" Annah usually left the children's blinds open at night because they lived in the country with no one behind them and the moonlight worked better than a nightlight.

"Simon, it can't hurt you. I'm right here and I will protect you. What did it look like?"

"It was a big furry creature."

"Like an animal?" Annah questioned.

"I guess so."

"If I got you a paper and pencil could you draw it for me?" Annah asked.

"Y..Yes," Simon smothered a sob.

"While you draw I'm going to get dressed and go take a look outside, okay?"

"Nooooo!" Simon wailed. "It will get you. You can't go. Please."

"Okay, sweetie, but I need to get dressed. How about if I let Ranger out?"

"No, Mommy. That monster will eat him. When Ranger started barking that's when the monster ran away."

Annah kissed the top of Simon's head, grabbed some clothes, and went back to the bathroom to finish drying off and drain the tub. With all the screaming and barking anyone that might have been outside was long gone by now. Once Simon had fallen back asleep she had every intention of going outside to check for footprints in the snow. If there were none it meant Simon was just having a bad dream and his screaming had caused Ranger to start barking. However, if there were footprints, it meant she needed to call the R.C.M.P. and Lachlan. Annah returned to her bedroom and Simon gave her his picture. It looked like a lion's face. It was round and had fur all around it. It reminded Annah of the conservation officers' regulation parkas.

"Could you see eyes?" Annah asked.

"Yes, eyes and paws."

"Paws?"

"Ya, like he had his paws beside his head on the window looking in."

"Were they furry, too?" Annah inquired.

"I don't remember."

"Could you see fingers, like we have or was it like mittens?"

"No, they were like paws or maybe mittens. Can I have some hot chocolate and can I sleep with you tonight?" Simon implored.

"Of course. You snuggle in and I'll go make some cocoa." Annah put the kettle on and then returned to Simon and Summer's room. She shut the blinds and decided to call Lachlan anyway.

"Hey, how's the nightshift?" Annah asked.

"It's quiet," Lachlan responded suspiciously. "What's going on? I know you're not calling just to hear my sexy voice."

"Simon woke up screaming that someone was looking in the bedroom window at him. Ranger was barking and scratching at the back door. I was in the tub and by the time I went to check nothing was there. Simon won't let me go outside to check for footprints. If he falls asleep before you get home I'll go out and check."

"I'm coming now. I was planning on leaving early but the paperwork is never ending and I kind of lost track of time. It's midnight already and Peter and the dispatcher are here. I'll be there in ten. Stay in the house 'till I get there."

Lachlan hung up and grabbing his coat and keys headed for the door.

"I'm out of here, boys. See you tomorrow," Lachlan called as he exited the station.

"Everything okay, boss?" Peter called after him.

"Yah, I'm just tired. It's been a long time since I pulled a twelve hour shift. I guess I'm not used to it anymore." Lachlan and Annah had agreed to keep the note quiet and since Lachlan knew this was related, although he trusted Peter above all the other officers, he was reluctant to confide in him. With a wave he closed the door and nonchalantly walked out to his truck. Once he was out of the watchful eyes of the station he floored it and shaved two minutes off of his usual drive time. As he pulled into the driveway one word Annah had said, suddenly slammed into his consciousness. Home. She had said "When you come *home*.....". He'd have to remind her of that later. First things first though. He grabbed his shotgun and a flashlight and made his way around the back of the house. When Annah heard him pull up she switched on the back door lights.   Simon had just fallen asleep, so she let Ranger out and grabbed her coat and boots and went to join him.

"Do you see anything?" she asked tentatively from the step.

"Yes, I do," Lachlan replied. "There are footprints in the snow leading from the bush up to the window and then around the other side of the house. Go inside and call the R.C.M.P. and have them send someone out here. I'm going to look around a little more without disturbing anything."

"Ranger took off "like a bat out of hell" towards the tree line. Do you think he'll be safe? Lachlan, please come inside and wait for the police. What if they are still out there watching us? If they are in the bushes they can see us even though we can't see them. You're a sitting duck with the light shining on you. Please," Annah beseeched.

"I'll go back around the front and come in that door," Lachlan agreed.

Annah closed the back door then grabbed the phone as she went to turn on the front light. While she was dialing the number for the Rocky Detachment she glimpsed something furry on the front step. Opening the inside door she stepped back in revulsion. Rainbow, the children's cat, lay on the top step with its head facing the opposite direction of its body. Turning the phone off Annah opened the outside door without disturbing the body and called to Lachlan.

"Lachlan!"   He walked around the corner of the house as she called out to him. "Stop! The cat......... Look what they have done to Rainbow."

Lachlan stood at the bottom of the steps careful not to interfere with the cat. With the front doors open he stepped over the cat
and into the house. He closed both doors and turned out the lights.
He pulled Annah into his arms and took the phone from her limp
fingers.

"You and the kids aren't safe here anymore, Annah. We need to
talk about an alternate place to live when I get off the phone. Keep an
eye out for Ranger. I don't want him coming back and dragging the
cat's body away." He called the police and explained the latest events.

An hour later a cruiser with two officers arrived. Ranger hadn't
returned yet. They photographed the trail of prints and position of the
cat on the stairs. After removing the cat and placing it in the trunk
of their car they returned to the house to question Annah. She gave
them the drawing that Simon had made and relayed to them what
he had told her. They confirmed what Annah and Lachlan had already assumed regarding the possibility of actually identifying the
footprints. Because the snow was fairly deep and fluffy there were
no actual prints, just holes in the snow where someone had walked.
The only telling feature was that they belonged to someone with large
boots. Unfortunately, that didn't narrow the field of suspects since it
would be pretty easy for a woman to wear a man's boot over top of her
own, to cover her tracks, so to speak. The police agreed with Lachlan
that for the safety of herself and her children Annah needed to move
someplace more secure or less remote.

Annah agreed to move into Lachlan's house which was already
equipped with a security system. He had motion sensor lights installed at various points along the driveway to the house as well as attached to each corner of the house. The only thing left to make things
safer was to hire a guard for her when he wasn't home and to instruct
the kids never to play alone and to stay close to the school at all times
during the day. The other option was to move altogether. Annah refused to do that. Lachlan just hoped he could actually keep her safe
here.

After taking the kids to school the next morning and talking to the
teacher regarding the need for close supervision of them, Annah returned to the house and made preparations for the move to Lachlan's.
She knew deep down that they probably wouldn't be returning to her

little home and it made her sad. For now she packed only their clothing and the food. She took her photo albums as well since they were the only thing of real value she owned. Lachlan called to inform her that an off duty R.C.M.P. would be showing up after lunch to act as her bodyguard.

As she was loading up a truck pulled off the highway and parked behind her. A very large, very imposing figure emerged from it and strode up towards her with his hand extended.

"Ms. Andersson?"

"Yes," Annah confirmed.

"My name is Officer Mike Sebastian. A Mr. Lachlan MacGregor employed my services to act as a bodyguard for you. I am an R.C.M.P. officer stationed in Rocky. I, as well as two others, will be guarding you when we are off shift from our regular duties. Is there something I can do to help you out? You appear to be moving."

"Yes, thank you, I am and I would I'd really appreciate some help." She shook his extended hand. "Please call me Annah."

By the time Annah and Mike had unloaded her truck it was time to pick up the kids. After returning to Lachlan's, the kids played with Mike while Annah started supper. Since Lachlan hadn't purchased beds beyond his own yet, the kids set up sleeping bags in one of the spare rooms. They played hide and seek in this wonderful new castle-sized playhouse with Mike and then sucked him into helping them with their homework. At six o'clock Lachlan arrived home and Mike left for the day. Annah served supper for the first time in what was unofficially her new home. The basement of the house was unfinished and several appliance boxes had been stored down there. The kids made a fort and played in it until bedtime.

After they were down for the night, which of course took longer than usual due to their new surroundings, Annah and Lachlan returned to the great room to sit in front of the fireplace and talk. Annah sat on the loveseat while Lachlan paced in front of her.

"I know that with everything going on you are going to feel like I am pushing you into something you're not ready for."

"But," Annah prompted. Lachlan stopped pacing, knelt in front of her, and grabbed her hands.

"Annah, I love you and the kids and I want you to marry me. Now that we are living together in this house let's make it official. I won't let you go back to the rental even after this is over, so you might as well just give in and give us what we both need. I don't care if you want a big wedding or a small one. I just want a promise that you'll marry me." With that statement he released her hands and reached into his vest pocket and pulled out a small satin bag. Taking her right hand he placed the bag in it. Looking down at the bag lying on her palm Annah held her breath. She knew that opening this bag was going to be one of those life-altering moments. Slowly she pulled the strings open and then shook out the contents. It was, as expected, a ring. The ring was white gold with an emerald nestled in the intricate folds. It was obviously custom made especially for her. Tears blurred her vision. Extending her hand to Lachlan she invited him to finish the ritual. He took the ring from her palm, kissed it, and slid it, wordlessly, onto her left hand. Then he pulled her off the couch towards to him and proceeded to kiss her, thoroughly sealing the deal.

⌒〜

The next two weeks flew by. Annah's days were filled with ordering necessary furnishings for Lachlan's instant family, planning a winter wedding to be held at the house, and everyday homemaker duties. The guards came every morning before Lachlan left and didn't leave until he returned. The next two weekends Lachlan took his new family to the city to shop for wedding supplies, Christmas trimmings, and house accessories. The wedding was scheduled for January 15th. This would give Annah time to clean up from Christmas and then get married. As they approached the middle of November Annah knew she didn't have a lot of time for getting everything done. Once the inquiry released its results she expected to be back at work within days.

There had been no more threatening incidents since Annah and the kids had moved. The findings of the inquiry were released on November 13th, six weeks after David's death. The verdict of the coroner's inquest stated that no negligence was found on the part of Lachlan, Annah, or any of the rescue officers. However, it was noted that if David had followed the procedures that Lachlan had implemented regarding the daily equipment check, the cut lines would have been discovered and that length of rope would have been disposed of. Unfortunately, David's own negligence led to his death. Annah was relieved but saddened by the results. The coroner and jury did pass down some recommendations for future rescues including tighter policies regarding rappelling procedures.

Annah was re-instated and the guards were released from duty. That didn't mean that the threat was gone. It just meant that with Annah back at work and them living with Lachlan the opportunity for someone to harm her was greatly reduced. Lachlan and Annah left for work at the same time every morning. She dropped the kids off at Larson's and then drove in to work. In the evening Annah left work at five o'clock to pick up the kids and Lachlan left at six o'clock. There was basically only half an hour a day that they weren't together or in close contact. Lachlan partnered Annah with Peter. Everyone appeared comfortable with the new arrangement.

Lachlan presented the staff with new two-way radios that were individual to each officer. They were to keep them with them whenever they left the station. Lachlan's radio was capable of communicating directly with specific radios like a private phone. Each radio had a GPS homing device built into it. The only officer that was aware of this feature was Lachlan. This allowed him to know where all of his officers were all of the time. Annah's radio also had a feature that forced her to check in with Lachlan every ten minutes when she was away from the station. She was aware of this and was to make sure that no one else found out about it.

Annah kept her radio strapped onto the outside of her coat sleeve. Every ten minutes the radio would vibrate silently for a few seconds. If she didn't send a signal back the system would send a warning to Lachlan. He could then manually override the automatic signal system and buzz her or call her. Annah promised him that the only way she wouldn't respond to the automatic page was if she were incapacitated. Although both the police and Annah suspected there may have been a third lover Lachlan was not convinced. His gut was telling him that one of the very officers that he would lay his life down for was behind the harassment. It sickened him to think this, but he had learned over the years to always trust his gut.

Friday afternoon Lachlan received a call from Dabria requesting a meeting. He had been anticipating this since the inquest findings had been made public. She had threatened him with a civil suit and she no doubt was about to follow through. Despite the verdict of no negligence Lachlan knew that Dabria believed that directly or indirectly Annah was responsible for David's death. Although her chances of actually having Annah charged with anything were zero, the publicity generated by the civil suit could have serious implications for Annah's career. The higher ups could put pressure on Lachlan to pull Annah out of the field and confine her to desk duty. Also chances were that no other station would ever hire her just because she was involved in press that reflected poorly on the entire conservation service. Under normal circumstances a civil suit would never occur. Because Dabria and David's families classified themselves as aristocracy and were extremely affluent the verdict that David's own inattention led to his death was unacceptable to them. Annah popped her head into Lachlan's office before she left and he informed her of Dabria's impending visit.

"Since I'm going to be later than normal could you please stay at Larson's and visit for a while. I really don't want you guys out on the acreage alone for too long without me there."

"Lachlan, I can't continue to live my life paranoid that someone is out to get me at every turn. We have all the safety precautions in place that are feasible. If someone is determined enough there will always be a way to sneak through our defenses. I will pick up the kids as usual and see you at home when you're finished."

Lachlan walked her outside. As she turned to leave he grabbed her in a big hug and kissed her.

"I love you," he stated simply as he released her.

"I love you, too. Now, get back to work."

Annah slipped out the door. Lachlan watched her walk to the truck and felt an unshakeable sense of foreboding.

He called her cell as he watched her get into the truck.

"What did you forget?"

"Call me as soon as you get home," Lachlan requested.

"I promise. Love ya," Annah signed off.

Annah changed out of the heavy regulation parka and put on her blanket coat. She pulled her radio out of the parka pocket and placed it on the seat beside her. After buckling up she pulled out onto the highway and made her way towards Larson's acreage. The Larsons lived just past Beaverdam. The highway curved around the side of a rock outcropping and gave one a perfect view of the small lake below. That was the site of the campground named after the large beaver dam that had created the lake. Annah always slowed down at this point since Big Horn Sheep and their babies were often found in the middle of the highway licking off salt.

Annah noticed a truck following her at a rather alarming rate of speed and tapped her brakes to alert the driver that she would be slowing down. Since the truck wasn't reducing its speed she pulled over onto the shoulder of the road, next to the guardrail above the lake, to allow the truck to pass. She hoped there were no sheep on the road tonight. If this fool hit one she could be involved in the accident as well. Before she could finish that thought the truck rammed her from the rear left corner forcing her through the guardrail and over the cliff edge. Although the plunge wasn't far, the frozen lake below could definitely kill her. Annah released her seatbelt and grabbed her radio before she hit the water. The radios had a distress button on them that when squeezed sent an immediate signal to Lachlan's control radio. As Annah hit the lake and broke through the ice she clutched the radio to her chest depressing the distress button.

CHAPTER 23

JUST BEFORE LACHLAN LEFT his office to collect Dabria from the waiting area his radio distress signal flashed. Striding back towards the radio he grabbed it and without checking the code his instincts told him it was Annah's. With his heart in his throat he immediately radioed her.

"Annah?" he barked, not even attempting to hide his concern.

"Someone pushed me off the road through the Beaverdam railing and I'm in the lake," Annah reported shakily.

"Is the truck filling with water yet?"

"Yes."

"Annah, clip the radio onto the sun visor with the open channel button on. Take a deep breath and concentrate on what I'm saying," Lachlan commanded. "**Do not** attempt to leave the truck. Trust your training. You know what to do while you wait for us. We're on our way. I love you!"

"I love you, too. Take care of my babies."

"**You** will be taking care of **our** babies after we get you out. Losing you is not an option for me, Annah! Keep listening to the sound of my voice."

Lachlan grabbed his coat and rushing from the office yelled to the officers in the station that they had a situation. "Annah went through the guard-rail at Beaverdam and is in the lake. The truck is already filling with water. We have *maybe* fifteen minutes to get her out alive. Let's move boys!"

Beaverdam was only about ten feet deep at its deepest point but with the lake being frozen Annah knew that getting to the surface without help was virtually impossible. The temperature of the water would inhibit her mobility enough that she would drown before ever reaching it. She took off your boots but left on her red coat. Although the coat would weigh a ton when wet, the wool in it would act as insulation and would keep her warmer than if she took it off. In the time it took to pull off her boots and crouch on the seat of the truck the water level was at the height of her chest. The truck was resting on the bottom of the lake at an angle, with the front of the cab facing down and the tailgate above the ice. Annah's only hope for survival lay in the chance that an air pocket remained at the top of the cab and that she could keep her head above the water. She backed herself into the corner of her driver's door, wrapped her arms around herself to keep her core as warm as possible, and let her head fall back to rest on the rear window. Her nose was as close to the headliner of the truck as she could possibly get it. If the water rose past this point she was done. All that was left for her to do now was to wait and pray.

———

The other officers knew that Annah was in deep trouble. Quickly grabbing their equipment bags and underwater rescue gear they headed out to the trucks and drove as a convoy to the accident site. Since it was only five minutes from the station, they prayed time was on their side. Lachlan continued to coach Annah as he drove.

"Baby, can you hear me?"

"Yyyyyyyes," Annah shivered uncontrollably.

"Good. We've left the station and Peter and Ken are getting geared up as we drive. We'll be there in less than five. Hang on!"

While John and Dan drove, Peter and Ken stripped and pulled on special dry suits for coldwater diving. Lachlan, leading the trio, stopped his truck by the break in the guardrail and using a high powered spotlight surveyed the lake. Due to the fact that the truck was closer to the road side of the lake than the campground side the rescue would have to be done down the cliff. This meant lowering both officers and the inflatable dingy they would need to rescue her. Conveniently her truck had cut a direct path through the snow down to the lake. Although this route wasn't going to make rescuing Annah easy, because of the uneven terrain, it was the fastest route to get to her.

Lachlan set up a road block with flashing lights to warn other motorists to slow down.

While the officers worked frantically to rescue Annah she focused on the reality of her situation. Hypothermia was an oft misinterpreted condition. There are three stages of hypothermia. The initial manifestations are uncontrollable shivering, loss of fine motor skills, quick shallow breathing and sleepiness as the body tries to keep itself warm. As you head into stage two your mind tricks you into thinking you are warming up and the urge to remove layers of clothing occurs. Annah was at that point and had to force herself to fight that urge.

Lachlan knew Annah was on the verge of stage two.

"Annah, we're here. How ya' doing, baby? You better have that beautiful red coat wrapped tightly around you. I know how much you love that coat and I **know** you don't want to leave it in the truck. Keep it close to you honey, so it doesn't float away in the water. I can see the tailgate sticking out of the water. Ken and Peter are going to enter the lake with the inflatable. When they get to your window Peter will break the window and pull you out. Can you still hear me? Whatever you do **don't** take that coat off."

"Hmmmmmmm," Annah mumbled. "Yes," she thought. "Keep the coat on!" She could hear Lachlan's voice and understand him but she was having difficulty making the necessary responses. She had been in the water almost ten minutes now and was well into stage two. Her fingers, toes, nose, and ears were all turning blue as the blood rushed to her vital organs. Although she was mostly numb she was cognizant enough to appreciate the fact that she hadn't drowned yet. Obviously the prayed for air bubble had materialized. "Keep the coat on! Keep the coat on!" became her mantra.

Lachlan was relieved to hear Annah make *any* sound. She obviously hadn't drowned which meant that there must be an air pocket. He didn't expect to hear from her again since he knew her ability to speak was obviously already compromised. That wouldn't stop him from continuing to give her hope by simply talking to her.

"Baby, the boys are climbing down the hill and will be in the water in two minutes." Annah knew that at fifteen minutes your chances of dying from hypothermia were very real. She was running out of time. Her mind drifted from the vision of Lachlan's face to the faces of Summer and Simon.

The inflatable was lined with blankets and bungee ropes to strap Annah in. There were also two axes to break up the ice and an underwater spotlight. Peter quickly descended the short drop and while he flipped his hiking boots off his dry boots Ken followed. Once both officers were poised at the edge of the lake with their masks and tanks in place and a rope linking the two of them together, John and Dan lowered the dingy. With a thumbs-up signal the men entered the lake where the ice had broken. A fresh skin of ice had already formed and was freezing the broken pieces back into place. Pulling the boat behind them they swiftly swam to the protruding truck.

"Ugh." Annah grunted. Stage three was setting in. The coat was forgotten as she struggled to keep her head above the water line.

"Annah, the boys are in the lake. Hang on!" Lachlan was reassured by Annah's attempt at speech.

Because the truck had gone in nose first but the lake had graduated sides the ice directly above the cab of the truck remained unbroken. Peter wouldn't be able to dive down right beside the window and bring Annah straight up. He would have to dive and pull himself along the side of the truck and determine that nothing was obstructing the path. Then he needed to break the window, pull her out, and swim with her towards the light that Ken was holding.

Ken grabbed the spotlight and turned it on. An R.C.M.P. cruiser pulled up and parked several yards down the road from the road block Lachlan had already set up. With his lights flashing and the giant searchlights trained on the lake, any approaching traffic should have no trouble seeing that they needed to slow down and stop.

"Annah, the boys are in the water right above you. I love you, baby. I'll see you in minute." Lachlan kept his field glasses trained on the spot where Peter and Ken had disappeared under the water and said a quick prayer. He would **not** lose the only woman he had ever truly loved. He would not!

Peter and Ken dove into the frigid hole. Ken held the light for Peter to see and Peter smashed the window with the point on the butt end of his knife. The window shattered. As the water rushed into the truck Peter grabbed Annah out and following Ken's light dragged her up to the surface. He and Ken promptly flipped her sopping wet, half frozen, but still breathing body into the dingy. They were at fourteen minutes and still counting. Although she was out of the water she was still in the cold. Annah lay at the bottom of the dingy unable to move so much as a finger. It was so bitterly cold that her clothing and hair were literally freezing into a solid mass. Ken pulled himself up into the boat as well. He wrapped her in the dry fleece and thermal blankets and strapped her into the bottom of the boat. Peter swam the boat back to the edge using his body and the axe as an icebreaker. Although he and Ken had just passed through this same path the lake had already formed a new skin of ice.

Annah could see the stars above her and tried to reach out and touch the shiny twinkling orbs. She hadn't moved an inch and yet she could feel them dropping star dust on her cheeks. Ken jumped out onto the ledge of the lake and reattached the ropes to pull the inflatable back up the cliff. Once John and Dan began to drag the boat back up, Ken turned around and assisted Peter up out of the lake. Both men slipped their climbing boots back on and began their ascent back up as soon as they saw the boat crest the hill and disappear.

The second the boat was hauled over the ledge and back onto the road Lachlan was beside it undoing the bungees. John and Dan helped him strip Annah out of her coat and all of her clothes. They rewrapped her in dry fleece and thermal blankets and Lachlan swiftly deposited her into the front seat of the cab of his warm, running truck. He stripped down and climbed into the back seat. Dan picked up Annah from the front seat and laid her on top of Lachlan in the back seat. Dan spread a fleece blanket and then a thermal blanket on top of Annah. He grabbed Lachlan's clothes and threw them into the front seat. Lachlan had left instructions that Ken was in charge while Dan drove he and Annah into Rocky to the hospital. Annah lay limply in Lachlan's arm. She was definitely breathing but was unconsciousness.

"Don't you leave me, Annah," he moaned with a shudder. He kissed her brow and held her gently but firmly willing her to warm up slowly. She was still in danger of having a heart attack. Dan drove as fast as he safely could to get Annah to Rocky. She was not out of the woods yet. She needed to be in a hospital.

Dan radioed ahead to the Rocky Mountain House Hospital so that they would be prepared for their arrival. Lachlan pulled her braid out from under the blanket so that is could thaw out and not add to the cold of Annah's body. She was very definitely blue but within several minutes her body started the uncontrollable shivering again. Lachlan almost wept with relief. She *was* warming up. Her breathing was becoming less shallow. The trip to Rocky was normally an hour. With the R.C.M.P. ahead of him and both their emergency lights flashing they made it into town in less than half that time. The staff was waiting as Lachlan's truck, with siren's now shrieking, zipped into the Emergency entrance. As the truck rocked to a stop they yanked the back door open and carefully lifted Annah out and onto a gurney. While they raced down the hall with Annah Lachlan jumped out of the truck and pulled his clothes back on. He rushed to follow her and was stopped at the door of her treatment room by a well meaning nurse.

"I'm sorry sir, but you can't go in there. Just give them a few minutes to assess her and then maybe I can let you go in."

Lachlan was about to push past her when Dan grabbed his arm.

"Hey, man. Let them do their job. Annah needs them right now more than she needs you hovering over her. Come on. We'll just pace back over here. Okay?"

Lachlan backed away from the nurse. "I'm sorry," he apologized, as he sank down against the wall and cradled his head in his hands trying not to break down. He inhaled deeply and smoothly but his breath shuddered out while he tried to keep it together. Dan went to get both of them some coffee and heavily laced Lachlan's with sugar. Despite what Lachlan may claim he was also in shock. Although it seemed like an eternity later the doctor finally left the room to talk to Lachlan. In reality it had only been about twenty minutes. By now he was up from the wall, had drank his coffee, and had paced several miles. Lachlan hustled over to her.

"So?" he demanded.

"She will be just fine," the doctor reassured him. "Holding her the way you did all the way into town helped to re-warm her slowly. We have her under heated blankets and are giving her a warm IV of sugar water. She is responding well and has regained consciousness. We want to keep her overnight and continue to monitor her but you can go in and be with her. We're going to move her into a regular room in about an hour. If you like you can stay with her overnight."

"Thank you, doctor," Lachlan pumped her hand enthusiastically. "Thank you."

"Before you leave tomorrow come and see me. I'd like to get all the details of the accident for my report. I've been told she was in the lake for over fifteen minutes. She's a very lucky girl. At this point there seems to be no permanent damage."

"I'll do that," Lachlan promised as she walked away and he hurried into the treatment room.

Annah was inclined on the hospital bed with an IV still hooked up to her arm and was covered up to her neck in blankets. Her hair had been pulled out of its braid and lay spread out across her pillow. She was pale but not blue anymore and weakly smiled up at him when he walked in. Lachlan leaned over her and very gently kissed her on the forehead. He sank into the chair beside the bed and cupped her cheek as he stared deep into her eyes. His eyes glistened with unshed tears as he haltingly spoke.

"I promised myself I would never care enough about another person to ever have to live through the hell I did when I lost Amy. Today that hell came screaming back. If I could I would bundle you and the kids up and we would move far away. But somehow I know you aren't going to go for that, are you? Annah I was so scared!" Lachlan whispered. Annah's hand came from beneath the blanket and as she covered his hand with hers Lachlan let loose and began to sob harshly.

The storm that raged within Lachlan had gentled by the time the nurse arrived to remove Annah's IV and move her to another room.

Lachlan's head lay on the bed beside Annah and her hand rested on it. She had fallen asleep. He quietly stood up and helped the nurse with the bed. After getting Annah settled in her new room he returned to the hall to update Dan and tell him to head for home. Waiting in the hall were Ken, Peter, John, and Dan.

Lachlan walked over to shake Peter's hand and ended up hugging him. "I can't thank you guys enough for saving Annah's life." He in turn gave each of his men a hug.

"No thanks are necessary," Peter assured him. "She's one of us. How is she?"

"The doctor says she'll be fine. They'll release her in the morning. You guys need to head home. If it's okay with June I'd like to stay and leave the kids with her overnight."

"It's all taken care of. We'll see you tomorrow. Give Annah our love. Oh, and her coat is in a bag in the back seat of your truck. We thought she might want to keep it since it probably saved her life!"

"Thanks." Dan threw Lachlan his keys and left with the others. The R.C.M.P. that had led them into town had asked Lachlan to call him when Annah was able to give a statement. As he walked back into her room he discovered Annah sitting up again and awake.

"How are you feeling?"

"Not so cold. And I think I'm hungry."

After Annah had something to eat she readjusted herself on the bed and asked about the children.

"Everyone is fine. So, can you tell me what happened," Lachlan prompted.

"I was slowing down because of the curve and the fact that there are often sheep on that stretch of road. I glanced into my rearview mirror and noticed a truck was fast approaching from behind me. I tapped my brakes to blink my brake lights to indicate I was slowing down. The truck continued to gain ground. I moved over to the shoulder to let it pass, hoping there were no sheep on the road for the truck to hit. Before I could check in my mirror again I was hit from the side."

"The side? What do you mean from the side?"

"The truck pulled into the opposite lane and literally swerved into the driver's side rear quarter-panel and pushed me through the railing. Lachlan, it was deliberate."

"Can you describe the truck?"

"It was red. I saw a flash of it as it passed by me. I can't tell you who was driving it. When it was behind me its bright lights were on preventing me from seeing anything other than the fact that it was a truck. Not much to go on, is there?"

"The police told me they found an abandoned red truck with damage on the front passenger corner parked in the Harlec Fish Pond parking lot. There were two sets of tracks in the lot. Since the pond was frozen over, there is a good chance that the other set of tracks belongs to someone who was waiting for the driver of the red truck, not some fisherman. Apparently the truck had been reported stolen only an hour before from a bar in Rocky. They're having it towed back to town."

"Speaking of towing, what's going to happen to my truck?"

"The police are coming out with a tow truck to trailer it back into Rocky."

"I don't suppose it's salvageable, is it?"

"No, Annah. It'll be a write off."

"I guess it was time for a new one anyway. The poor thing had almost six hundred thousand kilometers on it. Speaking of things, where is my coat?"

"It's in my truck. I'll get it to the drycleaners first thing in the morning. I don't want you ever leaving the house without it from now on."

"I knew right from the moment I first saw it that it was meant for me. Who knew it would save my life."

"Okay, back to the matter at hand. You can't side track me that easily, you know. If Dabria was at the station it obviously wasn't her driving that truck. Nicole and Matthew were both off today. We need to find out where they were and if anyone was with them."

"Are you saying that you think both of them are involved?"

"I think it's possible that all three of them are involved. Conveniently, Dabria's meeting would keep me at the station later than normal. Thank God, I implemented the new radios this week.

That brings up my next point. This has elevated beyond threats to attempted murder, Annah."

"I am well aware of that. However, I'm not sure what we are going to do to safeguard me any more than we already have."

"For one, you are never to drive or walk anywhere alone from now on," Lachlan commanded. "I forbid it."

"Yeah, well good luck with that one, Lachlan. That is extremely impractical. In view of the fact that my new very wet radio has a distress button and ten minute check-ins, I'm as safe as I can possibly be. I told you before I refuse to give into this."

"Damn it, Annah, I almost lost you today. I can't live with the loss of someone else I love. It would destroy me and you know it."

"Lachlan, you would have to go on because if something happens to me the children will be yours. And I know you would never abandon them. I'm changing my will tonight."

"You don't play fair."

"We both know life isn't fair. The only solution to ending this is to draw this person or persons out."

"Are you suggesting using yourself as bait?" Lachlan asked incredulously.

"I don't see any other solution. Do you? I plan on suggesting it to the police when I give them my report later. Do they want to talk to me tonight?"

"If you feel up to it I can get him to come down right now and get your statement."

"Let's do it. I'll call the kids while we wait for him."

By the time the R.C.M.P. was finished with her, Annah was ready to go back to sleep. Since she no longer had her IV in she invited Lachlan to climb onto the bed with her and she fell asleep in his arms.

CHAPTER 24

A͟ꜰᴛᴇʀ Aɴɴᴀʜ ᴡᴀꜱ ᴄʜᴇᴄᴋᴇᴅ out she and Lachlan returned to Nordegg to pick up the kids and head home. The police agreed with Lachlan that using Annah for bait was going to be a last resort. Instead they would install phone taps on the lines at work and suggested plainclothes officers follow Matthew, Nicole, and Dabria. Putting tails on Matthew and Nicole wasn't feasible since the area they lived in was isolated enough that everyone knew everyone else's vehicle. If a strange vehicle started following them around questions would soon crop up. Not wanting to alert Annah's tormentor to the fact that the police had drawn the conclusion that it was either one of the three or a combination of the three, the police chose to interrogate all the members of the station's staff regarding their whereabouts during the time of the hit and run.

Dabria's alibi was sound since she was at the station. Nicole claimed she was shopping in Calgary for the day and Matthew maintained he had spent the day at home. Another member stated they had seen Matthew's truck at his place both in the morning when they left for work and when they returned at the end of the day. Just because Matthew's truck hadn't moved didn't mean that he hadn't. Nicole's next door neighbor confirmed that she had left early in the morning and returned late at night but no one knew for sure where she had been. The second set of tracks in the fish pond parking lot were smaller than the first indicating a car rather than another truck. But again, because the snow was fluffy the police were unable to get an actual tire tread mark. All other staff members were accounted for during that time.

Lachlan and Annah spent the weekend at home preparing for Christmas. Annah and the kids made gingerbread houses and decorated inside the house while Lachlan strung lights around the outside and in some of the trees. It was a wonderful weekend.

Life returned to its recently new routine again on Monday. The only unusual occurrence was when Nicole gave Lachlan her notice. She told him her heart was no longer in her job and that she was returning to the city. Dispatchers were not an easy position to replace particularly right before Christmas. Lachlan wished he could talk her into staying both for that reason and because he at least could keep track of her when she was at work. Once she was done, there would be no way of knowing where she was.

Annah and Peter spent the week radio tagging animals and tracking previously tagged ones. Annah's favorite was a young female cougar named Thea. She and David had tagged her, weighed and measured her, and took blood samples in September. There had been a healthy mature male, dubbed Thor, in her territory and Annah hoped he had impregnated Thea. She was a three year old and it would be her first litter of kittens. The combination of the two cats would produce strong offspring. In the course of tracking Thor, Peter unfortunately discovered his remains, rather than the live magnificent cat he had encountered previously. He and an impressively large Big Horn Ram were both found dead at the bottom of a ravine. Since this was unusual, due to the fact that both animals appeared healthy, Annah and Peter photographed the area and performed a necropsy on both animals.

It was obvious both had recently died since no scavengers had begun feeding. The area around the animals suggested that a struggle had started farther up the mountain and that both animals had tumbled down into the coulee, since rocks and snow appeared disturbed and blood was splattered around. It was determined that the following scenario must have occurred. Thor stalked the Ram until they came to a place where he was able to rush him, leap on him, knock him down, and then sink his teeth into the Ram's throat without releasing his grip. The Ram obviously fought back and pulled the both of them over the ledge and down into the coulee. By then he had suffocated. Thor, however, received internal injuries from broken ribs as he plunged over the side and unfortunately he bled out. Their findings would be recorded including the date of Thor's death. The station had a family tree of Thor's dating back several generations. Thor, himself, had been the sire of several kitten litters over the past five years. Annah hoped he had been busy this fall since his death would seriously hamper the efforts of the conservation officers to not only maintain the cougar population but increase it.

Thor was the resident male for this area and he was known to service several females. Although an adult cougar's only predator was man the kittens often fell prey to bears and eagles. Thor's death was cause for concern. Lachlan requested that all the officers add tracking, tranquillizing, and testing all female cougars in the area to determine pregnancies and the number of pending litters, to their normal duties. Annah was to organize and compile the information that the officers brought back after each fieldtrip.

Annah relished the opportunity to be responsible for this project. The mountain lions were her favorite animal and she had done extensive research on them while still in school. This project would give her something to focus all of her attentions on while at work and reduce the number of opportunities for thoughts of frustration and of absolute terror to intrude. After hours, Lachlan and the kids filled up every spare moment she had, preventing those destructive thoughts from taking over.

It was now two weeks before Christmas and no one was any closer to determining the culprits behind the harassment. No other incidents had occurred and Annah was so caught up in her busy new life that she let her guard relax slightly from the high alert she had been on for weeks.

Most of the female cougars in the area had been tested and so far several of them had tested positive for pregnancy. Unfortunately, Thea was not one that they had been able to tranquilize. Although, they knew her range and had come across a couple of the remains of her camouflaged kills, so far she had successfully eluded them. Peter and Annah had tracked her to an area on Shunda Mountain that was not well known by the general public but easily accessible to the officers. Peter had gone out alone that morning and left Annah at the station to work on the information. Lachlan had a meeting in Rocky and was expected to return right after lunch.

The Monday following Annah's hit and run Dabria called Lachlan to inform him of her family and David's family decision not to pursue the civil suit. This withdrawal added to Lachlan's suspicion that Dabria, Nicole, and Matthew were all in on Annah's attempted murder. She could very easily have called Lachlan Friday night to relay that information rather than setting up a meeting with him. When he questioned her on that point, she claimed that she had wanted to apologize to him in person. Lachlan requested a meeting with the R.C.M.P. to discuss a plan for trapping the culprit or culprits. He had mulled over Annah's idea of using herself as bait and remembered seeing a female police officer that looked uncannily similar to Annah at David's inquest. He planned to ask the police if they would be willing to entice her into impersonating Annah.

At eleven thirty that morning Peter called the station for back-up. He had been tracking Thea and discovered that a kill site in her area had the remains of a deer tied to a tree. Obviously some poacher was baiting either a bear or Thea. All of the other officers were already out in the field. Annah requested that since she was his partner could she please join him. Peter hesitated but then decided that because he and Annah were partners then she was the obvious choice. Annah left the coordinates of where she and Peter would be with Mrs. Larson and headed out.

~

Peter signed off from Annah and was about to turn back to his running truck when he was struck from behind. He went down like a rock. He was trussed up like a Thanksgiving turkey and then dragged back to his truck and stuffed into the back seat. Still out cold he had duct tape smoothed over his mouth and blankets piled on top of him to disguise the fact that he was laying there. His truck was shut off, locked, and the keys stuffed under the front floor mat.

Twenty minutes later Annah drove down the same back road. As she approached Peter's truck she noticed a second conservation truck parked there. Obviously Peter had been concerned about the two of them dealing with this situation alone when it was such an isolated area and had called for more back-up. Annah parked behind the second truck and radioed Mrs. Larson that she was at the rendezvous site. Her radio vibrated at the same time and she signaled Lachlan that she was fine.

As Annah walked past the first truck she glanced inside. She moved on to Peter's truck and noticed there was something piled in his backseat under some blankets. She tried the door, but it was locked. Annah knew that something was wrong. Quietly Annah radioed Mrs. Larson and told her she had a feeling Peter was in trouble but not to call him. She told her she would contact her as soon as she knew something. She also told her truck number five was parked behind Peter's and asked who had signed it out. Mrs. Larson said it wasn't signed out and she thought it was still parked at the station.

There was a trail leading off to the right of Peter's truck with several sets of footprints and drag marks in the snow. Not wanting to startle Peter she buzzed him to let him know she was there without actually calling out to him. He buzzed her back, indicating that silence was necessary. She had her rifle with her and she proceeded with caution. As she rounded a corner she spotted Matthew crouched down with his rifle aimed farther down the path. He turned as she approached and signaled she stay quiet. When she was right beside him she crouched down and whispered to him.

"Where is Peter and what's going on? Did the poachers show up?"

"I just arrived and I haven't talked to Peter yet," Matthew responded. "I buzzed him and he buzzed me back so I was simply proceeding with caution. Edge over to that spruce at the next bend and I'll cover you and then follow," Matthew instructed.

"I thought you were off today," Annah commented.

"No, I'm supposed to be on afternoons. I just kept the company truck overnight because my truck wouldn't start yesterday. Could we maybe chat about this later? I think Peter may be in trouble. Go," Matthew gestured with his rifle.

Annah did as Matthew requested and as she turned around to wave him forward, he stood up. Instead of following her he raised his rifle and shot her.

CHAPTER 25

LACHLAN'S MEETING WITH THE Rocky R.C.M.P. had gone well. They agreed to consider his suggestion. It was almost noon and Lachlan was about five minutes away from the station. He knew Annah had left the station because his radio had sent him two signals in the last half hour. Since she hadn't radioed him that there was a problem before she left, he assumed she was with Peter and that everything was fine. He was about to find out how wrong assumptions can be.

Lachlan pulled into the parking lot and was collecting his gear as his radio went off and Mrs. Larson, unaware that he had just pulled up, asked his ETA.

"I'll be inside in a minute."

"See you in a sec."

Lachlan sauntered into the office with his arms full of treats from the Rocky Bakery and Annah's freshly dry-cleaned blanket coat.

"So what's up?" he asked as he deposited his load by the coffee counter.

"I may be over-reacting," Mrs. Larson hedged, "but I have a bad feeling that something is going on with Peter and Annah."

"What makes you think that?" Lachlan asked as the hair on the back of his neck began to rise and a sick feeling settled into the pit of his stomach. He quickly turned towards her.

"Peter called in and asked for back-up regarding a possible poaching situation. He asked for some of the other members but everyone was out this morning except for Annah. They were all a fair distance away from where he was. Annah talked him into letting her join him. She left about half an hour ago."

"She went out alone?" Lachlan grated.

"Lachlan, there was no one else to go that was close and it is her job."

"Please continue," he prompted curtly.

"She just radioed in and said she found Peter's truck along with truck number five. But no officers were in sight. The problem is truck number five isn't signed out by anyone and as far as I knew it was still here. I checked with Ken and Dan and they have trucks three and four and they have John and the new guy Mark with them. That leaves Matthew and the other two new recruits as possibilities."

"Have you tried to contact Peter?"

"No. Annah told me not to. She told me she wanted to maintain radio silence."

"Have you tried to reach Matthew or the other recruits?" Lachlan questioned over his shoulder as he hurried to his office.

"There is no answer on Matthew's house phone or his radio. I haven't tried the others yet."

Lachlan dumped his coat, briefcase, and miscellaneous gear onto his desk freeing up his hands to manipulate the various buttons on his own radio.

"Mrs. Larson, please radio Dan and Ken and instruct them to go to the fire road on Shunda Mountain and to indicate their ETA. Also radio the R.C.M.P. that we have a possible situation unfolding and to direct any officers in this vicinity to respond."

"Lachlan, what can you see that I can't?" Mrs. Larson asked as she watched him punching buttons on his radio and becoming tenser by the second.

"Peter, Annah, and Matthew are all at the same GPS coordinates but none of them are responding to their pages. Did Annah say if there was anything unusual about the parked trucks?"

"Actually she said that both were locked and that there appeared to be something in the backseat of Peter's that was covered up by blankets. She said there were at least two sets of footprints as well as markings in the snow that looked like something had been dragged."

"Okay. I'm out of here. Keep me apprised of anything you hear. Don't use open channels for talking to me or any of the guys and tell them not to use them either. Here is the privacy line for Dan's radio and for Ken's. Use them the same way you use mine when you call me. If someone else needs to reach me tell them to call the satellite phone. I want total radio silence on the common frequencies. If Matthew calls in ask him his location and if he knows where truck five is. Tell him we were calling him before because we were looking for the truck. Don't let him know that I know where he, Peter, and Annah are, or that there is any kind of situation going on." Lachlan grabbed extra guns and ammunition out of the locked gun cabinet in the storage room. He also grabbed the third set of keys for Annah's and Peter's trucks and truck number five.

"Call the new recruits into the office as well. I want all hands available because I have a really bad feeling about this one."

Lachlan ran the extra munitions out to his truck and then returned for his normal field gear and coat. Mrs. Larson had filled two thermoses with coffee and one with tea and handed them to him along with Annah's seemingly indestructible red coat. Then she hurried back to her phones, calling in Fred to help dispatch.

Lachlan peeled out of the parking lot with a shower of gravel raining behind him and headed for Shunda. Annah's safety signal should have gone off twice in the last fifteen minutes. Not only had it not but Lachlan had buzzed her repeatedly and she had not responded once. The location of the three radios was also not changing. Lachlan didn't know if that was a good sign or a very bad one. Normally the drive would have taken twenty minutes. Lachlan was determined to be there in ten. Those next ten minutes would be the longest of Lachlan's life.

Annah looked down at her leg and it registered that a tranquillizer dart was sticking out of it.

"Matthew, what's going on?" she demanded as she pulled the dart out and raised her gun, aiming it at him. With her own adrenalin pumping quickly through her system the tranquilizer drug swiftly started to work. Trying to maintain her stance propped against a tree Annah, unfortunately, started to slowly sink to the ground. Matthew approached her as the gun became too heavy for her to hold. He pulled the gun out of her unresisting hands and threw it back into the bush.

"What's going on is that you are finally going to get what you deserve, you little bitch!"

"I don't understand."

"I think you do. I know you guessed that David and I were lovers. But did you know that we've been together since we were eighteen years old. You thought you could just waltz right in here and take him from me. I let him have his women on the side because with each new lover he learned new things. He then brought that knowledge and the new techniques back to enhance our love life. David wasn't strong like me. He let his parents push him into that engagement with Dabria. But finally, he was ready. He broke it off with Dabria and that bimbo, Nicole. I was so happy. I knew that after years of my encouragement and faithfulness we would finally be together." While Matthew talked he picked Annah up and flung her over his shoulder. He carried her down the path farther into the forest. Although most of Annah's body was limp and useless she could still see and hear.

"But no! You wormed your way in. When we should have been coming out and telling the world about us, he tried to tell me he was in love with you. With you!!!! He loved me! He said he needed to end it with me, that you were his "soul mate". He said you weren't like the others. He said he'd been searching for you his whole life."

Matthew flopped her down onto a burlap gunny sack. Annah saw ropes hanging from two trees in the clearing that was actually a small plateau on the side of the mountain. The remains of a deer still hung from one rope. This was what Peter had found and radioed in about. She also saw a thermos stuck in the snow beside one of the trees. Could it be that Matthew had just wandered in on this and was now using it to his advantage or had he orchestrated the entire thing? Annah's partial paralysis prevented her from asking. Bending down over the gunny sack he tied her hands and feet together and then rolled her up like a jelly roll.

"I could never let that happen. David loved me. We belonged together. *You* should have been using those lines that day, not David. You're the reason why I'll have to spend the rest of my life alone. I hate you. But, I'm not the only one. Nicole hated you and so does Dabria. It's a shame that no one will know it was me that finally got rid of you."

Matthew cut down the deer that was hanging from the tree. He then hung Annah like a hammock in between the two trees. She was, thankfully, lying on her back but couldn't move and could no longer see with the burlap covering her eyes.

"Poor Nicole tried. She threatened you and tried to scare you into leaving. She ran you off the road with the help of some drifter from the oil patch. Oh, no...... wait, that's right, it was actually *me* that helped her," he chuckled, amused by his own ingenuity.

"Since our little schemes were unsuccessful, I then planned my own course of action. I no longer needed Nicole and I could accomplish what we set out to do on my own. How convenient for me that she quit her job. No one actually knows that she's missing yet. When they do find her they will also find a suicide note with a full confession. Who could have known that David's most recent little dalliance would end up helping to avenge his death?"

Annah heard him screw off the top of the thermos and could feel something warm and thick being poured over her. It had the metallic smell of blood. Oh my God, it was blood. She kept her mouth and eyes shut until the pouring stopped and hoped that the soaked cloth didn't freeze to her face and suffocate her. She knew that Lachlan would know she was in trouble and that with her radio still attached to her he would be able to find her. The issue was would she still be alive when he did. Hopefully, Matthew wouldn't shoot her. Cougars were not scavengers. They liked to kill their own meals. As long as Matthew left her alive she had a chance of surviving. So far, Matthew hadn't noticed Annah's radio occasionally vibrating. She wished

Lachlan would stop calling her. If Matthew saw the radio vibrate she was done.

"I think Dabria suspects that I may have had something to do with your little mishaps. But, she'll never tell. She loved David, too, and we've been friends since childhood."

Annah could hear him sweeping and smoothing the snow underneath her with a spruce bough, as he walked backwards away from her.

"I wonder if your cougar will be able to find your throat and end it swiftly for you or if she'll just start ripping pieces out of you. I watched her with the deer you know and she was merciful with them. I'll be watching you, too. That should give you some comfort that you won't be dying alone. If your cat takes too long to finish you off I might even assist her. I can't leave you lying here alive indefinitely, just in case someone finds you. I promise you it will be all over before nightfall. All officers secretly hope they will die in the line of duty. Don't we? Aren't you happy that your death will help your beloved cougars survive?"

With that last question Annah heard Matthew move back down the path continuing to sweep as he went.

⌒⌒

Matthew tried to erase all traces of them as he continued backwards down the trail. He forgot that Annah had pulled out the dart. Although her hands had been unable to hang onto her gun she had managed to clutch the dart in her hand and she had dropped it over his shoulder when he picked her up to carry her to the clearing. Knowing that he could be running out of time before a search started he did a quick but not thorough search on the trail and hurried back out to the trucks.

Annah had also locked her truck but each one had a spare key attached under the bumper. Matthew jumped in and moved her truck farther down the road to the main trailhead where there were already many footprints. He ran back and jumped in Peter's truck and did the same. He checked on Peter and determined he was still out cold. He pitched both sets of Peter's keys and Annah's keys into the bush hoping that when the search was finally launched no one would have the foresight to bring the third set of keys. He already had Peter's radio with him so instead of getting caught with it he pitched it into the bushes as well. Finally he ran back a second time and jumped in the truck number five and drove it to Nicole's place.

Nicole's house was only a mile farther down the road. That was one of the reasons Matthew had picked this spot to bait Thea. Matthew had left his own truck parked at Nicole's. Her neighbor had already left for work that morning when Matthew had shown up. He and Nicole had taken the company truck late last night and left it hidden at Nicole's. Matthew had seduced Nicole soon after David's death so that he could use her to avenge David. He recalled the things David had shared with him regarding her sexual preferences and used them to his advantage by pretending to seek solace with her over the death of someone they both loved. What she didn't know was that as of last night she had outlived her usefulness. Matthew was prepared to do whatever it took to punish Annah including steal, kill, and sleep with a woman. Matthew parked truck number five in front of her house and jumped into his own truck and drove to his lookout.

Matthew's lookout was a tree blind that he had set up to watch Thea. Because the plateau was open he could sit in the blind and with the scope on his gun or his binoculars he could watch the activity in the clearing as well as shoot at anything that wandered into it. Matthew was set up for a long siege. He had blankets and hot coffee as well as energy bars to keep him going. He also had a set of snowshoes just in case he needed to return to the plateau from his perch. Although Annah couldn't possibly know this he was really only about two minutes away from her. As he settled in he wondered how long it would actually take before someone sounded the alarm and a rescue was attempted.

CHAPTER 26

SOMETHING WAS GENTLY SWAYING in a burlap bag soaked in blood. The bag was tied like a hammock, between two large aspen trees on a small natural plateau, on the southwest slope of Shunda Mountain in the Canadian Rockies. The plateau was small, but level, and had provided the perfect feeding ground to lure a young pregnant cougar for the last couple of weeks. The serenity of the afternoon was uninterrupted except for the gentle breeze that ruffled the unfurled ends of the knotted nylon ropes hanging from the two trees. The warm afternoon sunshine and heat radiating from the bundle kept the blood from freezing in the crisp mountain air. The syrupy globules silently oozed from the warm bundle while it gently, ever so slightly, swayed. They seemed to transform into rubies frozen into the pristine, iridescent snow below. Thea scented the latest meal left for her and stealthily crept down the mountainside.

Annah was cold but not freezing yet since the blood Matthew had poured over her from the thermos hadn't been enough to soak through her winter coat and ski pants. Her hair was wet though and so was her face and a crust of red ice was beginning to form wherever the blood had landed on the burlap. The wet burlap was rough against her face as she moved her head to the side to try to breathe better.

The smell of the warm blood had made her gag, initially, but she was getting used to even that as it cooled off. She knew the scent of blood carried a long way and that there were many predators in this area. Besides Thea there was the very real threat of wolves as well as bears, bobcats, and badgers. Added to the animals, there was the danger still posed by Matthew. She knew he was hiding somewhere where he could see but not be seen. That meant that Lachlan or whoever found her first was also in danger.

She still didn't know what had happened to Peter and was afraid that Matthew had killed him as well as Nicole. Dying was not an option for Annah. She refused to allow Matthew to make her children orphans. She was starting to get some feeling back in her hands. If she could get the ropes off her wrists and cut her way through the rope attached to the tree at her head she might be able to partially roll behind the outcropping of rock beside the tree. If Matthew didn't have his sights trained on her constantly she might have a chance of freeing herself or at least protecting her head and upper body from getting shot. Methodically Annah worked the knots, slowly loosening them.

Lachlan spotted the trucks up ahead. He stopped behind Peter's and slammed his truck into park. His radio showed that Annah was somewhere on the right hand side of the ditch and that Peter was on the left. He needed to check the trucks first, since he had a feeling he might find Peter in one of them. Jumping out of the truck with the third set of keys in his hand he ran over and unlocked the door. Grabbing the blanket in the back seat he ripped it off revealing Peter still tied up but conscious. Swiftly he removed the duct tape from Peter's mouth and cut his restraints.

"So, fill me in," Lachlan demanded.

"There's not much to tell," Peter explained. "I came to check on the location of Thea, that female cougar. Her transmitter indicated that she has been using this area as a base. I came across a plateau where someone has been baiting. I radioed the station calling for back-up and the only one available was Annah." Peter put his hand up to stop Lachlan from interrupting him. "I know I should have told her she wasn't allowed to leave without someone else but there was no one else there."

"Peter, I'm not about to reprimand you for asking Annah to do her job. And being your partner in all respects is her job whether I like that fact or not. So then what happened?"

"I was just about to turn around to go back to the truck and wait for her when someone hit me from behind. The next thing I remember was waking up here. Someone came back here about five minutes ago and I pretended I was still out when he checked on me and moved the truck."

"What do you mean he moved the truck?"

"He moved two trucks and drove away in a third. He obviously wants you guys to think that Annah and I are somewhere down the trailhead leading up the mountain path that the hikers take. But that's not where I found the bait." Peter had moved around enough now that most of the circulation had returned to his cramped muscles.

"Am I right in assuming that Annah is now missing?" Peter questioned.

Lachlan nodded grimly.

Peter jumped down out of the truck and walked back down the road until he found the place where Matthew had used the pine bough to smooth over the trail. After Lachlan had checked over Annah's truck and determined that she wasn't inside he cranked a U-turn in his truck and followed Peter.

"I'm pretty sure I know who it is, Lachlan," Peter stated with a grimace. "The guy was wearing the same aftershave that Matthew does."

"Are you okay to track and back me up if necessary?" Lachlan asked.

"Absolutely," Peter affirmed.

Lachlan called in to Mrs. Larson to check on ETA's of his other officers and to give her an update on the current status of things. She was to inform the other officers to consider Matthew armed and dangerous if they were to come into contact with him. He asked her to apprise the police of all of the details. He then informed her that he and Peter would be following Annah's GPS beacon until they found her radio. If she wasn't with it, like Peter, then they would have to start a more thorough search of the area. Just as Lachlan signed off Annah's radio signaled him. He immediately signaled her back and holding his breath, waited for her to signal again. She did.

"Thank God, she's still alive," Lachlan announced to Peter as he staggered beside his truck and slumped to the ground with relief.

Using Morse Code he asked her if she knew where she was. She confirmed that she was down the path that he was on, but that Matthew was watching her, hidden from view and that he planned to kill anyone who interfered with her. Peter mentally recalled the specifics of the terrain on the plateau and relayed that information to Lachlan. He and Lachlan armed themselves. Lachlan radioed back to Mrs. Larson with the latest information and they proceeded cautiously down the trail. Just before they rounded the final bend they heard a shot ring out, a yelp, and then a muffled curse.

～～

Annah had managed to free her hands and page Lachlan. Once she knew they were on their way and that they knew the risks, she slid the knife out of her jacket pocket and carefully sawed at the burlap enclosing her. Suddenly, she felt another presence. The otherworldly cry and hiss of a mountain lion came from somewhere above her. A snarl and growl startled Annah by its closeness to her feet. Stilling the movements of her hands she hoped that the wildcat and the wolf would continue to concentrate on each other rather than on her. God, she prayed Lachlan would hurry. A shot rang out perilously close to Annah. The wolf yelped and loped off while Annah jerked and tried to stifle a curse.

～～

As Lachlan positioned himself behind a large spruce at the corner of the trail to cover Peter's approach he glanced down and found a tranquilizer dart sticking into the snow. He grabbed it and motioned for Peter to join him.

"This is one of ours," Lachlan confirmed. "Did you hear that? It sounded like a wolf."

"It was probably feeding on the deer remains," Peter suggested. "The plateau is just around that last bend. There is a rock outcropping to the left that will work as some cover. But it's a small space and you and I can't both fit behind it," Peter informed Lachlan.

Just then Mrs. Larson radioed that the R.C.M.P. were on their way but they were still ten or fifteen minutes out. The other conservation officers should be arriving within the next fifteen to twenty minutes.

"There have been shots fired and we may not have that kind of time. Peter and I are moving in for a closer look," Lachlan told Mrs. Larson.

"I'll go ahead. You stay and cover me," Lachlan directed Peter. "After you see me leave that bend, position yourself there, and I'll hide behind the outcrop."

Lachlan hurried over to the bend. He sunk to his belly and crawling around the corner quickly disappeared. Peter followed, crouched down, and waited for a signal. As Lachlan crawled around the bend he saw a hammock of sorts hanging in between two trees in the clearing. There was blood on the ground under it and the footprints of a wolf. One end of the hammock was almost close enough to reach out and touch. He quietly radioed Peter.

"There is something strung in-between two trees with some blood on the ground and wolf prints. Hang on, there's steam rising from one end of the bundle almost like exhaust from a breath."

Lachlan signaled Annah and saw a movement in the bundle. She returned the signal. Holding himself very still Lachlan whispered.

"Annah?"

She signaled him back on her radio. Slumping against the rocks, Lachlan in hushed tones, informed Peter that they had found Annah and she was indeed alive. Suddenly Annah's hands emerged from her enclosure and swiftly cut the ropes at her head. She thumped to the ground with a grunt and quickly rolled towards the outcrop. A volley of bullets followed her and Lachlan was unsure if she was hit. Her feet were tangled in the bag that was still attached to the other tree. The top half of her body and her head were sheltered by the rocks, but from the waist down she was exposed.

"My legs are stuck in that bag," Annah explained. "Is there enough room back here for you to pull me out?"

"There has to be," Lachlan declared. He grabbed Annah by the shoulders of her jacket and yanked with all his might. Annah's legs jerked out of the confines of the bag and she pulled them up to rest against her chest. Lachlan was wedged into the corner, unable to move. Annah repositioned herself so that she was basically curled into a ball on the ground with her legs tucked underneath her. Lachlan could now step over her and shelter the entrance to their refuge. A flurry of shots pelted the ground between the trees as well as the trees themselves. Bark, snow, and rock chips rained down onto the plateau.

"Are you hit?" Lachlan asked Annah as he tried to push her farther back into the crevice.

"I don't think so, but my legs are still partially numb so I wouldn't necessarily feel it and there's so much deer blood that I can't tell if I'm bleeding or not. Let's just go with "I'm fine" for now. Is anyone with you?"

"Peter is just on the other side of this lovely refuge we're in.," Lachlan informed her before radioing Peter. "Peter, I have Annah and she seems fine. Can you see where the shots are coming from?"

"I have the general location but I'm not in a position to get off any safe rounds."

"Now that he knows we're here I can't send Annah back out to you. Her legs are still numb from the tranquilizer. Get yourself back to the trucks and act as liaison for the R.C.M.P. I'll call Mrs. Larson and let her know you will be her contact for the other staff. Although it's cramped in here I can't see him being able to get a clear shot in unless he stands right in front of us. So, we're safe for now."

"Lachlan, you know it's Matthew, right?" Annah quietly stated.

"Oh, and Peter, Annah just confirmed that Matthew's our man."

"Got Ya. I'm heading back now."

Lachlan looked down at Annah and reached out his hand to her.

"My god, girl, I thought you promised me you were going to stop getting into situations like this."

"Oh, come on Lachlan, you know you love it. It's a rush to be able to come charging in and save the damsel in distress. It's just part of your whole chauvinistic persona."

"Baby, every one of these little escapades that you drag me into is taking years off of my life. Once we get married you're going to stay at home like a good little wife and have babies for me."

"Maybe someday. But, for now I was born for this and you know it. You know Thea was here hanging over top of me in a tree just before Matthew shot off a round and scared the wolf away. That was Matthew's plan, by the way, to have Thea eat me. He killed Nicole and left a suicide note with her saying that she had initiated all of the harassment and ultimately was responsible for my death as well."

"What else did he have to say for himself?"

"He and David were lovers and have been for years. He was the third lover that David indicated he needed to deal with. I would never have guessed. Matthew claimed David tried to tell him he was in love with me, that we were soul mates. Matthew said the cut ropes were meant for me so he obviously was responsible for them, too. Ultimately, he killed his own lover."

"So, he has been trying to get rid of you ever since."

"He and Nicole. It was a joint venture."

The forest had been quiet now since Peter had left. There had been no more shots.

"How are the legs? Do you think you can stand yet?" Lachlan asked.

She nodded and with the hand that he was still holding, he pulled her up. She swayed against him and he wrapped his arms around her to steady her. A twig snapped to the right of the crevice. Annah froze. Lachlan had two hand guns and a rifle with him. He shoved one hand gun into Annah's hand and pushed her to lie back on the ground. Lachlan straddled Annah's outstretched hands waiting for Matthew's imminent confrontation. Matthew jumped in front of the crevice with his gun blazing. Lachlan ducked and dove at Matthew knocking him down as Annah shot him in the knee. Matthew had clipped Lachlan on the right shoulder.

Both men crashed to the ground. Lachlan knocked the gun out of Matthew's hand. Annah jumped to her feet and followed them as they rolled out onto the plateau. At the end of the plateau was a drop of about five meters. As the men rolled back and forth Annah prayed that they didn't roll over the edge. She was unable to get off a clear shot to further injure Matthew so that he would release Lachlan. Suddenly, unexpectedly, Matthew was able to pull a knife from his boot and slash at Lachlan. It was enough to make Lachlan relinquish his hold on Matthew. That shift gave Matthew the advantage and he pushed Lachlan over the edge.

Annah shrieked a blood curdling, "No!!!!"

Matthew turned back to her and stood up. They faced each other, one with a knife and one with a gun, both with rage in their eyes.

"I told you before I will do whatever it takes to punish you even if I have to destroy everyone around you first," Matthew roared.

Annah braced her legs and with arms outstretched aimed Lachlan's gun at Matthew.

"You don't have the balls to pull that trigger. You pretend you have the guts of a man but you're soft. You weren't made to kill. You were made to protect and nurture," he spat sarcastically mocking her. "What a shame you won't be around to nurture those soon to be orphans of yours."

"Matthew, you know that in nature all mothers will protect their family to the death. I am no different. You take one more step towards me and I will shoot you."

Before Annah finished her statement Matthew rushed her with his knife extended. Without conscious thought Annah pulled the trigger. Before Matthew could stab her she was pushed sideways and hit the ground hard enough to knock the wind out of her. An R.C.M.P. officer rolled off of her and quickly pulled her up to a sitting position to make sure she was okay.

Suddenly, there were officers filling the clearing. She couldn't see Matthew. But neither could she see Lachlan. Brushing the policeman's hands away she scrambled to her feet and headed for the ledge. A police officer was already standing there looking over and talking. Annah hustled over to him.

"Lachlan," she peered down at him. "You're hurt!" The drop was shorter than she had feared. Lachlan was standing up holding the shoulder that Matthew had first nicked with a bullet and then slashed with his knife.

"I'll get Peter and Ken to come pull you up." As she turned away the police officer grabbed her arm and suggested she sit down and keep taking to Lachlan while he went and got help. Gratefully, Annah sunk to the snow.

"Are you okay, baby?" Lachlan called up.

"I will be as soon as they get you back up here," Annah looked Lachlan straight in the eye. "I shot him, Lachlan," Annah stated with horror lacing her voice. "I didn't want to, but I think I might have killed him."

Just then Peter and Ken appeared, ready to bring Lachlan up. John helped Annah take her jacket and ski pants off and into a dry coat. He plopped a toque on her frozen head. Once Lachlan was brought up and his shoulder wrapped, he pulled Annah into his arms and held her tightly.

"Let's get you someplace dry and warm." As he turned her around he pulled her close into his side and walked her out of the clearing preventing her from viewing Matthew's tarp covered body.

"I don't know if I will ever forgive myself, Lachlan," she whispered to him. "Matthew was right, you know. I was put on this earth to nurture and protect, not to take a life."

"Annah, we are all put on this earth to protect the things we love. You were just protecting your own. I, for one, am thankful you're on my side. If Matthew had been able to kill you he would have turned around and finished me off and then where would Simon and Summer be? Don't be so hard on yourself and don't forget he killed Nicole with no remorse. Come on. I've got to get this shoulder checked out and then I want to head home and hug our kids."

When they reached the trucks Annah returned John's jacket to him and seeing her blanket coat in Lachlan's truck she stripped down and wrapped herself in its welcome warm folds. Once they arrived back at the station, Annah quickly showered and dressed in a clean uniform to drive Lachlan into Rocky to get stitched up.

EPILOGUE

A SECOND CORONER'S INQUEST HAD to be held in the Rocky Mountain House Provincial Building regarding the unnatural death of a conservation officer. In most municipalities this would be unusual. In a community of seven thousand it was unheard of. This time the findings indicated that the bullet that killed Matthew Johnson was fired from a gun that one of the R.C.M.P. discharged, not from Annah's. It was determined that the gun had been fired in the line of duty to stop a kidnapper and murderer from murdering another victim. An autopsy on Nicole proved what Annah had claimed, that she did not commit suicide. She was murdered and all evidence pointed towards Matthew.

After sifting through the contents of Matthew's and Nicole's houses there was no evidence to suggest that Dabria had been involved in Annah's harassment or the two murder attempts. The events of the last six months had dramatically changed her life though. Two of her life-long friends were now dead, her wedding dreams destroyed, and three families of Calgary's elite had suffered staggering, irreparable blows. All three of the childhood friends' families requested that Matthew and David's sexual orientations be kept confidential. Annah felt David's family had suffered enough. She promised to never discuss the events or comments that Matthew had made to her on his last day beyond the statement she had made to the R.C.M.P.

She and the remaining officers from the Nordegg Station that had worked with Matthew attended his funeral. Lachlan had been right when he said that every one of them would do whatever it took to protect their own. Matthew loved David and although he crossed the line, he believed that he was avenging David's death. As Annah had learned the day that she pulled that trigger, we all have the ability to kill when our lives or loved ones are threatened. Despite Matthew's actions over the past several months he had been a good conservation officer and an asset to the Nordegg Station. Therefore, for the sake of his family it was only right that the other officers recognized Matthew's contributions and achievements while serving in their station.

Annah was able to move forward with a clear conscience after hearing that it wasn't in fact her bullet that had killed Matthew. She and Lachlan were married in January. Jennifer and Dane stood up with them. Simon was the ring-bearer and Summer was the flower-girl. She had a small white fur muff draped in red velvet roses just like her mother. Although, they had planned on a small wedding it didn't end up that way. Annah had talked Lachlan into inviting his brother, his sister and her family, and his father. Not surprisingly, they all came, as did Nanny, and Annah's family from Saskatchewan and St. Albert. They also invited everyone from the station. The house was filled to capacity for the wedding and they ended up having a reception in the Nordegg Community Hall.

It had snowed all night and the ground was covered with a new layer of fresh white powder. Annah and Lachlan were married on the landing at the top of his massive staircase. This allowed the guests to sit in the foyer and the great room and watch them exchange their vows. The late afternoon sun streamed through Lachlan's two story floor to ceiling windows and seemed to bathe him and his new bride in an almost blessed glow. After the nuptials were exchanged Lachlan and Annah posed inside and out for pictures while their guests journeyed to the hall.

After a buffet fit for a king and queen and a night of dancing and laughter Lachlan and Annah headed to Rocky to spend their wedding night. Once they were finally in their suite Lachlan presented Annah with his gift. It was black pearl earrings in a box of sand.

"Okay. I get that the earrings go with the necklace, but what's with the box of sand?"

"You can leave your blanket coat behind since we'll be spending the next two weeks alone in the Mediterranean. Nanny's staying to babysit. Your favorite necklace is already packed."

"Lachlan, this is so exciting. What a perfect gift!" she squealed. "Are we on a cruise ship?"

"No, I thought we'd only do day cruises while we're there. Is that alright?"

"It's perfect. The ship might have been a problem anyway," Annah giggled as she handed her wedding present to Lachlan. Wrapping her arms around her waist she tried to quiet the butterflies. She had wrapped up a pair of baby-sized hiking boots. Although Annah and Lachlan had been using birth control no method is one hundred per-cent effective. She hoped Lachlan would want this gift as much as she did. Lachlan opened the box. With tears in his eyes he pulled Annah to him.

"When?" Lachlan whispered hoarsely as he hugged her close and kissed her reverently.

"Sometime in August," Annah responded.

"I can't wait." Lachlan turned Annah around and undid the hun-dred buttons running down her spine as he kissed her neck and shoulders.

"So, if I hadn't propositioned you last year, do you think we'd still be in this place right now?"

"Of course, we would. I would still have hired you and I've wanted you since the moment I ran into you. Sometimes you just can't mess with fate. We're meant to be together, Annah. You know that. Once I get you out of this contraption I'm going to show you exactly how I plan to spend the next hundred years of our lives together," Lachlan vowed.

As he peeled the white satin dress off his new bride and flung it onto the red blanket coat draped over the chaise lounge, he did just that.